D1006808

Justice for the Damned

Also by Priscilla Royal
Wine of Violence
Tyrant of the Mind
Sorrow Without End

Justice
for the
Damned

Priscilla Royal

Poisoned Pen Press

First Edition 2007

10 9 8 7 6 5 4 3 2 1

Library of Congress Catalog Card Number: 2006900752

ISBN: 978-1-59058-330-2 Hardcover

Poisoned Pen Press
6962 E. First Ave., Ste. 103
Scottsdale, AZ 85251
www.poisonedpenpress.com
info@poisonedpenpress.com

Printed in the United States of America

Whether it makes one cry or sing,
justice must be carried out.
　　—Marie de France, c. 1170, "Lanval," l.
　　437-8 (translator unknown)

To Peter Goodhugh with gratitude
for your kindness and help from the beginning.

Acknowledgments

Christine and Peter Goodhugh, Ed Kaufman of M Is for Mystery in San Mateo, CA, Henie Lentz, Dianne Levy, Sharon Kay Penman, Barbara Peters of Poisoned Pen Bookstore in Scottsdale, AZ, Robert Rosenwald and all the staff at Poisoned Pen Press, Marianne and Sharon Silva, Sisters in Crime, Lyn and Michael Speakman, and the staff at University Press Bookstore in Berkeley, CA.

Chapter One

This early May morning in 1272, near the feast of Saint Melor, dawned with such sweetness that the Fontevraudine monks and nuns of Amesbury Priory rushed from Chapter with far more eagerness to their assigned tasks than they had felt heretofore.

Although a few were laggard, those for whom early rising would always be akin to the wearing of hair shirts, none regretted this coming of soft spring. The fog from the River Avon swirled like thick smoke through their cloister garth, but it came with a pleasing scent, suggestive of tender, bright flowers and the coming warmth of lengthening days.

Indeed, there was such happiness amongst the monastics of the ancient priory that some began to sing, their voices so filled with reverent joy that the force of their fervent celebration must have breached the surrounding stone walls and surged into the secular land beyond.

As Prioress Eleanor of Tyndal walked slowly out of the Chapter House and into the tranquility of the nuns' cloister, the cheerful voices of her fellow religious began to grow faint in her ears. She hesitated, leaned against a pillar, and glanced up at the wooden roof over the walkway. Although the stone felt cold through her woolen habit, she found comfort in the familiarity of its gouged and pitted surface. She shut her eyes and slowly breathed in the sharp river scent that clung to the twisting wisps of fog drifting through the shrubs and walkways of the gardens before her.

"Home," she sighed and lowered herself with unsteady care onto a bench so worn that the stone looked polished in the soft light.

Although she had been head of her own priory for almost two years, learning to love the storm-battered East Anglian coast where she now lived, Eleanor had spent most of her twenty-two years in the midst of this gentle place of rolling fields, a land enriched as much by ancient myths and rumors as it was from the silt left by the meandering Avon. It was here at Amesbury Priory that a six-year-old Eleanor had arrived, grieving with the silence of those whose mothers have died too soon.

She glanced down at the cloister walk itself. The sight of the hollowed-out paving stones brought back the memory of the day she had joined other little girls who were hopping from one worn depression to another and making a game of it. She smiled, acknowledging the spot with a nod. Was it not just there that she had balanced herself on one foot, surrounded by her new friends, and laughed for the first time since her mother's death?

Fragments of other memories began to march through her mind like some liturgical play performed on a holy day. There were images that brought sadness: a friend's eyes turning dull as she died from some mortal fever; another waving before leaving the priory forever, taken away by her family for an arranged and profitable marriage.

Grief there was, but there was far more joy in these unvoiced thoughts. Hadn't they loved frightening each other with stories about the pagan spirits which surely haunted the ancient fort across the river? Some claimed it was Roman, others that King Arthur had built it as a defense to the lands of Camelot. Whatever the truth, the place was rife with mystery enough to spark their young imaginations like flint.

And there was the time she had tumbled from that tree, age-gnarled even then, and had found comfort in the arms of the novice mistress. Sister Beatrice, her father's elder sister who had dedicated herself to God, had folded her close that day and kissed the bruises to make them well, kisses that never failed to ease whatever pain she felt.

It was here at Amesbury that Eleanor had begun her woman's courses and found her own religious vocation. No matter how fond she might grow of Tyndal, this would remain that irreplaceable spot where the world had been mostly joyous, safe, and full of love.

Women's courses? Eleanor winced as a severe cramp stabbed her lower belly. She shifted to ease her aching back. Why must she suffer the return of this affliction brought to women by their Mother Eve? Had she not endured enough with that near-fatal ague she contracted in late winter?

"Apparently not," Eleanor groaned. "I should have known my monthly bleeding would arrive now." This must have been her particular torment, inherited from the mother of all women, for her courses always seemed to come whenever she undertook a long journey. Despite the short remission granted from this pain after her illness, she had come at least prepared for the return of her bleedings. After all, she concluded with wry amusement, curses only gained in power when they were unexpected.

Another sharp spasm hit her with such force that she bent forward. As the cramp eased, she remembered that she and her aunt were in agreement on this matter. Neither of them doubted that Eve's grave sin was cause enough for God to scourge women with painful courses, but they did conclude that Eve herself would never have passed this down to her daughters if she had had her say about it. In fact, Sister Beatrice had once added that God had surely exempted the Virgin Mary from this monthly woe. In spite of her pain, Eleanor smiled.

Slowly the prioress straightened. The potion brewed from willow bark that Sister Anne had given her was beginning to take effect, but the cramps had exhausted what little strength she had possessed upon rising for prayer earlier this morning. She closed her eyes again, the need for sleep rushing through her with almost irresistible force. Clutching the rough edge of the cold stone bench, she forced herself to look at the earth around her.

Delicate but determined shoots of young flowers, some with tiny blue buds or lovage-green leaves, were escaping the freezing prison winter had made of the earth. "My spirit must take courage from this sight," she said, but her body was unmoved by her determined pronouncement.

Whether or not her soul greeted this eager life with joy, a deep weariness had taken residence within her, an indifference that suggested God might be easing her toward death. Was she ready for her soul to part from its casing of dust? Did it even matter whether or not she was? Her eyelids heavy with fatigue, Eleanor bent her head, and her spirit began to slip into a pool of black humor as if weighted with an iron chain.

Before it had sunk far, however, her ears caught the sound of familiar and cherished voices. Her spirit brightened.

Two women, deep in conversation, were coming toward her. Both were unusually tall for their gender, but it was the younger that looked up at the elder. The former, Sister Anne, was a most talented healer as well as Eleanor's dearest friend at Tyndal. The latter might hold no higher title than novice mistress at Amesbury Priory, but all who knew Sister Beatrice had learned that she was servant only to God.

"You look pale, child," the elder woman said as she stopped in front of her niece. "You must eat meat to regain your strength. Sister Anne agrees."

Although Sister Beatrice had spent six decades on earth, her soft skin retained an almost youthful hint of rose. The creases of age might be shallow in her high forehead, around her sea-blue eyes and the corners of her thin mouth; nonetheless, two dark furrows formed a deep V between her gray eyebrows, lines that had been there since infancy. While the frown warned lesser mortals that she was possessed of a mind whetted by reason, it also hid her very warm heart, a mixed blessing to a woman who understood the nature of love more than most and considered rational thought a weapon to be used only against fear or evil.

"I took a vow," Eleanor replied. "Meat overheats the blood."

Beatrice raised one eyebrow. "Overheats the blood, you say? Neither Sister Anne nor I think so. After all these weeks, you are still too frail. Meat should bring the warmth you need and restore balance to your humors."

Years ago, the Baron Adam had jested that God must have branded his elder sister with her perpetual scowl because she showed ill grace by frowning at their suffering mother who had just given her birth. This remark aside, he valued his sister and taught Eleanor that the wise rightly knew they should fear her aunt and fools would soon learn the price of thwarting her. As the niece now noted her aunt's deepening frown, she reminded herself that her father had rarely been proven wrong.

"With respect, dearest Aunt, I must decline." While others might see this woman as both frightening and formidable, Eleanor found only warmth in her. Beatrice had reared her niece with as much sweet love as if she had been the child of her own body, yet neither had ever pretended that the devotion of an aunt could replace that of a dead mother. Nevertheless, the love between them was profound.

"Meat is allowed under The Rule," Beatrice replied. Her tone suggested that further argument would be pointless.

"Might you not compromise with a beef broth, my lady?" Sister Anne interjected, her eyes twinkling with a mischievous look. "Should you choose not to do so, I believe you and your donkey would be of the same mind."

The two women, who had been looking at each other with a certain familial stubbornness, blinked and turned wide-eyed toward the sub-infirmarian of Tyndal.

Eleanor laughed with a merriment few had heard since her illness.

Beatrice's expression changed into one of confusion. "Donkey?" she asked. "An ass that speaks? Or, if such a miracle did occur, how could the beast talk with any reason?"

With affection, Eleanor squeezed her aunt's hand. "I'm afraid I have disobeyed one of the Commandments and shown disrespect toward a parent. I named my fine mount after my father. When Sister Anne wishes to tell me that I am being obstinate

beyond reason, she reminds me that the donkey would agree
with the position I have taken."

The novice mistress put a hand over her mouth.

It was a gesture Sister Anne had seen her own prioress use, but
one that rarely succeeded in disguising the underlying laughter.

"Irreverence," Beatrice said, "but not disrespect. I know how
much you love your father." She turned to Anne. "There is truth
in the donkey's naming. As you may have noticed the winter you
were at Wynethorpe Castle, my brother possesses a fair share of
mortal obstinacy, a quality which I most certainly lack!" The
sparkle in her eyes betrayed the jest hiding in her words, but
her look now shifted to concern as she looked down at Eleanor.
"You will agree to the broth?"

"I shall willingly concede on that but would not eat meat
otherwise."

The sub-infirmarian of Tyndal and the novice mistress of
Amesbury looked at each other in silent conference, and then
replied in unison: "Agreed."

"Your failure to eat much of anything since your arrival has
troubled me, child. I fear you have not recovered any of the
health you lost."

"Health is difficult to regain after such a hard fever, my lady,"
Anne replied. The words may have been intended as an explanation, but the tone expressed her own ongoing worry.

"Not *my lady*, rather *sister*. I hold no high rank at Amesbury,"
Beatrice said absently, still scrutinizing her niece.

"You are the temporary head of this priory now," Eleanor
replied, nodding approval of Anne's courteous use of title.

"Only because our sub-prioress died just before Prioress Ida
was obliged to travel abroad for some weeks on priory business."
The novice mistress flicked her hand, as if the responsibility
had landed on her like a pesky fly, and continued the study of
her niece.

Eleanor shifted uneasily. Under Sister Beatrice's careful
examination, she felt like a little girl again, one who could hide
nothing from this aunt. Of course, she had felt as weak as a babe

after her illness and needed her aunt's strength and comfort. Why else had she returned to Amesbury Priory if not to be pampered like a child, regain her woman's strength, and seek advice on a sin that deeply troubled her?

"Prioress Ida will name a successor when she returns," Beatrice was saying to Anne.

"Might you not…" Anne's gesture suggested an advancement in position.

"Never. I was quite clear that I would only take on these duties because there was no other reasonable choice. When our leader returns, someone else must be named sub-prioress, and I shall remain novice mistress, a position I have held for more years that our prioress has stood upright upon this earth." Beatrice's thin lips twitched with amusement at some private thought.

Her aunt's words suggested an admirable monastic humility, but whatever she willed had the force of a king's edict. Perhaps more so, Eleanor thought, now that the current occupant of the throne was rumored to be dying. In any case, her aunt had not grown meeker since Eleanor had left for Tyndal. For all she knew, Sister Beatrice had arranged for the election of the current prioress to head Amesbury after the death of Prioress Joan. That would not surprise her at all.

"Enough said on temporal matters." Beatrice caressed her niece's cheek. "Sister Anne and I have decided that your diet should not only include this broth to restore your humors to their accustomed balance but also a tonic. Your sub-infirmarian has mixed a most interesting one with lichens…"

The sound of running feet interrupted the conversation. As the three women looked toward the Chapter House, they saw the face of a very young novice appear at the doorway.

The girl glanced around in evident distress. When she saw the threesome, her eyes grew round with relief. "Sister Beatrice!" she shouted, raised the hem of her woolen robe up around her knobby knees, and bounded toward the novice mistress.

Just before the girl skidded to a halt in front of her, Beatrice straightened herself into a model of proper sternness. "Soft!"

she said. "You are no longer in a castle filled with warriors and hounds. This is a priory, dedicated to God, a God that loves hushed speech…"

The girl's manner instantly grew solemn as befitted the gravity of a messenger. "I ask forgiveness, Sister, but Brother Porter is very upset. He said I must beg you come to the gates with due haste." The child stopped, gulping air as if she had been holding her breath along with the message from the moment she had been sent to find the acting prioress.

Beatrice laid a calming hand on the girl's shoulder. "Slowly, now. Tell me what has happened."

"The ghost! Last night he saw it!"

"Brother Porter?"

"Nay! Wulfstan has come!"

Astonished, Eleanor stared at her aunt. "Ghost?"

"Satan, it seems, has given our founder leave to trouble us." Beatrice hid her hands in the sleeves of her robe. "Queen Elfrida's spirit has returned from Purgatory."

Chapter Two

Brother Thomas longed to weep, but his eyes remained dry. They stung as if he had rubbed them with salt. Had he no tears left, he asked himself, or had he become like the woman known only as *Lot's wife*?

He had always assumed God had turned that insubordinate creature into a pillar of salt for defying Him. Now he wondered. Might He have forbidden Lot's family to look back on the annihilation of their city out of mercy, knowing that mortals could not survive the grief such slaughter of loved ones would bring? If that was the truth of the tale, Lot's wife had not turned to salt for her sin of disobedience. Instead, the cause was her infinite tears of unbearable sorrow.

As he now mourned his own bitter loss in utter silence and with no hope of comfort, Thomas was beginning to understand what this unnamed woman might have suffered. "Must it ever be so?" he whispered as he seated himself, cross-legged on the ground. Pounding his fist into the forgiving earth, he pressed the back of his head into the rough bark of a tree and shut his aching eyes.

ᏬᎷᎣ ᏬᎷᎣ ᏬᎷᎣ

He had not wanted to come to Amesbury Priory and had fought against doing so, but his black-clad spy master refused to yield or compromise.

"I cannot go to Amesbury!" Thomas had cried out, still gasping from the other news the man had brought.

If the priest had had lips, he might have smiled. "A change of scenery will do you good," he said, sipping wine from a beautiful goblet that had once been used by a less than saintly Tyndal monk whose current residence was probably Hell.

Despite that small, gold cross attached to a silken cord around the man's neck, Thomas wondered if the priest was one of Satan's own. Surely he needed something larger to remind him that he was supposed to serve a Lord who exemplified compassion.

"First you tell me that my father is dead, and then you send me off to hunt manuscript thieves. Will you not leave me alone so I might grieve a while?"

The man in black shrugged. "Why such grief? Although your father might have been most generous to you, a bantling seeded in a serving wench, your choice of bedmate surely killed his little fondness. You are a sodomite, a sin much akin to murder in the opinion of some. Surely I need not remind you of that? I am kind to set a task for you, my son. Sorrow without distraction becomes an indulgence that festers into sin." He let his words sink in as he swirled the wine in his goblet, then sniffed at it. "Your prioress has an exceptional wine merchant."

"And what sick brother am I to visit this time?" Thomas spat. "If you continue to send me on these errands, even the Devil himself will find it hard to devise enough plagues to afflict my mythical family. Or," he lashed out, "shall I tell Prioress Eleanor that my father has died at Berkhamsted..." He pointed to a hypothetical location on the table. "...which is why I must go to Amesbury?" He banged his fist on another location far to the west of the first. "Do you know that her aunt is novice mistress in that priory?"

The man in black said nothing, continuing instead to study the color of his wine.

"Wouldn't Sister Beatrice find it odd that a monk from Tyndal had arrived and was showing much interest in the Amesbury Psalter when Prioress Eleanor did not even know he was there?

Might I suggest that one of your other underlings be the wiser choice to catch the thief who wants this precious item? How do you even know...?"

"We received warning." The man in black savored the last of his wine, then stared into the empty goblet with evident regret. When at last he looked up, he blinked, and his expression slowly developed into mild surprise. "Did I not tell you? Your prioress will be traveling with you," he said. "It is all arranged."

ᎧᎧᏦᎧ ᎧᎧᏦᎧ ᎧᎧᏦᎧ

The raucous cawing of a large crow dragged Thomas out of his miserable reflections, and he glanced up to see the cause of such avian rage. What he witnessed brought him to his feet in horror.

Lying flat on the severely pitched roof of the priory library and scriptorium, a man clung by his fingers to some invisible groove in the slate covering. The great black bird swooped at him, circled, and flew once more at the man's head.

"Help!" Thomas shouted, but there was no one near to heed his cry. He ran to the wall, searching the ground with frantic haste for some fallen ladder.

Above him, he heard a scrabbling sound and next a voice: "Thank you, Brother! You scared the fiendish fowl away. I am safe enough and most grateful to you."

Thomas looked up.

The young man, now standing with both feet firmly planted on the narrow scaffolding, was lean, muscular, and dressed only in his braes. Although his naked chest was still heaving from the exertion and his long brown hair was dark with sweat, the fellow was grinning.

Despite his pounding heart, Thomas returned the man's infectious smile. "A miracle!" he shouted back.

"One peril of my occupation, Brother, but one to which I have become accustomed. King Henry may have given the priory ten cartloads of lead, but this roof has too steep a pitch for that and the slate was badly installed. Nails have rotted.

Leaks occur. There are manuscripts within that could be damaged. I do my best to keep that from happening." He put his hands on his hips and gestured with his head in the direction of a nearby tree. "The crow has a nest there. I had come too near her young. When she flew at me, I lost my footing." He bent backward and fell. The scaffolding groaned, and the wooden walkway bent alarmingly.

Thomas cried out, instinctively raising his arms as if he might truly and safely catch a man falling from such a height.

The roofer jumped up, laughing like a boy caught in an innocent lark. "That slip was but a jest. The monks lead such dull lives. I do them some service with a harmless scare from time to time. Something must be done to keep their humors from growing too sluggish."

"I fear that *kindness* was lost on me, friend, for I am not from Amesbury."

"I did not think I had recognized you. I beg pardon, Brother...?"

"Thomas of Tyndal. And you?"

"Sayer." As a gust of wind shook the scaffolding, the man kept his balance like a sailor on a ship. "Were you to slip over these walls for a bit of joy in the town, as some of the religious in this priory have been wont to do, you would hear me called anything from a fellow most fond of japes to an irresponsible and heartless knave. You may believe most of that but never that I am heartless." He slowly tightened his braes around the waist. "And might you be a monk who finds he prays more diligently after refreshing his sense of sin?"

A feeling, akin to that of a virgin boy alone for the first time with a girl, inexplicably hit Thomas. A lump formed in his throat. He swallowed. "And if I am?" he asked as an idea forced the discomfort aside.

"I must warn you that the Saxon queen, who founded this priory as penance for her own misdeeds, has returned to torment the monks here. Some say that the wicked ways of the religious have angered her, and she roams the path from priory to village on many a night, bringing the fear of Hell to all she meets." He shrugged. "Now the monks stay inside and pray for her earlier release to Heaven as they were paid to do." Sayer's grin destroyed any righteous meaning to his speech.

Either this Sayer was only repeating gossip or else he was telling him that he knew how to provide men, weary of hot dreams, with soft flesh for pleasuring. Might he also know something about men who lusted after precious manuscripts as well? "Yet she might not trouble strangers to the priory for these would not be beholden to her." Thomas wondered what the man would say.

"You may be correct, Brother, for her quarrel should only be with those who promised to stay on their knees praying for the peace of her soul. If that is the case, a stranger could seek me out at the inn without fear of her wrath. I can be helpful—and discreet."

"Especially if graced with a flash of the king's face?"

"I love King Henry, Brother. He looks most noble on silver."

"Such loyalty is no sin," Thomas replied and smiled back in spite of himself. If Sayer provided whores for monks, he might well know others who worked outside the law. Thomas groaned in silence. Such a man would be useful if he could ever determine how to get outside the walls without provoking either suspicion or gossip that might get back to the ears of Prioress Eleanor. Coin would also be needed. Once again he cursed his spy master. The man was a fool to think a monk in the company of his prioress was suited to this sort of investigation.

"In the meantime, do not worry about me, Thomas of Tyndal. The fog might make this surface slippery, but God must love those who repair priory roofing. I have yet to fall to my death." Sayer tossed his head, his hair falling back to frame his beardless face.

Somewhere beyond the priory walls, a man shouted, his words lost in the breeze.

The sound made Thomas blink, and he realized he had been staring at Sayer. A handsome fellow, one that would have little trouble finding women to bed, he thought, then felt his face grow hot with embarrassment. He should not make such an assumption. After all, the roofer might well have a wife.

He quickly raised his hand to bless the man in farewell. As he walked away, his neck began to prickle as if someone was watching him. He spun around and looked up at the roof.

Sayer was carefully removing a piece of slate.

Chapter Three

Although the morning had promised warmth, the day remained quite chill. Accompanied by her aunt and Sister Anne, Eleanor retreated to the lodgings belonging to the prioress of Amesbury. There they found a lively fire. A servant quickly brought both wine and cheese for refreshment and just as promptly departed to allow the women private conversation.

As they all rubbed their hands near the fire, Eleanor looked around at her temporary residence, rooms she had rarely seen when she was a young novice and nun. When she had been brought to these chambers some days ago, Eleanor had commented with due courtesy on how comfortably appointed the quarters were. In this she had spoken the truth, for her own at the East Anglian priory were quite poor in comparison.

Three of the stone walls in this public room were softened with well-crafted and colorful hangings, whereas Eleanor had but one near her bed at Tyndal. Above the door here hung a smaller embroidered cloth which depicted Adam and Eve leaving Eden, a work that must have given Prioress Ida pause for thought each time she left the tranquility of her quarters for the chaos of the world without.

Against the other two walls, full-length tapestries kept any cold at bay. One illustrated the falling walls of Jericho, beside which stood a blond Joshua bearing a shield with three lions. Eleanor wondered if this had been a gift from King Henry or his queen in honor of their son, Edward, who was on crusade. The other showed a matronly Virgin holding the infant Jesus; the mother's face vaguely resembled that of the prioress in charge during Eleanor's youth.

Close to the fourth wall stood an altar and an elaborately carved prie-dieu, the wood of which glowed with a reddish cast in the firelight.

A comfortable enough room, Eleanor thought, yet she had discovered one lack. The Amesbury Psalter was missing, an elegant, illuminated work that had always been used by the prioress for her own prayers. Or so she remembered.

She turned to her aunt. "Does the priory still possess the Psalter done in Salisbury? You sometimes used it to teach us to read."

"Rarely, child, rarely." Beatrice shook her head. "Prioress Joan agreed that I might do so only as a reward for those most diligent in their work." For a moment, she fell silent as if lost in a past memory, then she sipped her wine. "It would never have left this room, but one corner is torn. Prioress Ida sent it to the library and scriptorium where a monk more talented than any of our own will come to do the needed repair."

"I must take you there to see it," Eleanor said to Anne.

"An excellent walk for us both on a warmer day," the sub-infirmarian replied as she rose and offered a plate of cheese to the other two women.

Eleanor shook her head in refusal and turned to Sister Beatrice. The novice mistress was examining the contents of her mazer, but her expression suggested that the quality of the wine was not her concern. Had the news brought to her by the man at the gate been so troubling? The prioress settled into her chair, grateful for the support of the firm wood. Her back ached.

"Did you learn something distressing from the laborer?" Eleanor asked.

"I did not expect to hear that Wulfstan, of all people, would see a ghost coming out of the reeds by the river." Beatrice raised her hand in a gesture of disgust. "Had it been almost anyone else, I would have assumed that the vision was a wisp of fog that wound around a winter-killed bush or even a large bird. We have a crow nesting in a tree near the library. He may have seen it flying out of the fog near the river, but I am troubled indeed. Wulfstan is a steady fellow, not given to imaginings."

"You said that he was not the first to see such a vision?"

With evident dismay, Beatrice shook her head. "All it takes is for one person to see something that frightens, something inexplicable, and rumors of ghosts multiply like mice." She put down the wine and rested her chin against her folded hands. "Although I thought Wulfstan a more sensible man, he has apparently been infected with the same affliction shared by others who work on our lands. Even some of our own monks have run to us of late, claiming the priory itself is haunted."

"When did this begin?" Eleanor asked.

Beatrice rubbed her hands together, reached again for her cup, and listened to the snapping flames before answering. "The sightings started some time before you arrived. At first, they were mere annoyances, but now they occur almost every night or early morning. Many say that some spirit from Hell has a quarrel with our priory. I fear that we must do something soon to dispel these ideas. The villagers are becoming fearful and our own monastics…" She smiled. "Ah, well! At least some of our monks have become more ardent in their prayers out of dread of this ghost. Perhaps I should bless the shade!"

"Has the spirit injured anyone?" Anne asked, politely ignoring the suggestion that any Amesbury monk might be less than devout.

"Some have suffered scrapes and bruises in their rush to run away." Beatrice sipped her wine and set the cup down on the table.

"You said in the cloister that the creature had taken the shape of the priory's founder?" Eleanor winced as her cramps returned.

"Most of the witnesses maintain that our ghost is that of Queen Elfrida, wife to King Edgar. Others, fewer in number but vocal enough, claim it resembles a local woman who drowned herself in the Avon and was buried in unsanctified ground. Mistress Eda was her name."

"What cause has either spirit to trouble this priory?" Anne asked.

"According to legend, Sister, Amesbury was founded by Queen Elfrida in atonement for her part in the murder of her stepson, Edward the Martyr. For over two hundred years, our monastics have prayed that her soul might have ease in Purgatory and ascend quickly to Heaven, but some villagers believe we have become so sinful ourselves of late that her ghost has grown angry and returned to rebuke us."

"Sinned? How?" Eleanor asked. "Are we not all sinners?"

"Our religious community has had some weak-fleshed members, although no more than many others. As a double house, and one run by women at that, we are especially prone to these rumors. Most in the village know us too well to accuse us of habitually wanton behavior, but I will not hide the truth here. The inn did attract some of our lay brothers and the occasional monk."

"Surely Prioress Ida has dealt with this problem?" Eleanor replied.

"She learned from Brother Jerome about a break in the wall on the monks' side of the grounds and promptly had it repaired before she left. I have since discussed the matter with our prior, and he believes that the repair has solved the problem. Where the mended wall might have failed to ensure chastity, the tales of this wandering spirit have succeeded. This, I have confirmed with a trustworthy source in the village itself. The inn has seen no tonsure for some time."

"Thus the spirit of your founder should be satisfied and leave you in peace," Anne said.

"Not yet, for Wulfstan claims he saw her last night." The novice mistress' tone conveyed her vexation.

"Might the thing be the wraith of the woman damned for self-murder?" Anne glanced briefly at her prioress, who was leaning forward, quite attentive to the conversation. "What quarrel had she with the priory?"

"Other than the burial, Mistress Eda had none. Before her death, she suffered from a growth in her womb. The disease resisted prayer and the aid of mortal medicine, both of which we gave her. One day her husband found her missing, and her body was soon discovered floating in the Avon."

"And who adjudged the death self-murder?" Eleanor asked, glancing at the food on the table.

Anne reached over and passed her some cheese.

"The crowner did, based on evidence given by several villagers."

"Yet someone believes the decision was in error or else the rumor would not be rife that Mistress Eda is the ghost." Eleanor smiled at Anne in thanks and took a piece.

"Her childhood friend, Mistress Jhone, is the source of that, and the widower agrees with her. Few others concur." Beatrice watched her niece eat one bite of cheese and then another.

"Mistress Jhone and the bereaved husband think...?"

"...that Mistress Eda slipped, but was so weakened by her illness that she was unable to pull herself from the water."

"Why did the crowner's verdict find otherwise?" Anne said, casually placing the plate of food closer to her prioress' elbow.

"Everyone here knew that Mistress Eda hated the river and would never have walked there willingly. When she was young, she had taken her younger brother down to the Avon but fell asleep in the sun. The boy decided to go swimming and drowned. She never forgave herself," Beatrice replied. "After she grew ill, all knew her pain. When her body was found, they concluded that she had given up all hope and turned against God in her suffering. Satan, they said, must have seen his chance to gain her soul and lured her to the river in the guise of her brother."

Eleanor now tore off a small bit of bread and nibbled at it thoughtfully.

"All these rumors and tales are nonsense." Beatrice slammed her fist down on the table. "There is no ghost. No matter what is claimed, imagined, or believed, Saint Augustine taught us that there is no communication between the world of the living and that of the dead."

"Spirits seen are more likely Satan's imps dressed up as mortals to fool us than truly tortured souls of the dead," Eleanor finished. "Although you taught me to seek out mortals more than imps when evil has been done."

"And I have not changed my mind. Mortal and flawed as we are, we see what we expect to see and in the guise we most fear. In using our frailties against us, Satan is a most clever creature." Beatrice's anger gave way to a merrier laugh. "Nor have I forgotten what I taught you, dearest one! I am not yet so aged that my memory has begun to drift into that tranquil land many find before death."

"Were I even to suggest such a thing, my father would come roaring to your defense all the way from Wales!"

"He and I have always butted heads like goats, but that is how we show our love for each other. As for our haunting, I do suspect the ghost is made less of spirit than flesh, but, if the acts were intended as a jest, the game has turned cruel. Those who work hard in the priory fields now fear to take the shorter path to the village along the river and return home even wearier. Honest men should not be made to suffer so."

"Then you must dispel these rumors and the growing fear." Eleanor smiled at her aunt with fond expectation.

The novice mistress looked heavenward and gave an immense sigh. "I would, but I have no time to devote to this pagan nonsense. With Prioress Ida gone, I must continue with my old duties, plus hers, and a few other tasks as well. The spring planting season is full upon us…"

Eleanor blinked. "Might the prior take this matter in hand?"

"He could, if he were not such a fool and inclined to believe in ghosts himself." Beatrice folded her hands and placed them in her lap. Still gazing at the ceiling, her features slowly formed into what one might call a study in perplexity.

Anne and Eleanor looked at each other in silence. The sub-infirmarian raised one questioning eyebrow at her friend.

"If you will allow it, Aunt, I might look into this matter for you," Eleanor said, her voice showing an enthusiasm that had been much lacking of late.

The novice mistress waved one hand in a dismissive gesture. "You are too weak."

Eleanor's face turned scarlet. "I am *not...*"

Anne laid a hand on her friend's sleeve. "Might I make a suggestion? You could conserve your strength but still help."

The aunt continued to look upward as if in deep thought, then replied with a measured hesitation. "How so, Sister?"

"Accompanying us was Brother Thomas, a brave and clever man who has been of great service to your family as well as Tyndal in matters of justice. Might Prioress Eleanor set him to the task of finding the source of these apparitions?"

Eleanor paled. "I would rather not..."

"Ah!" Beatrice brightened. "A most original idea! My noble brother was uncharacteristically fulsome in his praise of your monk as I recall." Her lips twitched and her eyebrows rose. "I, too, found your Brother Thomas quite memorable." The novice mistress' expression could only be described as appreciative. "A man with hair the color of Satan's own fire and a body so muscular that Sir Lancelot would be jealous? I would guess he might be bored with no better company than our aging and placid monks on the other side of the priory. Perchance he would welcome a bit of innocent adventure outside the walls, searching for a jester who must have strayed from court?" She clapped her hands with a merry vigor. "Set him to the task, child, and report to me on his success. Or failure. I do think you could help me so much in this matter without exhausting yourself. Meanwhile, I can see to the planting of our herb garden..." Her voice trailed off as she gazed with affectionate delight at her niece.

Eleanor bowed her head. Although the gesture spoke of respect to her aunt, it succeeded in hiding her troubled expression.

"It is a task that should be started soon," the novice mistress declared, rising with evident stiffness from the table. "Now, I fear, I must go to our infirmarian for something to give me some ease. I am an old woman whose joints ache more than I would wish, and I need something to help me sleep."

"It shall be done." Eleanor rose as well, kissed her aunt, and watched in silence as she limped away.

Suddenly, Anne leapt up and turned to Eleanor. "I might have a remedy for your aunt..."

"Go to her then." Eleanor gestured toward the disappearing nun. "Quickly!"

"Sister," Anne called out, running after the elder nun. "We have found something at Tyndal that has proven successful..."

When the two tall nuns were far enough from Eleanor to speak without being overheard, Sister Anne asked, "Do you think she is strong enough to handle this matter?"

Beatrice nodded. "My niece has ever been one to gain strength from a challenge. Did you not see pink return to her cheeks and a sparkle to her eyes? She even ate more than has been her wont. This task may be just the medicine she needs, and it is an easy enough one with your Brother Thomas doing the work of investigating. If I had thought otherwise, I would not have whined so about my trifling duties and aged joints. Now return before she suspects we are conspiring!"

But when Anne reentered the room and Eleanor greeted her with one eyebrow arched, the sub-infirmarian of Tyndal knew full well that she and the novice mistress had utterly failed to deceive.

Chapter Four

With that supple grace common to youth, sixteen-year-old Alys spun on the heel of her soft leather shoe and marched precisely five steps away from her mother. "I cannot accept this, and I shall not." Despite her resolute tone, her eyes were moist when she turned to face the woman she loved but longed to disobey.

The tumult in the daughter's heart was lost on her mother. Mistress Jhone, widow of a local woolmonger, was glowering instead at a round young man standing nearby.

Bernard, a maker of gloves, shifted uneasily and lowered his very pink face.

Turning her glare from him, Jhone now cast the full force of her disapproval upon her daughter. "A child's duty is to obey her parent: *honor thy father and thy mother.* I did not create that law. It comes from God Himself!" Although the mother's face was wan, her robe of rough brown russet suggested that her widowhood was recent and a disobedient daughter was not the sole reason for her pallor.

The young man stepped closer to the wall, glanced upward, and squeezed his eyes shut as if in rapt concentration. Although the glover could have been praying for protection against possible flying objects, he might have been thanking God as well, for the two women seemed to have quickly forgotten his presence.

"A duty in which you must be quite conversant, Mother," replied Alys. Her voice projected a determined gentleness, but the clenched fist she pressed to her breast hinted that her meaning was less than docile. "Sadly my grandparents died before my birth, but I must assume, from your certainty in this, that you did marry as your parents demanded." She breathed in deeply as if taking in courage, then asked: "Can you claim to have been happy in your obedience?"

Bernard nervously cleared his throat. If he meant to remind them that another was in the room, someone who should not hear this quarrel, his effort was wasted.

"You choose to remember your father only when he was…" Jhone closed her eyes and sucked in her lips if willing some unwelcome thought away. "Your father may have been ill-tempered from time to time." Her voice quivered. "The strain of running a successful business is hard on a man." This, she spoke with firmness.

Alys gave her a look that was both disbelieving and disdainful.

"Yet he was a worthy man, provided well for us, and loved you as much as I, even though you have now willfully decided to forget that." The mother's mouth trembled with suppressed emotion, and she absently brushed one thin hand over her abdomen. "Cruel daughter that you are, I am still grateful that God allowed at least one of the children your father gave me to live."

With sympathetic courtesy Bernard nodded, a gesture that the elder woman noted and acknowledged with a distracted smile.

Alys was also now gazing on the glover, but her look was not disinterested. Instead, it had a particular warmth to it, the meaning of which did not much please Jhone.

The widow loudly cleared her throat.

"Well and good, Mother, if that is what you believe," the daughter said, tearing her eyes away from the young glover with evident regret. "A child does owe obedience to her parent, but surely our obligation to God ranks higher? If you will not allow me to marry as my heart wishes, please permit me to join this Order of Fontevraud. Although I am sure Master Herbert is a most honorable man, I regretfully find marriage with him somewhat less than agreeable. I would rather leave the world and spend my life praying for your soul—and that of my father." The girl folded her arms. A soldier could not have had a straighter back.

"Surely there is a third way…" The young man reached out as if pleading for at least one of the women to listen.

Alys waved at him to remain silent. "I would not be the first in the family to ask this, Mother. You have told me that your parents were willing to let your elder sister take holy vows instead of entering a marriage she did not want." Certain that she had presented an unassailable argument, she smiled with satisfaction.

Jhone's eyes widened with horror. "Need I remind you, however, that my sister never took those vows but instead wed Wulfstan, a man of whom they most heartily disapproved? Had they been stricter, she would have vowed herself to a successful merchant and led a comfortable life instead of what she has suffered!" Her eyes glazed briefly, and she spoke the next words with a sweet but pleading tone. "Is it so wrong to want you settled into a prosperous marriage? May I not look forward to grandchildren? These wishes are not sins."

"I would agree, but only if I become Bernard's wife." Alys' face flushed as she looked back at her beloved whose face quickly matched her rosy color. "Why do you object to our marriage? We adore each other so."

Jhone's pale face turned a rough and angry red. "This is a matter for private discussion!" she growled, staring at the glover as if he had just walked in on this conversation unbidden.

Master Bernard bowed with nervous grace. "I will take my leave most willingly…"

"Nay, you shall not!" Alys barked, then beamed at him with love. She turned to her mother. "I can think of no reason why he and I should not marry. Since he has asked most courteously for my hand, he has the right to hear from you in plain speech why his suit is unacceptable and Master Herbert's so persuasive."

"Later might be best. I can return when..." Bernard edged toward the door.

Jhone's back stiffened. Although her lips twisted into a chill smile, disdain burned hot in her dark-rimmed eyes. "My disobedient daughter may have chosen to forget that it was her father's last wish that she marry Master Herbert, but I have not. Of course I must follow my dead husband's direction. Surely you can understand my obligation as a proper wife in this matter, Master Bernard?"

The glover nodded quickly, then glanced at Alys with silent apology.

She turned her head away as if he had just denounced her.

"Were my husband still alive, Master Glover, he might have explained that your youth and failure to show great success in your own trade were strong arguments against your suit. My dead husband's wool venture was profitable, and my daughter's husband must not only assume this undertaking but build on it. Neither you nor Master Herbert is knowledgeable about wool. That is true, but my husband left a trusted man to help run the business until a sound tradesman can take over the management of it and learn what is needed. This requires a man who has proven he knows how to manage a profitable enterprise. You clearly lack this experience. Master Herbert, on the other hand, has proven his skills in his vintner trade."

"So say you! Bernard is not poor. He has just begun in the business his father left him, but you can see how prosperous he looks." Alys gestured at her plump beloved as if arguing the benefits of buying a fat sheep. As her eyes focused on the man himself, her expression softened with love. "Modest in dress, but..." She blushed.

"This boy makes *gloves*!" Jhone shouted with evident exasperation. "Master Herbert is a wine merchant with vineyards in Gascony. He has gained respect amongst merchants beyond our shores and could improve on what your father began with the contacts he has made." She waved at the young man as if he were so insubstantial that her gesture would make him disappear.

"What is wrong with gloves?" Alys protested.

"May I explain…" Bernard began.

"Fa!" Jhone spat, doggedly pursuing her argument with this daughter who remained so illogically enamored of something other than a secure living. "A glover and his family will starve the first time crops turn black from drought and no one can buy such pretty trifles. Wine and wool are things we all must have. Not only does Master Herbert have the more secure business and better connections, he is of more mature years." She put her hands on her hips. "Must I remind you that he provided well for the wants and fancies of a prior wife?"

"We can all drink beer and wear homespun cloth if bad times come." The girl's voice dripped with contempt. "I would rather a man whose hands are as soft as his gloves than one with horny, old paws. Marry him yourself, mother, if you like him all that well!"

Jhone leapt forward and slapped her daughter, then stared with horror at the red mark her fingers had left on her only child's cheek.

Bernard put his hand behind him against the wall and moved toward the door. Quickly he looked over his shoulder. The door was shut. He closed his eyes.

Tears streamed out of Alys' eyes, and she fell to her knees in front of her mother. "I beg your forgiveness! Can we not make peace in this matter? I want to be your most dutiful daughter, but I yearn just as much to become Bernard's wife."

Jhone clutched her hands tightly under her breasts, a gesture that might have suggested grace and dignity if the knuckles on her fingers had not been quite so white. "You must obey me, child."

Alys shook her head as she rose to her feet.

The mother now turned a beseeching gaze on the young man. "And you, Master Bernard? Surely you understand my obligation in this matter. Will you not show charity and support this poor widow by withdrawing your plea? I have no quarrel with you other than this unwise suit."

His eyes shifted away from hers.

"If you hesitate to do this," she continued softly, "I beg that you ask yourself if you would not make the same decision as I must for a much beloved daughter."

"We would not demand such a terrible sacrifice from any child of ours!" Alys cried out before Bernard could reply.

Jhone stamped her foot in outrage. "You shall marry Master Herbert!"

"Before you drag me to his bed, I will enter Amesbury Priory as a novice!" Alys pounded her fist on a nearby chair.

As the two women glared at each other with equal obstinacy, the now forgotten Bernard, maker of soft gloves, leaned against the hard wall and silently prayed for peace.

Chapter Five

Wulfstan was an angry man. Had he been less so, he might have felt pain as he stomped along the path to the river, jolting his aging joints as his feet pounded the earth with the force of his just resentment.

"I did see the ghost," he muttered. When he reported this earlier in the day, Sister Beatrice should have listened with both courtesy and respect. Had he not proven to her over the years that he was a reliable man? Instead, her frowning silence had proclaimed her utter disbelief.

Wulfstan snorted. How dare the nun so casually dismiss what he had seen? He was no woman, prone to irrational fantasies and likely to faint if a shadow took on some writhing shape. He had, most certainly he had, seen the ghost.

He shivered. The evening was chill. Now he began to feel the pain in his knees and shins as well. "Fa! This is the priory's fault," he growled, and spat on the damp earth.

Maybe that difficult wife of his would at least have a hot stew ready when he got home. Last night, after the fright the ghost had given him, as it would any mortal man, he had sought ease from her body; but his wife had pushed him off, whining that her courses had come and she would have none of his urges for at least six days.

Or so she claimed. Wulfstan shook his head, his mouth imitating a peevish look. "I will not be humiliated by bearing a red-haired child so the village can mock us for sinful intercourse," he muttered in high-pitched imitation of his reluctant spouse.

Grumbling to himself, he remembered when she could not have enough of his *urges*, but after the birth of their sixth, she had found far too many excuses to deny him his rights as husband. Tonight he should demand his marriage debt. If he recalled correctly, and he was sure he did, her courses had come quite recently. She must have been lying last night. Women did that, or so his father had told him.

He shivered again but trudged on. From the sound of the Avon, he had reached the part of the path that passed close to the river bank. As he looked up, he could see a few specks of light from Amesbury Priory. Aye, he was getting closer to home. There had better be a warm hearth waiting for him, Wulfstan thought sullenly, or else he would administer a beating to someone for cert. He rubbed a hand under his dripping nose.

With sudden apprehension, he saw how near he was to the place he had seen the ghost. Quietly, he cursed the stubborn pride that had sent him back along this path where the spirit had appeared to him. Last night the phantom may have turned away from him, disappearing into the mist and rushes without causing him harm, but the memory of her black form made him uneasy. Perchance the first sighting had been but a warning. The second time, might she not carry him off to Hell?

Wulfstan quickened his step.

Without a doubt, monks had warm enough hearths, he said to himself, attempting with small success to turn his thoughts away from specters. Not much better than women, they were, groveling on their knees and weeping over their sins to God while others sweated on the land so they could eat. Yet that was not enough for some! He knew about those who had slipped through the hole in the wall to warm their little cocks in the dark chambers of whores. "No wonder Queen Elfrida has returned from Purgatory," he muttered.

He shook his head with indignation. "So why should her spirit trouble me?" he growled, his breath gray against the growing dark. He, Wulfstan, had done her no harm. She should haunt the monks that had lengthened her time in Purgatory when they chose lust over prayer.

The hairs on the back of his neck rose. He looked around. Nay, it was not yet dark enough for ghosts to be fluttering about, troubling the likes of the honest living. Nevertheless, he could not stop shaking, and his temper began to cool in the darkening light.

Maybe he had no wish to swyve that wife of his tonight after all, he thought. He did not want any red-haired child either, and she had been a good woman to him in so many ways over the years. Briefly he smiled. Aye, she always made sure one of the children put wood on for a fire, and she would have a hot meal waiting for him. And, if he mentioned the ache he had, she would even rub his shoulders with that balm…

A movement on his left caught his eye.

He stopped.

A tall, black figure stood by the priory wall.

Monks! Even with the wall repaired, this one had discovered a way to get through. He cursed. Once more, the inn would gain from the ale the man drank to dull his guilt before he found soft breasts to fondle.

The figure remained motionless, watching him.

Wulfstan glared.

The dark and hooded shape glided toward him.

"Off to play at thrusting like a gelded goat," Wulfstan said in a low growl, then raised his voice. "Others might stay silent, but I shall go to Sister Beatrice about this!"

The figure halted in front of him.

Wulfstan stepped back. "What were *you* doing…?"

The first burst of pain was unbearable, but Death came with compassionate speed.

Chapter Six

The cresset lamps in the prioress' chambers flickered unevenly and cast moving shadows on the faces of the four monastics.

Prioress Eleanor was seated. The others remained standing.

"I'm told you have a talent for clever investigations, Brother," Sister Beatrice said. Soft though her words may have been to the ear, her piercing gaze sharpened their meaning.

Thomas lowered his eyes, but this had nothing to do with modesty. The novice mistress reminded him of the cook who had raised him, a woman who could read everything in a boy's soul, including those secrets left unformed by word or image. The man began to sweat.

The silence lasted a heartbeat too long. Mercifully, his prioress broke it. "Brother Thomas is humble," she said, her voice tender as the May air. "I shall respect that virtue and confirm myself what you have heard. Not only has his pursuit of justice been of great value to my priory, but it saved our family's honor..." She began to cough, bending forward with the force of it.

How thin she is, Thomas thought, watching Eleanor gasp for breath. As he saw the quick glances now passing between sub-infirmarian and novice mistress, the monk knew they shared his concern that this once energetic young woman was still so wan and frail.

When the prioress' fever had spiked to dangerous heights just after Twelfth Night, Sister Anne had remained by her bedside, sending him orders for herbs and potions. Dark-eyed with worry and ashen with fatigue herself, Anne confided her worst fears when he delivered the medicines to the nuns' cloister door. Then Eleanor's fever broke at last, and Tyndal's religious offered grateful prayers that their respected leader had spurned Death's skeletal hand.

Or had she but delayed her acceptance?

Although he had realized from the day he arrived at Tyndal that he owed Prioress Eleanor a liegeman's loyalty, he was surprised to discover that his sense of duty had deepened with warm affection. She had always treated him with kindness, and, after he had been forced to tell her something of his past before her illness, she had shown him sensitive compassion. Aye, he thought, he very much wanted this woman to live.

Eleanor straightened. A worrisome flush painted her cheeks, but Thomas saw a sparkle in her eyes he had not seen since last autumn and a look not unlike that gleam in a huntsman's eye when he saw a fine boar he wished to kill for dinner.

"My lady is most generous," he said, bowing. Since he had no reason to believe her look was directed at him, he welcomed this sign of returning vigor with joy. Thomas found his prioress' iron will and determination most daunting, but he admired it as well. For once he was not embarrassed by the tremor in his voice. Relief was the cause.

Sister Beatrice tilted her head to one side, her lips easing into a reflective smile. "My niece would not have praised your actions out of a magnanimous spirit, nor would my beloved brother of Wynethorpe. He liked you, he said. That remark, from a man more likely to bark reproach than sing approval, has greater value than the gift of a furred robe from King Henry."

"I am honored," he replied and once again bowed his head, but this act of humility masked amusement. The convent nun and her warrior brother did share a fondness for candid speech.

Beatrice nodded approval. "Courtesy has now been given its due, I believe. We have a problem to solve." She gestured at the monk. "Do you believe in ghosts?"

Thomas blinked. "Ghosts?"

"Aye." The corners of the novice mistress' thin lips twitched upward.

"Forgive my hesitancy, but I am amazed. This is the second time today I have heard such spirits mentioned. Sayer, the roofer, warned me that one was troubling the priory, but I did not take his tale too seriously. He seemed a very merry fellow and quite fond of jokes."

"Indeed he is. Now I would hear what you know of the restless dead."

"Saint Augustine did not believe in them, nor do I think our Brother Aquinas would from what I have been told. Although there have been sightings of saints as well as demons in the guise of humans, there does seem to be general agreement, amongst the wise scholars of the Church, that the dead remain with their own. I bow to their superior knowledge."

"Such sweet phrasing is worthy of a bishopric, Brother." Beatrice raised an amused eyebrow. "Within that speech, I conclude that you do not personally believe in these spirits who some claim rise from their graves after dusk?"

In spite of himself, Thomas grinned in reply.

"Excellent. I concur. Yet others have declared that we have such a phantom nearby, insisting that they have seen it on several occasions. The sightings have become more frequent of late, and there is panic growing in the village as well as amongst our monastics."

"What form has this spirit taken, to whom has it appeared, and when?"

"A man who wastes no time." Beatrice clapped her hands with satisfaction. "I like that!"

Thomas stared at her for a brief moment. Nay, he was not back at Wynethorpe Castle, and he was not facing Baron Adam.

As if acknowledging his thoughts, the novice mistress shook her head. "Our nuns have not seen the creature at all. Some of the men, who work in the nearby priory lands and live in the village, have. Several lay brothers and monks as well. Although they say the spirit has no face, they think it wears a woman's robe.

The majority claim the shade is that of our alleged founder, Queen Elfrida. Based on such imprecise details, I might not conclude that King Edgar's long dead wife has come to us all the way from Wherwell Abbey, but many believe they have seen a crown on her head. The description of that has been both varied and vague."

"You told me others say the ghost is that of a local woman." Eleanor learned forward, resting her chin in her hand.

"Who has also been described as wearing a crown, but this one is made of fiery nails for her spirit comes from Hell," Beatrice replied. "In either case, the shade appears at twilight, when men are returning from work in our fields, or else very early in the morning, especially when the fog rises from the river. She walks along the road by the Avon, although some monks have claimed to have seen her within our walls on priory land."

"So said your roofer." Thomas glanced over at his prioress. "He seemed to think the ghost was the queen."

Beatrice closed her eyes in a brief attempt to hide her disdain for the whole debate. "The first sighting was before Prioress Ida left on her journey," she continued. "A worker saw a woman on the path and, noting her veil and plain dress, thought it odd that a nun would be walking alone outside the walls, especially at that hour. When she drew closer, he saw she had no face. Others have reported that she came from the river, her attire wet as if she had just emerged from the water."

"Which might explain why a few think she is the local woman."

"One reason certainly," Beatrice replied to Eleanor. "Opinions on that vary, but one man went to offer aid. When he saw she had no hands and nothing where a face should be, he ran away."

Thomas began to pace, then asked, "Why do some think the ghost of a local woman would haunt the area?"

"Mistress Eda was the wife of a vintner in the village. After she drowned in the Avon, the crowner and his jury determined that she had committed self-murder. We then buried her in unconsecrated ground. Despite his verdict, there are those who still believe she died by accident and has been wrongly accursed."

"I can understand why the villagers might conclude that the ghost is the vintner's wife, if her corpse was dishonored in burial, but why do so many think your founder has returned?"

"Our young rogue, Sayer, did not give you a clue?"

Thomas felt his face flush. "Aye, he did."

"Come, now, Brother! Surely you know there are those who come to a monastery with little longing for the life, and that others arrive with a vocation but must struggle with the flesh more than they imagined? Our priory has had our share of these and, like any villager who saw them at the inn, Sayer knows them well—as do those of us who are responsible for this priory's reputation."

"He did tell me as well that these monks had repented."

"And he is right. Our prioress made sure the break in our wall was repaired. Those monks who chose to lie between the legs of Eve's daughters instead of praying on their knees for the queen's spotted soul have been punished and now have renewed enthusiasm for the chaste life."

"That the creature continues to bother the priory argues in favor of those who think she is the vintner's wife," Eleanor suggested.

"Or else there was some delay receiving the news in Purgatory that Prioress Ida had destroyed the easy path to sin?" Anne did not betray, by either tone or expression, whether her words were said in jest.

"There is no ghost," Beatrice snapped, the V between her eyes darkening.

"The *alleged* spirit has committed no violence?" Thomas asked with careful emphasis.

Eleanor's brief smile expressed her approval of this speech.

"An older man fainted, but a companion soon found him. Our Brother Infirmarian treated him and he survived."

"Have most of these sightings occurred outside or within the priory walls?" he continued.

"Nearly all without."

"The king's justice..."

"Lest you think our local sheriff should be interested, I must lay waste to any hope. According to him, no harm has been committed; therefore, there is no crime. Even if some ill had befallen someone, he says that all ghosts fall under Church authority, not secular justice. Besides his evident laziness, he has not the intelligence of your own local crowner, as my niece has told me. I would not trust our fellow to know a ghost from a bed sheet."

Sister Anne chuckled.

"If the ghost prefers to walk outside the priory, I may be of little help in this matter, Sister. Since I am a monk…"

"That is easily remedied." Beatrice poured a measure of wine into a footed mazer and handed it to him. "We can let you out the gate. Monks do travel the roads, and a late arrival might find his way to the inn. You are not known in the village."

"Sayer might recognize me." Thomas hesitated before quickly adding, "We did have some conversation. I was walking nearby and had cause."

"And he does spend time at the inn. Nay, blush not, Brother. I know he provided both women and drink for our weaker brethren. Since you are a stranger to this priory, I would not be surprised if he tried to tempt you, for the rediscovered piety of those monks has surely cost him. Perchance he even cursed this *ghost* for that."

"If he sees me, I cannot play either a virtuous or a traveling monk. He will think I have come for sinful purposes. How then shall I…?"

"Let us hope he is not at the inn, but, if he is, I must trust you to be as clever and true to your vows as my niece assures me you are. There may be no ghost abroad, but there is something malign out there. Whether it is simply mischievous or truly evil, there must be an end to this matter."

Thomas shifted uncomfortably under her steady gaze, before nodding his concurrence. Although he was grateful that his prioress had given such strong witness to his virtue, he had caught something in the aunt's tone that suggested she was not quite so certain about him. Even though her precise words did not betray this, he felt he was being tested.

The assignment to find the truth behind a ghost would make his undertaking for the Church easier, and, with Sister Beatrice's permission to leave the priory, he would not have to sneak out or come up with some questionable disguise in order to find this unknown manuscript thief before the Amesbury Psalter disappeared. In order to assuage any doubt she might have, he must present his response carefully to avoid showing any eagerness to escape the walls, an enthusiasm that might be interpreted as worldly.

Thomas twisted his hands nervously. "I long to obey, as my vows demand, but do not wish to do anything that might bring dishonor to this priory. If you want me to go into the village, I must do so with the modesty expected in one of our vocation." He held his breath, awaiting confirmation of his hopes.

"That I do and with a bit of coin to buy ale or otherwise ease truth's birthing amongst those who might talk to you of local matters at the inn." Beatrice nodded sympathetically. "Ah, Brother, I know this is not an effortless thing I ask of you, but Satan is cunning and Man must use both prayer and God-given wits to defeat the evil he brings to the world. While our sheriff has chosen to visit a distant manor just now for a hunt," the novice mistress snorted, "innocents both within and outside our walls have grown fearful of walking abroad. We cannot allow this to continue, and we have only ourselves to stop it."

Thomas exhaled.

Eleanor sat back in her chair with evident fatigue. "If you see this strange and even unholy shade, Brother, try to note what you can but take care. If the being is one of Satan's, it has the full power of the Prince of Darkness at its disposal. If the creature is mortal, it may have some malign intent. I beg you not to endanger yourself in this quest."

"My niece has properly reminded me that there is physical as well as spiritual danger here. I fear that I have been so blinded by my belief that the dead do not walk the earth that I failed to issue her very wise warning. If nothing untoward approaches you, however, a visit to the inn should prove helpful."

Thomas glanced over at his prioress.

She nodded.

The exchange was not lost on Sister Beatrice, and pride in her niece's authority briefly shone in her eyes. "The inn is the perfect place to hear gossip, and I will instruct our porter to let you out the gate at an hour most religious should be in bed. This plan is a dangerous one, and I know I am sending you into a world where Satan will delight in testing you. Your devotion to justice and your calling must strengthen you. I trust you will remember you are there only to serve God. Had we some other choice…but we do not. Surely, if you dissemble as well as you did…"

Thomas wiped a sudden light sweat from his forehead.

"…when you faced that murderer in Tyndal, you will be convincing as a wandering monk with news to exchange. Some of the inn's visitors should be quite willing to tell you things they might not a local man. With God's grace, your mission may be quickly accomplished, and you can come back to our priory without suffering from your experience." She raised a thoughtful eyebrow.

"I delight in honoring my vow of obedience and am happy to do as required, praying that my actions result in peace returning to these sacred walls." Thomas put his hands together in the attitude of prayer and bowed his head.

"As for your findings, do not come to me, for I fear my many extra duties keep me from giving this matter the proper attention." Sister Beatrice drained her mazer and smiled at her niece. "On this question of ghosts, Prioress Eleanor shall act on Amesbury's behalf."

Brother Thomas could barely contain his glee over this good fortune.

Chapter Seven

The next morning's mist was a light one. The yellow sun had already warmed the nearby outcropping of blue and lavender flowers, soft as a bishop's linen, and their fragrance filled the air with an agreeable scent that almost masked the stench of rank filth and rotting weeds along the river bank. Nor did the air bite the skin as was sometimes true before the midsummer sun finally vanquished all remnants of the darker seasons. In sum, the day seemed quite filled with tenderness.

Alys, however, was unmindful of the morning's promise. Had she been passing a dunghill, her expression could not have been more sour; her face was reddened as if winter's chill still ruled.

"Is it not a lovely morning for a walk, mistress?" Master Herbert slowed so he would not outpace the sullen young woman at his side.

In the distance, a crow cawed, the grating sound heard clearly above the rush of the river's waters.

"My daughter most heartily agrees!" Jhone's tone was flat with forced enthusiasm. "And would have answered herself were she not dreaming of how happy she shall be upon your marriage." Although she remained some feet behind the wooing couple, the sharp rebuke in these last words was not softened by the separation.

Alys said nothing, and the color in her face now darkened even more. She stopped and kicked at a rock in the path. The force sent the stone flying over the tall grass and into the river.

Herbert folded his arms and studied the flight of the rock with a thoughtful look. When he saw the splash, he turned around and motioned Jhone to turn away.

"Oh!" the mother exclaimed softly, reading his meaning well. Studying the ground as if she had dropped something, she began to walk slowly back toward the village.

The vintner stepped close to Alys and reached for her hand.

The girl folded her arms into the sleeves of her robe.

He bent to her ear and whispered: "I may be twice your age, but my breath is still sweet and my rod can give much joy to one who has known only callow boys."

Alys glared, and her nose wrinkled with disgust.

"My first wife was pleased enough with me as husband, mistress. Take heart in that. Few of us marry as we wish, but many find joy nonetheless. You will forget Bernard's fumblings in time."

Alys raised her hand to strike.

Herbert stepped back. "Ah, see how modest your daughter is!" he called out with merry laughter. "I promise her a tender wedding night, and she blushes with such innocence."

Jhone turned around and waved brightly at the couple. To herself, she prayed that she could get her still virginal daughter into this merchant's bed before the girl gave up that virtue to her precious glover.

Alys froze, her mouth open to protest, and her hand still raised. Then she shuddered, spun around, and raced off toward the priory.

Herbert watched the young woman hurry away. As his gaze dropped below her waist, his tongue circled his lips. Although this union had been arranged for economic benefit, he seemed to have concluded that some of Alys' other charms might be equally compelling. He shook his head and strolled back toward the widow.

"Your daughter is fortunate to have you as an example of wifely virtue, Mistress Jhone," he said as he reached her side. "You were a most worthy spouse to your dead husband, and he spoke often of your thoughtful obedience and sweet modesty, qualities all Christian women should share. He may have spent many hours drinking with his friends at the inn, but he always went home to you. Not once did he dishonor your marriage by bedding another woman, although there were many to tempt him." He smiled down at her. "As his close friend, I can confirm his fidelity."

Jhone bit her lip.

"Are you sure you will not reconsider my offer?" Herbert's breath brushed the widow's ear.

"You are generous to offer marriage to a poor widow of my years, sir," she whispered hoarsely, "but I cannot remarry. To share another man's bed would be like putting horns on my dead husband's brow. Nay, I shall go to him at death as faithful a spouse as I have been since we wed."

"The Church would give its blessing. Remarriage is no sin."

"To some it is, and I am one who believes it so. Which man would I call my earthly lord, and at whose side should I stand on Judgement Day? Nay, Master Herbert, my daughter is the better choice and more likely to bear you sons as well. Remember that I bore my husband only one living child and that a daughter." She winced as if stabbed with a sudden pain.

The vintner's palm lightly touched Jhone's waist but did not stay. "Your late husband gave you no sons, mistress. With due respect to my old friend and your honored spouse, my seed has proven stronger. My dead wife, may God have mercy upon her, bore three sons for me, but they all died soon after birth. She was weak of body, I fear. Even all the daughters failed to thrive." He rubbed the corner of his eyes with one finger. "I wish that had not been true, but you were her childhood friend and saw how quickly my beloved Eda grew frail."

"She suffered so!" An unrestrained tear slipped from the widow's eye. "No, I could never take her place in your bed. To do so would be a betrayal."

"Betrayal? Never! Nor would she think such a thing, even though her soul twists in Hell's fires. Your fidelity to her memory has been constant enough to prove your loyalty. You are amongst the few who share my belief that she was wrongly accused of self-murder and should have been buried in sanctified ground."

"I pray daily at her grave."

"Just so! On my own hope of heaven, I swear it would please our Eda to see us comfortably wed to each other. May I not persuade you to take me as spouse?" He bent to kiss her.

Jhone turned her head away from the vintner's lips, although the slowness with which she did so suggested some reluctance. "You need sons, sir. Your seed should be planted, not in the weak body of this aging widow, but in a strong girl like my Alys..."

"...a daughter who appears inclined to reject my suit and join this Order of Fontevraud where Eve rules Adam. A most unnatural Order methinks, although I believe it is much favored at the king's court." Herbert stepped away to put a more respectable distance between them.

"Fear not! My daughter shall take vows for cert, but they will be earthly ones as your wife at the church door."

"So you say, yet she continues to refuse marriage with me with unwomanly determination."

Jhone's face flushed. "She will be persuaded. As for her plea to become a nun at this priory, I swear that I shall not allow such a thing."

Herbert frowned as if deep in thought, reached for her hand, and placed it lightly on his arm. "Nor would I, were she my child. This priory is most undeserving of her, a cursed place I think. Although I have said that the spirit haunting this priory must be our Eda, longing for proper burial, I cannot discount those who say the founding queen has returned to condemn those false monastics for their lewdness."

"Yet the priory has been of assistance to the village. My sister's son and husband both earn their bread there, along with many others from Amesbury. Prioress Ida is known for her generosity to the poor, feeding their bodies and praying for their souls."

"She is a chaste and honorable virgin herself, but we cannot ignore with what disgrace priory monks follow Satan's song over the broken wall to the inn where they satisfy their unholy lusts."

"That is surely past! My sister told me the wall has been repaired and no one has since…"

"Your sister says? Forgive me, but I cannot give credence to her opinions. Honest though she may be, your sister is not known for her judgement in worldly matters. Did she not resist, like your daughter does now, when your parents proposed an honorable marriage many years ago? Did she not instead marry a rogue, a man who once spied on tradesmen, men traveling to make fair profit, for the purpose of sending masterless men to rob them of their wealth?" Herbert let his words sink in. "Nay, I am not convinced that the priory has ceased sinning and have long questioned the competence of its leadership. How wise was it, for example, to give work in priory fields to a man like your sister's husband?"

"Wulfstan was never found guilty of any crime…" Jhone quickly lowered her head as if apologizing for her quick speech. "I thought the priory kind…"

Herbert patted her hand. "What sweet, feminine charity you show! Even though he was never arrested for his foul deeds, most of us know your brother-in-law was a felon." Sighing, he continued. "The old prioress, who is most assuredly in Heaven for her charitable spirit, may have been ill-advised to hire such a man, but I cannot dispute her soft-hearted motives in doing so, nor yours in defending them."

The two fell silent as the May sun enfolded them with amiable warmth. To their right, a row of yellow-cheeked Great Tit chicks, evenly spaced along a tree branch, filled the air with raucous protest over an unacceptable parental delay in their feeding.

Jhone's lips curved into a brief smile at the sight.

"Very well, I trouble you no longer with my pleas, although I trust that you will tame your wayward Alys and keep her from following the ill-advised example of her aunt."

"I shall."

"And teach your daughter how to serve a husband as you yourself did with your dear spouse? That is not so much to ask in return for my devotion and the sharing of my wealth."

"You may count on it, sir."

"And persuade her that convent vows are not for her?"

She nodded.

"I shall be most thankful to you for all of this and will demonstrate my gratitude in a more tangible form as soon as the marriage takes place." His lips smiled, but his eyes lacked the glow of comparable joy.

A scream shattered the peaceful morning.

Jhone picked up her robe and raced toward the river. The vintner was not far behind.

When they reached the trembling Alys, the pair quickly saw the cause of her horror. A dead body bobbed gently in the tangled growth at the edge of the Avon. Although each of them knew most of the townspeople of Amesbury, none could identify whose body it might be.

The corpse had quite lost its head.

Chapter Eight

"He is my father." Sayer stumbled backwards as if the pale, headless body had pushed him away with spectral hand.

Thomas put a comforting arm around the son's shoulders but quickly drew it back when he saw Sayer's eyes narrow with anger.

"We feared as much," replied Brother Infirmarian. "I recognized the broken arm I had set some years ago. The bone had broken the skin just there. Wulfstan was lucky to have survived that one."

"A cruel kindness since he lived only to be murdered." The son's voice was flat.

"The deed was a most foul thing," Sister Anne said. Standing behind Thomas, she frowned in thought. "To behead a man after killing him is a devilish act."

Brother Infirmarian shrugged, then gave her a sheepish look. "I treat the living and leave the cause of death to God, but Sister Beatrice told me that you have skill with both."

"Beheaded. Stabbed. Pushed into the river to drown. What does any of that matter? My father is dead. He should have gone to God as an old man with a cleansed soul and whispers of love in his ears." Sayer stared at the body now fully covered on the trestle table. Tears had yet to dampen his cheeks.

Thomas felt a kindred sting in his own heart. He, too, was bereft of any final word with the man who had sired him. "Your mother..." he began.

"She will live."

"I pray she will! My concern was..."

"She has a plot of land." Sayer's hands formed fists. "We need no charity."

"Nor did I think otherwise." Thomas' voice softened. "Does she not have you?"

The bright anger in Sayer's eyes faded, leaving only a muted but flickering glow.

"I knew not if she had been told about your father's death." Thomas looked first at the other monk, then at Sister Anne. "That was my question."

Brother Infirmarian shook his head.

The young man put his hands over his eyes, pressing his fingers into his brow as if he suffered an intolerable pain. "Will you bury my father in sanctified ground?"

"There is no reason to do otherwise," Brother Infirmarian replied. "Although he was not shrived before his death, we will surely pray for his soul. In that you may find comfort..."

"What if the ghost killed him?" Sayer interrupted.

Brother Infirmarian's eyes opened wide with horror. Clearly he had not thought about this complication. "If Satan seized his soul..."

"Ghosts do not kill," Thomas snapped.

"I would not be so certain," the son replied, his voice as cold as the corpse on the table. Then he turned his back on them all and strode out of the chapel.

ᏯᎢᏯᏅ ᏯᎢᏯᏅ ᏯᎢᏯᏅ

"Not Wulfstan!" Jhone put her hand to her mouth, her eyes round with shock.

"You were acquainted with him?" Thomas asked as gently as he could.

Herbert answered for the woman beside him. "He was married to Mistress Jhone's sister."

"What will Drifa do alone?" she whispered. "Their children!"

Realizing it would be cruel to question a woman lost in the distress of both murder and its consequences, Thomas turned to the tall, dark-haired man. "How could this have happened?" he asked.

Herbert shrugged. "Who knows? Our laws are lax, and evil men are everywhere. Any one of them might have met this man on the road and killed him for some little thing. Of the man himself, I can say little. He was free, of course, but a poor creature with few skills, unless thievery…"

Thief? Thomas blinked at the word.

"Even if the tales were true, all that was many years ago!" Tears slipped down Jhone's cheeks. "He had long been an honest man. I beg you to show compassion!"

"I did not mean to do otherwise, although I could never include him amongst those I would call upright men."

"I am not unmindful of this dreadful thing you have just seen," Thomas said, "but if Wulfstan had enemies or was engaged in something outside the law, please tell me now."

"Why?" Herbert asked. "Surely this is a matter for secular law. The body was found beyond the priory walls."

Thomas cursed himself for not thinking before he spoke. Quickly he tried to cloak his odd demand with some reason. "The sheriff is delayed. If you give me the details now, I will pass them on to him when he arrives, and you will not be troubled by questions from him." His mind raced. If Wulfstan had the reputation for thievery, could he have been part of some band that planned to steal the Amesbury Psalter? Had something gone wrong that had resulted in his murder? Maybe not, but he had to know whether or not this was a possibility.

"As Mistress Jhone has said, my comment dealt with events long ago." Herbert's lips curled into a sneer. "I did not respect the man, but I know of no crime he committed in recent years."

"Old sins sometimes return to haunt." Anything, Thomas thought, just tell me anything.

"He labored on priory lands," Herbert continued. "You must ask Prioress Ida, or Sister Beatrice in her stead, about his service. For my part, I have not heard any tales to suggest his work was not diligently done or that any of his fellow laborers had issue with him."

"No rumors? No suggestion of problems or worry?"

The man folded his arms. "I will be happy to talk to the sheriff when he returns."

Jhone suddenly looked up at Herbert. "There was that one matter…" Her voice was just above a whisper.

With an abrupt gesture of his hand, Herbert interrupted her. "Nay, mistress, do not even mention that petty thing. It would never have resulted in such a brutal killing." He scowled at Thomas. "I fear our brother here merely longs to satisfy some worldly interest in gossip, for he has no authority in this matter. You and I shall talk further in private, once you have recovered from your shock, and I will discuss what is needed with the sheriff."

"I meant only to save you distress," Thomas said through clenched teeth.

"And have forgotten charity, a virtue all monks should both learn and practice? Perhaps your intentions were benign, Brother, but your questions are impertinent and inconsiderate. As you should see, Mistress Jhone is too upset to remain here." Herbert waved at the monk with barely concealed contempt. "To humor you, I will say this. Please listen carefully for I will not repeat it." The merchant bent forward as if talking to a child and enunciated each word slowly. "Neither of us knows any mortal who had such a wicked hatred for the man that they would slay him in so foul a manner." He stepped back. "Does that satisfy your small curiosity?"

Thomas felt his face turn hot with humiliation. How dare the merchant speak to him in this way? Bastard I might be, he shouted to himself, but I am no churl! In thoughtless fury, he spun around and faced the pale Jhone. "You have no idea who might have done this either?" he snapped.

The woman looked up at the vintner with pleading eyes.

Herbert's face darkened.

Instantly, the monk regretted his action. Like a coward he had attacked a weak and innocent person.

"For a monk who claims to love compassion, Brother, you have a harsh enough tongue. I think we have humored you enough." Herbert took the widow's arm with tenderness. "Come, mistress. We have answered all we need of this monk's rude queries." Firmly, he turned the woman away from Thomas, but not before giving him a thin but triumphant smile.

The monk denounced himself for his burst of temper that had allowed the merchant's easy victory in this battle of wills.

When the couple reached the entry door to the small chapel, however, Herbert suddenly stopped. Looking back at the monk with a thoughtful expression, he said in a tone that was almost conciliatory: "You might ask if the ghost killed him, Brother, and if her spirit had some quarrel with him."

The words were like cold water in Thomas' face, quenching all his fury in a trice. As he watched the pair leave, he stared with growing uneasiness at the sunshine streaming through the open door. If he hoped the brightness would present him with a real killer instead of murderous ghosts, he was disappointed. The light revealed only dust motes that drifted about with unruly grace.

Chapter Nine

Leaning back into her chair, Eleanor stared at Adam and Eve in the tapestry above the chamber door and pondered the news of Wulfstan's murder.

Her first reaction had been outrage. Not only was her beloved priory troubled with this vile and unlawful act, but had she not come here to escape death? For the last two years, she had been forced to deal with murders and had nearly died of a fever herself. Could God not grant her some respite?

Quickly, her indignation had turned to shame. A man had been slain like a criminal and his wife and children left to grieve. He was a laborer. Would they have food and shelter now that he was dead? How could she put her own selfish concerns first?

For this sin, she spent an hour in prayer, time she yearned to increase, but she had grown too weak to concentrate longer on God.

Despite her mortal frailty, He had been merciful, sending both understanding and the calm of forgiveness. With the peace she felt descending on her, Eleanor became convinced that God had no quarrel with her longing to escape worldly violence, nor had He deemed Amesbury Priory worthy of this foul assault. Even her wish to turn her back on Death's grinning arrogance was innocent enough.

Her failure lay in not directing her anger against the Prince of Darkness. Death had been a pawn of Satan in this murder.

Was it not her duty to deny the dark angel his pleasure in wronging the innocent? She should find a way to bring justice to the bereaved family. In so doing, she could restore order to priory life as well. Surely God would grant her the tranquility she herself prayed for later.

As she had gripped the prie-dieu and painfully pulled herself from her knees, however, she doubted her ability to do anything to resolve this issue. What a pitifully weak creature she had become! Once seated, she shook her head in despair. Nay, she did not have the strength to fight the Devil in this situation. Someone else must do it.

Suddenly her foot grazed something next to her chair and she glanced down. The object was a woven basket, fitted with a smooth cushion that was coated with brindle-colored hair. It belonged to the greyhound Prioress Ida kept as companion, a dog she had taken with her on her journey.

Eleanor studied the basket.

Her own creature, a great orange cat left at Tyndal to protect the kitchens from pillaging rodents, would never tolerate such a soft thing, she thought. Ignoring snow or wild storms, he went out each day to hunt vermin. Had he been born a man, he would have been the perfect knight, embracing any hardship in the performance of whatever his liege lord might require.

"Dare I be less dutiful than my cat?" she asked herself in a voice tinged with both humor and self-mockery. "Here I sit, in the warm comfort of these rooms, like a pampered pet. I should be ashamed!"

She rose from her chair and walked with determination to the chamber window. Leaning to her left, she could see just a bit of the River Avon now flowing with enthusiasm, free from winter's icy grasp. The Saxon cross was invisible from here, as were those strange hillocks across the river that she remembered from her youth.

Were the barrows sacred or profane? Opinions amongst adults were varied, but a younger Eleanor and her childhood friends had loved frightening each other in the dark with tales of pale spirits that danced on the mounds and longed to capture a young Amesbury novice.

Did they really believe in such phantoms, Eleanor now wondered, or was it mostly pretense? "Maybe it was both," she said aloud, "for there seems to be a place in all mortal souls that longs for ghosts even as we fear them or logic dismisses them."

Now she must seek the truth about wandering souls. Her aunt may have discounted the current ghost as both playful and quite mortal earlier, but the murder of Wulfstan had changed that. The spirit had been accused. It had ceased to be an innocent thing.

Had an angry soul escaped from Hell and killed Wulfstan? Or was the specter the diabolical creation of a mortal who wished to hide behind engendered fear to slay with greater ease? If she succeeded in discovering the truth, would she be faced with a nightmarish sight so horrible that no human could survive it, or with a craven killer deserving of the hangman's rope?

Her grip on the window weakened. She turned away and went back to sit in the chair placed near the fire. Leaning her head against the carved wood, she almost slipped into sleep, then forced her eyes open. How could she engage in battle against such foes when she could not even stay awake?

When would she regain her strength? she asked God. Was she not a grown woman? It had been many years since she had been a babe that needed a wet nurse to watch, feed, and bathe her. She had suffered from too much frailty over the last many months, not just as a result of her illness but from her sinful soul as well.

"And I am tired of it," she declared. "Weary of it all!"

Without doubt, her aunt was quite able to deal with the nature of the ghost without her help. If anyone could get that sheriff to do his job and investigate whatever lay behind the malicious acts, Sister Beatrice was the one. But Eleanor knew full well why her aunt had fashioned the original plan with Sister Anne to involve her in the investigation.

Even as a girl, Eleanor had loved solving problems, and her aunt would have known that this phantom was the very thing to strengthen her niece's hold on life. "We may all yearn for heaven," the novice mistress had once said to her, "but our hearts desire with equal passion to keep loved ones on earth." By setting her this task, her aunt had hoped to bind Eleanor firmly to the world she had almost abandoned.

Now that the specter had turned deadly, however, her aunt might change her mind about her niece's involvement, but that did not daunt Eleanor in the slightest. Her resolve hardened, and she sat upright. She had a duty to honor.

Willing herself to her feet, the prioress rose and looked toward the chamber door. Rather than just sit and muse on ashes in the hearth, she would take her sub-infirmarian's advice and start walking to improve the balance in her humors.

"It might be harder to regain health than lose it, as Anne so often says" she said, stiffening her back, "but I am a Wynethorpe, a breed as strong-willed as any of Angevin descent."

She would walk.

srne srne srne

As the May sun warmed her face, Eleanor lost all doubt. The dead did not come back to trouble the living. Raised on the works of Saint Augustine, Eleanor had never quarreled with his logic. Even after she had attained enough education to allow some disputation, she had found him persuasive in this matter. Because of this, she was reasonably convinced that the spirit had a man's body.

Or a woman's? Before the murder, she would have concluded that this sort of jape was more likely a boy's game. Now she must ask what kind of a woman was capable of killing a strong man like Wulfstan and beheading him. Had not the shape been described as a queen or a local wife? "How very odd," she muttered. It was difficult to imagine many women able to commit this particular crime—and even harder to see how a man, one easily mistaken for a weak woman, could do so either.

Maybe she was wrong to assume the ghost and the murderer were the same. The specter had been accused by both the dead man's son and those who had found the body, but this charge might be based solely in shock and grief. Not to separate phantom from killer might be a mistake and in defiance of reason. She needed more facts.

Meanwhile, Brother Thomas had been charged with identification of the ghost when she and her aunt believed the creature was annoying but not threatening. Would he be in danger now? A chill shook her. Her own decision to find an answer in this was one thing, but she did not wish to put the monk in peril.

She clenched her fist, once again cursing her weakness. Had she not given in and brought the monk to Amesbury, this would not be a concern. She had not wanted him here at all. After her fever had burned all lust from her body, she had hoped to escape from the man, while she was still free of her sinful passions, and seek the wise counsel she knew Sister Beatrice would give.

This she would have done had she not had a visitor before she left Tyndal. It was a man she had seen before, a priest who sometimes brought Thomas news of family matters. The last time, he had summoned Thomas to a sick brother's bedside. On this occasion, he had come with word that the monk's father had died at the beginning of April.

How had this priest managed to change her mind? Closing her eyes, she pictured the man's concerned look as he told her the news, explaining that the monk would not travel to be with his family for reasons that were never made quite clear.

"It is such a pity that he cannot be distracted from his grief," the man said. "A journey would bring him much benefit," he finished, his eyebrows rising as if surprised that he had come up with the idea. Then the man's expression changed, his eyes intense with a gaze much like that wolves used to stun rabbits into stillness.

What a strange image, she thought at the time, considering the man's priestly vocation.

"Are you not traveling to Amesbury, my lady?" he asked. "God would surely be most pleased if you showered pity on our poor brother and took him with you."

Having suffered her own mother's death, Eleanor understood the sharpness of Thomas' pain and suspected that his particular anguish might have been even bleaker due to an estrangement. She may also have been so weakened from her illness that she had little strength to argue against this reasonable request no matter how much she wanted to refuse. Whatever the cause, she had agreed to the priest's suggestion.

Her decision had delighted Sister Anne, who held the same opinion that a change of scenery might chase away some of the monk's dark sorrow. Although Eleanor feared that his presence would only add to her grave weariness, she reminded herself that she would not have to see him at all after their arrival until the time came for their return to Tyndal. Not at all, that is, until the appearance of this cursed Amesbury ghost…

A hand, gentle but firm, came to rest on her arm.

"You should let me know when you are going to take exercise." Sister Anne's expression was troubled.

Lost in her musings, Eleanor had not realized she had walked all the way into the cloister garth. Fatigue made her feel momentarily faint, and her comfortable chair seemed so very far away. "I am not a child's plaything," she snapped.

"Some toys may be unbreakable. You are not. Have you forgotten how close you came to death last winter? Nor have you recovered either your strength or customary weight. None of this can be ignored without risk." Anne shook her head to silence her prioress' expected protest. "Would you not chastise any sub-infirmarian who disregarded these details with another patient?"

Eleanor looked down at the hand on her arm. It was the same one that had held her head so she could sip broth and drink watered wine, a hand that had soothed her feverish brow for weeks to keep her in this world. She looked up at her friend with deep affection. "I would that."

Anne's expression softened as she saw a healthy color return to her friend's cheeks. "You promised to show me some of your favorite places at the priory. If they are not far, would you take my arm and guide me to them?"

In companionable silence, the two nuns started walking slowly toward the parish church.

"Has Brother Thomas told you much about his father's death?" Anne suddenly asked. That their thoughts were often in accord might be one of the comforts of their friendship, but a slight tremor in her friend's hand made Anne look down with concern.

Eleanor's face betrayed nothing. "Nay," she replied, pausing to point out a lush bed of mint that had been carefully enclosed to prevent any undisciplined spread in the monastic garden. "I hoped he might have confided in you."

"He has not. Although he has grown gaunt with grief, he refuses to speak of it. It was not until he was asked to investigate this ghost that he brightened for the first time."

With a thoughtful frown, Eleanor gently disengaged herself and walked toward the mint, bending to pick a leaf. "I was told that his father died near St. Albans," she said, inhaling the bracing scent.

"I had not heard that. Our brother told me only that he prayed his father had been shriven in time."

Eleanor put the mint leaf into her mouth and chewed it with evident enjoyment. "He did not ask leave to spend any time with his family, either then or when we passed nearby on our way here."

"Maybe they are no longer in St. Albans?"

Eleanor nodded. "My aunt told me that Richard of Almayne died near there as well. What a sad coincidence. I wonder if Brother Thomas' father was in the service of our king's most noble brother?"

With that question, the two women fell silent, for both knew that the absence of Thomas from any ceremony to honor his father might well be proof that he not only merited a bar sinister but had somehow lost favor with his sire.

"There it is!" Eleanor said in a low voice as they entered the parish church. With a show of strength that both amazed and pleased the sub-infirmarian, the prioress pulled her friend toward a corner and pointed out a much worn stone. "This part is so ancient that some believe it dates to Queen Guinevere's death. Others say Queen Elfrida ordered it set as the cornerstone of her new abbey when she presented the relics of Saint Melor. It is his feast day we shall celebrate…"

Suddenly she fell silent, gesturing to Anne to do the same.

At the nearby altar, a young woman knelt, sobbing as if her heart had been shattered with grief.

Chapter Ten

"My name is Alys," the girl said, wiping her cheeks dry with her fingers. "I live with my widowed mother in Amesbury village, just beyond the bridge in a house near the inn."

"Come walk in the nearby garden," Eleanor said. "Your prayers must have drawn us to you. Speaking of your sadness might give you some ease."

Although her look lacked any disdain, Alys' expression reflected much doubt.

Eleanor read the look well. "No cloister ever put a wall around a woman's heart, and surely I have been on this earth only a few summers longer than you. I might understand your plight." Her laughter was soft with caring.

The young woman had the grace to blush. "I meant no discourtesy, Sister."

"Nor did I think otherwise. This is Sister Anne. I am called Eleanor. We are both members of this Order but not of this priory, rather visitors from another daughter house on the coast near Norwich." She gestured in the direction of the priory gates. "Anything you wish to say leaves Amesbury with us."

"Your words are sweet like balm on a wound, Sister Eleanor, but the cause of my grief is well known." Another tear crested in the corner of the young woman's eye. "You have not heard the news, methinks, but a man was found murdered outside this priory." With firm determination, she tossed her head to chase any tears back. "The man so cruelly slaughtered was my uncle, Wulfstan. I was the one to discover his body."

"God grant you solace! I heard the story, although not your name until now. We were horrified. No one in the priory could imagine who might have so hated your uncle that he was driven to do such a terrible thing."

"It must have been Satan's imp. My uncle has no enemies, or rather no more than any man does who has reached his age. Although my mother claims he is a rude man, he is always sweet-natured to me."

Eleanor noted the young woman's use of the present tense. *How we do cling to our loved ones even as Death drags their souls away,* she thought.

Tears resumed their course down Alys' cheeks. "I weep for his son, my cousin, as well. Sayer must be bitter with grief for he had quarreled with his father just the other night. My uncle is quick to anger but does not stay so for long." She sobbed, then resolutely faced what had happened. "The time was too short, and they were never able to make peace!"

"I pray your cousin will find consolation. Surely the argument was minor and soon forgotten?"

Alys brightened a bit. "I do not know the cause of their disagreement, but it must have been a petty thing. Sayer is a sweet lad."

Eleanor hesitated, feeling her fatigue. Her usual quickness of mind was another casualty of her illness, and the moment to pursue any more questions under the guise of innocence passed. Taking a deep breath of regret, she continued. "You have been quite brave in this matter. Were you out walking with your mother and affianced…"

The girl covered her face and moaned with renewed anguish.

Anne and Eleanor stared at each other. What had Eleanor said to expose even greater grief? Had Brother Thomas failed to tell them something?

"Please forgive me," the prioress begged, clasping the girl to her for comforting.

After a few minutes, Alys calmed. "You said nothing amiss, Sister. I sorrow most for my uncle's death and hope God will have mercy on his blemished soul. I pray as well that my mother, whose husband died most recently, may find ease. Yet I have a secret grief as well."

Anne stepped away so they could speak privately.

"I will keep your tale in confidence," Eleanor said.

"My mother wants me to marry a man I hate!" she burst out. "I confess that my feelings may do him some injustice. Were my heart not joined with that of another, I might feel…" Giving up the struggle to find a word, she went on. "I can view no other man with joy. If I did not say so, I would not be truthful."

Eleanor liked the young woman for that. Her blunt speech reminded the prioress of Gytha, her maid at Tyndal and a woman not much different in age. "Will you join us?" She gestured toward the gardens where she knew she could sit.

Alys agreed, her face slowly regaining its natural rosy color.

The trio set off along a path, the stones worn deep by the rough elements and soft shoes of many nuns over even more centuries. With silent discretion, Anne dropped back to examine a yellow-flowered Planta Genista, the Broom plant doubtless placed in the garden to honor the current king's grandfather who had rededicated the priory to the Order of Fontevraud.

Eleanor drew Alys into a corner of the garden, bounded by a trinity of ancient yews. "A woman has the legal right to refuse a husband, for cert, but our parents often see things with more wisdom than we do," she said. "Do not misunderstand. I have not chosen to ignore your grief, but you seem a sensible woman. I would hear why you have concluded that your heart is wiser than your mother."

"I long to do as commanded, Sister, but I fear I am much confused. I do not understand why my parents decided Master Herbert must be the only choice. He is older, although not without favor, and dresses well, which speaks of wealth. I can see the merit in that. My father, before he died, had apparently found in him a proper match for me."

Eleanor laid a sympathetic hand on Alys' arm.

Gaining solace from the supportive touch, the young woman continued. "My Bernard is the son of a glover in the village, one who had an established business when he died last year..."

"...a man closer to your age who has not yet acquired much or any wealth?" The failure to add the word *profitable* had not escaped Eleanor's notice.

"But one who will in due course! Of that I am confident. If my parents had found him so unacceptable as a husband, why was he never discouraged, even barred from coming to court me? Surely our blushes must have spoken the truth of our desire to marry. We did nothing to hide our feelings. We had no cause. Yet, after my father's death, my mother became obsessed with this vintner and now claims Bernard is unsuitable!"

"Did your father never speak of this arrangement to you?"

"No."

The prioress noted with curiosity that the girl's eyes remained quite dry when she spoke of this recently deceased father. "Was his death sudden?" she asked softly. "Perhaps he did not have time..."

Alys turned away from Eleanor. "He and I spoke together as little as possible. What he wished to convey to me, he usually did through my mother. You need not waste comforting words on me, Sister. Although I sought to obey the man's will, as one must a sire, I bore no love for him. For that I shall gladly serve my time in Purgatory, but I cannot feel repentant." She pressed tight fists into her thighs, before continuing in a hoarse whisper: "He beat my mother when he drank more than he ought and mounted her with as little tenderness as if she were a common whore rather than his wife. My first memory of them both was this."

The cruelty in the tale hit Eleanor's heart with brutal force. She closed her eyes but could not stop herself from exclaiming, "You poor child!"

When Alys turned back to face the nun, all adult defiance had faded from her voice, replaced with a child's confusion. "When my father died, I thought my mother would see Bernard's fine qualities and how kind he is to me. My mother is a loving woman, Sister! After she had suffered so, I was sure she would wish just such a sweet man as husband for her daughter, but I was mistaken. She holds to Master Herbert as if her very soul depended on our marriage. Had I not known otherwise, I would now think my mother, not my dead father, had chosen him for me."

The deep exhaustion, which Eleanor had tried firmly to will away, now returned with unavoidable force. Quickly, she gestured toward the stone seats. When they sat, Eleanor hid the trembling of her body by bracing herself on the stone and bending toward Alys as if encouraging the confidential talk. "What lack do you see in the man your mother is so set on?"

"Oh, he has enough of his teeth left," Alys said, her anger glowing in the bright spots on her cheeks, "and his breath does not reek of the grave!" She wilted into the seat with utter defeat. "I cannot explain my objections. When I am with him, he makes sure my mother is in attendance. He has never tried to dishonor me, yet he whispers things in my ears that I do not care for. When I protest, he claims I have misunderstood, and his reasons are well expressed. I often conclude I am misjudging him." Her lips twisted as if she had just tasted something foul. "Nonetheless, I draw back from him and cannot bear even the touch of his robe. I am unable to explain further, Sister. Truly I cannot!"

"What sort of things does he say?"

Alys flushed, her face now completely scarlet. "He has suggested that Bernard and I have already bedded."

"Have you?" Eleanor asked gently.

The young woman turned her head away as if she were confessing her sins. "I have fondled him most lovingly, and Bernard has kissed me in such a way that I have almost swooned. Yet, on my faith, I am still a virgin." She glanced at the nun beside her as if to gauge her reaction.

Eleanor compared one sweet summer eve at Wynethorpe Castle, before she took final vows, with her lustful dreams at

Tyndal and knew just how innocent these two young people were of mortal sin. She nodded.

With pleased surprise, Alys smiled.

"Was the vintner married before?"

"Aye, for some years, but his wife drowned. Master Herbert has always claimed she slipped. Others say she committed self-murder, for she was in much pain from a running sore in her womb that refused to heal. The crowner believed she had willfully drowned and so her soul was cursed and her body laid in an unsanctified grave."

This would be Mistress Eda, Eleanor thought. The other ghost. Yet she could see no way to turn her questions to restless spirits when this girl needed a compassionate ear. "Might the vintner be unaccustomed to wooing after years of marriage? Could he have meant well and intended only to show that he understands the passions of youth?"

Alys shrugged. "As I have said, I cannot explain why his words trouble me. When he murmurs in my ear that he is capable of riding me until I scream with joy, I should conclude that he means to convey how skilled a lover he will be. Yet I hear only that I will *scream*. In that prospect, I find neither comfort nor joy."

Surely the man was not cruel, Eleanor thought, and is unaware of the violent mating between the girl's parents. Yet there was something in the way Alys had repeated the man's words that troubled her. "This Master Herbert may not possess skilled phrasing, but surely... Was he not acquainted with your father?"

"Aye, and must have known full well what manner of a husband he was to my mother. Only she believed that she hid the bruises from the neighbors, and, if I could hear her piercing cries outside the house, they did as well. Master Herbert cannot be ignorant of any of this."

After hearing this tale, I shall always be grateful that I knew how tenderly my parents loved each other before my mother's cruel death, Eleanor thought. Children are not without ears or eyes, although many seem to think they are.

Alys looked up at the sky in shock. "Sister, I did not hear the bells, but the time must be past None! I promised my mother that I would accompany her to prayers, and she will be worried." She reached out her hand and grasped Eleanor's much smaller one in hers. "I thank you for listening to my woes."

The prioress squeezed the hand that held hers. "Should you wish to speak further, ask Brother Porter to summon Eleanor of Tyndal."

Watching the girl rush away along the path to the gate, Eleanor knew she had not served her well. She must seek the young woman out on the morrow, before fatigue had dulled her wits, and provide wiser and more comforting advice.

Anne helped her rise, and the two walked slowly back through the gardens. Alys' sadness over the death of her uncle reminded Eleanor of the black humors cursing Brother Thomas.

He should go into the village to seek the truth behind these apparitions, she decided, and do so tonight. The sub-infirmarian had been right about the eagerness that had returned to his eyes when Sister Beatrice suggested he find meaning behind the ghost. If she did not have to snatch that joy from him, she would not. A crowded inn was safe enough. The task should not pose any danger.

Before Wulfstan's death, the hauntings had been benign. Why would they have suddenly turned deadly? She could see no apparent reason, which surely suggested there was no connection between some jape and murder. The sooner the two things were separated, the better. Cautious fear of a mortal killer was reasonable, but rumors of ghosts often allowed Dread to let loose her most foul child, Panic.

She had already warned the monk to take care lest the spirit turn out to be a man or imp with malicious intent. Now she would order him to leave the inn if he began to suspect that the phantom and slayer were the same, or if he learned something that pointed to the murderer's identity. Under no circumstances was he to investigate further. She would not allow it. That was the work of the sheriff.

After all, Wulfstan had been killed outside religious walls. Once the ghost had been revealed as a man, the sheriff would no longer have his pretence of an argument and must drag himself back from his boar hunting.

Eleanor brightened at the thought. Then she might consider her own duty to Wulfstan's family done and retreat to her sanctuary from the world's violence with a clear conscience. She grew eager to resolve this matter quickly.

Chapter Eleven

Thomas waited for Brother Porter to open the massive wooden gate and wondered what the old monk thought of this strange command to let him go into the village when he should be at prayer.

"God be with you," the porter whispered.

"Pray for me," Thomas replied with sincerity, noting only benevolence in the old man's eyes. With a sigh, he wondered if he would ever be capable of such unquestioning obedience.

At least the air was mild tonight, he noted, as he walked toward the bridge leading to the inn. Had God tempered it as a kindness, wishing to remind all mortals that the season of life was upon them despite Wulfstan's cruel death?

Looking around, the monk saw nothing that resembled any ghost. He felt a momentary disappointment, almost as if he had been found unworthy of some crucial test. Reasoned arguments may have proven that no such spirit could exist, but he, Thomas, was troubled by Sayer's fears and even by the merchant's suggestion. Men of accepted wisdom have been wrong before, he thought with some irreverence, although he would not voice his fleeting doubts about wandering souls to either Sister Beatrice or her niece.

When he reached the bridge, he stopped. He would have no problem finding the inn. Even at this distance, he could hear the laughter, shouts, and snatches of song. A memory flashed through his mind of another inn, one in London where he and Giles had often found a woman to share for an evening. Something twisted painfully inside him. He struck his heart with his fist, and the image shattered like some fragile object.

"I should never have decided to go to this inn as a traveling monk," he muttered aloud as he started across the Avon. Belatedly, he realized that he had been wrong about a disguise. He should have hidden his tonsure with a hood and dressed as a farmer on pilgrimage. In religious robes, he would stand out in the crowd, and the sight of monks at an inn either shut men's mouths or opened them with rude jests. It was too late to return, and he strongly doubted that either his prioress or her aunt would approve of a secular disguise.

He ground his teeth in frustration. Was he wasting his time tonight? He would certainly try to discover what was behind this haunting of the priory, but his real purpose was to find out anything he could about threats to the Amesbury Psalter. His prioress was troubled over Wulfstan's death, but she had no idea that the man was reputed to be a thief or at the very least had associated with robbers many years ago.

When he told her about the conversation with Mistress Jhone and Master Herbert, he had omitted that bit of information. He understood her clever mind well. After all, he was forbidden to tell her of his mission, and he feared she might begin to ask too many questions if she knew this detail. Although it was unlikely she would conclude the Psalter was in peril or guess his involvement in its protection, he could not chance it. Her mind was capable of amazing leaps of logic, an observation he had had frequent opportunities to make during the last two years.

Fortunately, Prioress Eleanor seemed most concerned that Wulfstan's death was being linked to the phantom and shared his own suspicion that the ghost was but a boy's sport, a mischievous act beginning to turn nasty. As for murder, she had forbidden him to pursue any such thread on the reasonable assumption that it was the sheriff's job to do so, despite the man's blatant disinclination to investigate much of anything.

Thomas was grateful that Amesbury's sheriff had decided to go off hunting. This gave him time to look into any possible relationship between the murder and this manuscript theft. It troubled him that he would be disobeying his prioress. Had he been able to explain what he had been sent to do, she might well have approved and aided him in his task. Once again, he cursed his spy master for refusing to inform her of his role for the Church.

Even if he resolved the ghost issue tonight, Thomas decided he must keep this knowledge to himself, at least for a short while. If he claimed that someone, who might know the facts about the jape, would be at the inn the next evening—or even the next—he could provide reason for being outside the priory again if need be. The deceit would be innocent enough, but he did hate lying to Prioress Eleanor, whom he held in such high regard.

Thomas spat. He could do little as he willed in this matter. Had he been able to choose what action to take first, he would not be on the way to the inn. He would be visiting Jhone for answers to some questions without the presence of Herbert, a man he strongly disliked.

A loud splash startled Thomas, and he stopped by the side of the bridge to peer into the darkness. Had a dead limb from some winter-damaged tree fallen into the river, or was the cause something more sinister? Seeing nothing, he shuddered and continued on.

Of course he did not trust the man. Herbert was of the prosperous merchant class, a greedy lot as far as the monk was concerned, demanding prompt payment of debts from those for whom coin was scarce. No student or poor clerk liked them, and Thomas had been both. As far as he was concerned, the fellow would say anything to make a profit. When Herbert mentioned the ghost, Thomas could not imagine what gain a wandering spirit might bring, but he would not dismiss his belief that there might be something.

His strongest reason for disliking the tradesman was the indisputable fact that he had bested Thomas in their battle of wills. His honor had been befouled, and he was disinclined to let that pass. "I should turn the other cheek as a monk with a true calling would," he muttered aloud, "but I likely shall not and, without question, not tonight."

He was falling into a black mood and disinclined to benevolence. Satisfying his pride must wait, of course, until he had pleased his masters in the Church, but he would make sure the eventual restitution would be even sweeter for the delay. In the meantime, he had been granted freedom by Sister Beatrice that allowed him to look into the Psalter theft. For that he would have to be grateful even if he was annoyed by the restrictions placed on him.

He shrugged his shoulders. He would make the best of the situation, discovering what he could. If he listened with discretion, he might still hear something of use. Maybe he would learn more from ale-loosened village tongues in gossip as the night wore on than from anything Mistress Jhone might tell him. After all, the shock of seeing her brother-in-law's headless corpse was surely cause enough for horror. The merchant's snide comments aside, Thomas had no wish to increase the poor woman's pain.

Deep in thought, the monk arrived at the village side of the river and headed toward the inn. Suddenly a movement caught his attention, and he paused to peer into the shifting patches of shadow.

Two men emerged from a gloomy lane just in front of him. One he did not recognize, but the other he most certainly did.

Keeping a safe distance, he slowly followed.

The men leaned toward each other in earnest but whispered conversation before stopping some yards away from the inn door.

Thomas slipped into the darkness between two houses.

"It would not be wise if we were seen together," he heard Sayer say to the plump young man beside him.

"Aye, you have the right of that. This matter is too important to have anyone suspect we are in it together. Yet are you sure...?"

"I am your man on this and shall not fail you, but let us not seem friendly or be seen to speak together in public."

"Aye. Go into the inn, although I shall follow in a while and find myself a quiet corner. This talk of plots and plans has made me thirsty." He put something into Sayer's hand. "Something for your thirst as well, my friend."

As the roofer opened the inn door, enough light fell on the other man's face for Thomas to note his features well.

A merchant by his dress, the monk thought. If this one had some guilty secret he wanted no one else in the village to discover, he might welcome the distracting company of a stranger. Were Thomas particularly fortunate, the man might even find some comfort for his troubled soul in talking to a man of God.

Chapter Twelve

A spotty-faced serving woman gaped when Thomas walked in, licked her lips, and tossed her head in the direction of the rooms upstairs. He lowered his gaze and inched into the mass of sweating men.

One burgundy-cheeked fellow, a wooden tankard of brown ale in hand, stared pointedly at the monk's tonsure, poked him in the ribs, and made a lewd gesture. Feeling his face turn hot, Thomas transformed his blush of outrage into an expression of sheepish unworldliness. The man snorted but let the monk edge by.

If God were willing to grant him just a little grace, Thomas thought, He would lead him to the plump merchant and keep him away from Sayer. If He were truly merciful, He would let him get answers to his questions and allow him to escape this place before he broke some lout's jaw.

When he had at last untangled himself from the milling crowd, Thomas found himself in a comparatively quiet corner of the hostel. At a small table, next to a large pitcher of wine, sat the round young man with dimpled pink face.

He was in luck.

The man rested his cup against his lips as if interrupted by a thought in the act of drinking. Something heavy crashed overhead and he blinked, raising his pale brown eyes and studying the ceiling, fearing perhaps that those carousing above might fall into his lap.

Thomas smiled. "May I join you in what passes for solitude in this worldly place?"

The young man's eyes came to rest on the monk's tonsure. "You are new to the area, Brother?"

"Aye," Thomas replied, happy to answer this one question with truthfulness.

"There is the priory of Amesbury across the river. You would find more congenial company there." He examined the monk with some curiosity. "Your habit is not one commonly seen on the king's roads. Is your Order…?"

"…that of Fontevraud. In truth, I knew about the priory, since I bring a message of greeting from another daughter house, but my journey has been long. The hour is now late, and I fear the gates have been closed." Thomas looked around him with wide-eyed amazement. "I thought I might clear the travel dust from my throat before I found a stable in which to sleep, but I have long been out of the world. I had no idea that this inn would be so…"

"Popular?" The man's laugh was merry and utterly devoid of ridicule. "Forgive my discourtesy, Brother." He gestured to a seat opposite him. "I am Bernard of Amesbury, a glover in this town. Will you join me in some wine?"

Although this Bernard was as sober as he had looked, he turned out to be a most sociable man, much inclined to talk as he poured Thomas a generous cup of wine. The stout fellow might be a merchant, but Thomas warmed to him as he sat back and listened to the glover tell him about Amesbury and its unusual environs. With more drink, he thought, the man's tongue would surely loosen, and he could pose some questions.

"There is a great stone circle not far away. If you came to Amesbury by the western road, surely you saw it."

Thomas shrugged. It was just as well, he decided, to remain vague about his journey. Even though they had traveled from the east, he had heard talk of this circle on the way. "The sun was setting, and our party was hurrying to reach the village before dark. I noted it but little. A strange pile of huge rocks?"

"Perhaps you were wise not to tarry, for many believe it a haunt of Satan and his minions. The plain on which it sits is bleak enough for hellish things, and there are always robbers to beset lone travelers even if the Devil is not about."

"Robbers, imps, or both? What is your opinion?" Thomas carefully sipped his drink and was surprised to find that the wine was a pleasant one. He hoped he was not sampling Master Herbert's wares.

"Lawless men are everywhere in England, Brother, but I cannot believe the stones shelter imps." Bernard shut his eyes and smiled as if falling into a pleasant dream. "It is a wondrous place. Sometimes I have imagined that a knight of the Round Table raised it as a monument after King Arthur's death on Salisbury Plain, or else Brutus of Troy came here, hoping to rebuild the city of his father. When the days are at their longest, I ride out to watch the light playing amongst the stones and how the shadows dance. I feel no fear, even when I walk to the center. Instead, there is only profound silence, one that is as calming as if God had blessed the place. I doubt any evil lives there." He laughed, dimples plunging deep into his cheeks. "I burden you with my fanciful thoughts and beg pardon!"

"Nay, Master Bernard, do not apologize, but please forgive me if I ask this: do you write verse? Singing well-turned phrases at court might serve both you and your gloves well!" Thomas grinned with genuine pleasantry. "I have heard that King Henry and his queen happily part with coin and gifts for finely crafted art. Business might come your way as well."

Bernard quickly sang the one English line from *Dou Way Robyn*. His voice grated like a saw on metal. "That may prove my lack of talent in the art of music, Brother. In truth, one of my neighbors has forbidden me to sing, lest my voice hurt the ears of his pigs. He claims the sows would miscarry should they hear me."

"Surely your neighbor jests."

"He is my sister's husband."

Thomas laughed and took another appreciative sip of the wine. "Your stone circle does intrigue me. If there are no imps in residence, our party had only lawless men to fear. We must have been most fortunate to avoid them."

"They do not bother large or armed groups, nor those from our village. I suspect they are local men." The glover's expression soured. "Were there not some honor amongst them, we would be severely troubled. Our sheriff fancies boar chasing more than he does the pursuit of men who break the king's law."

Thomas raised an eyebrow. "A corrupt sheriff?"

"Nay. A lazy one."

The monk fell silent as he pretended to drink. Since he had gained little from the discussion so far, he had to turn the discussion into another path. "Your priory here is famous in our Order. Was it not founded by a Saxon queen who murdered her stepson and sought forgiveness for her sin?"

Bernard brightened. "Queen Elfrida. She died not long before King William came from Normandy, yet many claim the site is far older than that. Others in England may say that Queen Guinevere died elsewhere, but we in Amesbury insist it was here. After all, it would have been fitting that she live her last days in penance near the place Mordred slew the king she wronged."

"For cert! The presence of such an ancient place of faith should be the reason the village is little disturbed by evil, even if your sheriff is lax. The prayers of so many monks and nuns would surely save you from all demons."

As the monk had hoped, Bernard's expression turned gloomy. "One would think so, yet a strange spirit now troubles us."

Thomas leaned back, gazing at the glover with expectant curiosity.

Bernard bent across the wooden table, his voice lowered as if he feared someone would overhear. "Some weeks ago, men first reported seeing a ghost near the River Avon, just around dusk or early dawn. Soon after, a few monks claimed that the phantom had drifted within the walls of the priory as well." Bernard sat back, drank deeply from his cup, and stared in silence at a spot over Thomas' shoulder. "This morning a man's body was found, beheaded. Now men say that this ghost must be a most vengeful spirit for it has turned murderous."

"Why has this hellish thing come to Amesbury? What sin could the village or, God forbid, the priory have committed that Satan would let loose this creature from his domain?" Thomas shook his head. "Pardon my questions but I am filled with wonder at your story!"

Bernard gave him a thin smile. "Forgive me if my words offend, Brother, but some from the priory came to this inn to satisfy worldly longings. Did you note the reaction to your presence? I hope no one approached you with base intent?"

"I fear I might not understand their meaning if they did, Master Glover, for I came to my vocation as a youth…" Thomas lowered his head to suggest modest innocence while praying that the lie that should have shone in his eyes would remain hidden.

Bernard straightened his back. "The lapse in monastic chastity was but a momentary one! Since the grandfather of our current king cast the sinful Benedictines out and invited those of your Order to take their place, this priory has been steadfast in God's service. If He was offended by the weakness of a few, He would have been pleased when Prioress Ida swiftly made amends and chased the Devil back to Hell. I do believe, if Queen Elfrida's spirit was the one loosed by Satan as some have claimed, that she would have returned to Purgatory by now and not slain this man."

"You do not believe a ghost killed him?"

"There is another spirit that might be abroad, that of a local merchant's wife. She drowned in the Avon. Although some believe she committed self-murder, others think she was unfairly condemned by the crowner's jury to be buried in unsanctified ground as a suicide."

"So her ghost might blame both village and priory for her place in Hell." Thomas rested his chin on folded hands. "Was the murdered man the one who brought witness against this dead woman?"

"He had no part in the verdict," Bernard snapped. "I do not know why she should have any quarrel with him."

Thomas sipped more wine, unsure of where he should go from here. "Might the killer be mortal?" he asked at last, deciding that the direct question might not seem strange.

"Wulfstan had no enemies."

How can a man be slaughtered so brutally, yet have no foe? Thomas wondered. "Then he must have been killed by this heinous phantom of a woman."

The man's knuckles turned white as he gripped his cup. "Eda was ever a virtuous creature. Although no mortal can live without sin, she came near enough in her devotion to God's commandments. I cannot believe she would ever commit such a crime, even after suffering the tortures of Hell."

Thomas blinked at the sharpness in tone. The boyishness had fled and left behind an angry man.

The glover silently filled the monk's cup and poured a modest amount of wine for himself. His hand was steady.

The man is quite calm, Thomas thought, almost too calm.

Suddenly, Bernard slammed the cup down on the table and covered his face with his hands. "Cursed be that priory! It brings grief to mortal men."

Stunned at the outburst, Thomas sat back. What contradictory views of the priory! After what he had overheard between Bernard and Sayer, he wondered if some wish for vengeance was the cause of this passionate cry. Might a clue to the identity of the ghost be found in it or even something about the Psalter theft? He reached out and touched the man's arm in sympathy but said nothing. Silence was the better tool for bringing truth to a man's lips.

"Ah, forgive me, Brother," Bernard said at last, his now exposed eyes wet with tears. "I should not burden you with minor woes. You asked about ghosts, but I cannot imagine who would stalk innocent men and kill them so cruelly. I can only suggest that it could not be sweet Eda."

Sincerity colors that speech, Thomas decided. "Are there any strangers in town or at the priory, Master Bernard? Might the phantom be found amongst them?"

"Our town is known for hospitality, else we would not have this well-stocked inn, nor is the priory ungenerous to travelers. There are always strangers here, but they come and go. A few in their late years have made accommodation with the priory for care in exchange for lands or other wealth, but I cannot see any silver-haired man or his hunched dame playing a cruel spirit that beheads innocent men."

"No younger strangers who have shown a special interest in the priory?"

"Other than you, Brother? Nay."

"And I but long to learn more of the Evil One's devious ways!" The monk folded his hands and lowered his eyes. "Does anyone local have a quarrel with the monks and nuns there?"

Bernard snorted and quickly swallowed his cup of wine. "You are looking at the only man who might."

Thomas' eyes widened with hope.

Chapter Thirteen

The glover rose hastily from his seat. "I have grown too merry, Brother, and must seek my bed. Morning comes early for those of us who live by trade, and gloves need a steady hand at stitching if they are to please a woman's critical eye."

"Nay, not yet!" Thomas reached out in genuine supplication. "Your words have struck fear in my heart. If this priory has brought grief to mortals, I question whether I dare approach the gates without meeting with evil spirits."

"Do not be alarmed. My remark was but a common complaint amongst men who have no wives but see so many eligible women encloistered. Take my words as the poor jests they were. The wine made me forget that becoming a nun is a holier choice than wedding a man like me."

"I hope one of those who chose God did not betray your hopes…"

The glover shoved the nearly full wine pitcher toward Thomas. "I will not offend your ears with the meaningless speech of a sinful man, Brother. Please finish this and remember me in your prayers." With that, he dropped a coin into the monk's hand, bowed, and disappeared through the crowd.

Thomas hit the table with clenched fist. "I have let myself be fooled by a boyish face," he growled. "I should have pressed him harder. Surely this glover has some quarrel with the priory. Does it involve a woman?" He stared at the coin the man had donated to him. It was not the meager offering of those given to the token gestures of superficial faith. "No one who fears for his soul, like this man may, plans to steal a nun for his bed. Nay, if Master Bernard and Sayer have some plot together, it must mean profit for them both. After all, the glover is a merchant and the roofer is a rogue."

Growing gloomy with frustration, the monk tilted the pitcher and contemplated the large quantity of wine remaining. Quickly, he downed what was in his cup, poured another, and listened to the raucous joyfulness that filled Amesbury's best hostel.

Had Thomas been possessed of a more selfish nature, he might have viewed such merry crowds with envy. Were he a man of greater faith, he would have leapt upon this table and screamed abuse at the people, describing how they would look as they tottered on the maw of Hell. He was neither, however, and all he could feel was distance from any kind of happiness, a profound melancholy that he blamed only on himself.

"I have failed," he muttered, finishing the wine he had just poured and replenishing his cup. Now that the glover had escaped him, he felt defeated and did not know what he should do next. Without a clear purpose to occupy his thoughts, Thomas grew increasingly uneasy sitting in the inn. "I should never have come here," he said to his crudely wrought mazer.

In his days as a clerk, he had often partaken of an inn's particular joys. The darkness of his prison may have dimmed the shimmering lure of enjoyable ale and willing women, but Thomas would never pretend his past had been other than what it was or that he had become a monk as penance. Perhaps, he thought with some bitterness, he was too sober to find the women here as attractive as they had seemed when he and Giles had shared them.

He finished the cup, poured another, then another, and tried to force such memories away. He did not succeed. With the energy of some dark will, the past roared back into his soul. Even his normally quiescent flesh had inexplicably hardened, mocking his long impotence.

Thomas summoned the serving wench. With only a brief glance at the coin in his open hand, she put another pitcher in front of him. He drank deeply.

A voice began to hiss in his ear. Was it his dead father? "No son of mine would ever release his seed in another man's body," it echoed with contempt. Thomas shook his head and the voice faded, replaced by laughter. Surely that belonged to the Prince of Darkness.

"We haven't seen any of your vocation for some time, Brother."

Thomas looked up.

The innkeeper stood over him. As the man bent his head in the direction of a woman beside him, his grin seemed unnaturally wide.

Thomas turned his head carefully from one side to the other. "I am a monk," he enunciated carefully.

The pair disappeared.

He finished his cup and poured more from the new pitcher. A soft wall was slowly surrounding him, and the noise of the inn began to fade. The wine was acting like a balm on the deep bruises in his soul. He closed his eyes. When he opened them, the world was muted, blessedly so.

Thomas looked into his cup. He should not be drinking like this. Did he think he was still some boyish clerk, unburdened by a man's responsibility? Whatever his pain, honor was at stake. Both his prioress and his spy master had set him tasks, and he had given his word that he would carry them out. Maybe he had learned nothing from Master Bernard, but surely there were other men here with looser tongues. He shoved the pitcher away and focused his aching eyes on the figures in front of him.

Many in the crowd had grown quite cheerful with drink. In one corner, several sang with ragged harmony. Despite the press of bodies, with little room for privacy, two men sat nearby, heads almost touching as they spoke with some apparent urgency.

What were they talking about? Women? Thievery? Crops? Were any of them plotting to steal the Amesbury Psalter?

Thomas sat forward and pretended to sip his wine. Could he ease himself toward the pair and listen in on what they were saying? If he heard something of interest, how could he join them?

He swore under his breath. Even if he posed as a wayward monk, and a drunken one at that, he would learn nothing. Like the red-faced man who had mocked him when he first arrived, these men would never treat him like a fellow. Instead, they would surround him, taunting with ribald jests, pressing and grabbing at him, jabbing their fingers...

"God save me!" he gasped as reawakened pain and humiliation raged through his soul like flames shot from Hell. Grabbing the pitcher, he threw back his head and gulped the wine, praying that would extinguish the inferno, but the fire seemed unquenchable. He set the empty jug down and, trembling, covered his face with his hands.

He knew he must leave, but he could not move. Satan had stunned his will. Thomas tilted the pitcher back once more. It was empty. He dropped it. In despair, he tried to pray, but his charred soul had grown numb with tortured memories.

A hand pushed a tankard of ale toward him, and a man slid onto the bench beside him.

"I am pleased to see you here, Brother, and quite admire your cleverness in discovering a way out of the priory." Sayer's face was red, his look unfocused.

God had most assuredly forsaken him. "Nor am I surprised to find you," Thomas replied softly.

The young man gestured at a nearby serving wench. "You can do better than that one," he said. "Every man has her."

"She does not interest me." Thomas had not even noticed her.

"A monk who is particular about how he breaks his vows?"

"Most are not?" A cold spot of sobriety was emerging just behind his eyes.

"Contrary to common jest, few of your monks ever leapt over the wall, and most of those were so shocked when their feet touched profane earth that their manhood wilted." Sayer put his hand on Thomas' shoulder. "The others jumped on any willing woman, after which they ran back to the priory, cupping themselves as if their sex might fall off from the sinning." His words slurred.

"I am not looking for a woman."

"What are you looking for, monk?" The man's hand slipped down Thomas' back and came to rest on his thigh.

Thomas froze, shock now chasing off his remaining drunkenness.

Sayer stared across the room and drank his ale in silence. His fingers briefly stroked the monk's leg with a light caress.

Why had God so abandoned him? Sweat began to pour down Thomas' sides. Was he not on a quest for His Church? With his last ounce of mortal will, the monk silently removed Sayer's hand. All speech had turned to ash in his throat.

Sayer's expression did not change. A passing serving wench slammed a full tankard of ale in front of him. Without a word, he drained it dry and dropped it on the table. As the vessel tumbled onto the floor, the roofer swayed for a moment, then passed out.

Thomas sprang from the bench and elbowed his way through the crowd, not caring what pain he might cause any man. He had to get as far from Sayer as he could. Although the inn was hot, Thomas knew the heated air was not the cause for the sweat that now bathed his entire body. Surely it was rage that filled him, he thought, but something within him laughed.

Thomas rubbed his coarse sleeve over his face and leaned against a rough support beam. His humors were just out of balance. That was the reason for his strange mood tonight. He had had no time to mourn his own father, then Sayer's had been murdered, and the roofer's grief rekindled his own unhappiness. He had had too much to drink. Sayer had as well. Surely the man had been too drunk to know what he was doing. With God's grace, he thought, Sayer would not even remember meeting him at the inn this night.

As he pressed his back against the beam, Thomas breathed in the rank stench of inn air, finding comfort in the smell of living men. Satan had best take his imps back to Hell, he growled to himself, for he would not fall prey to them again. He had work to do and valuable time had been lost.

With all that now firmly decided, he shouldered his way through the inn door and plunged into night's restless and less-defined shadows.

Chapter Fourteen

It was following the midday meal that Eleanor set off for Amesbury village.

In the morning she had risen with an unusual eagerness to face the day, and, when she joined the others for prayer, she felt a fresh surge of strength. Like any mortal who has stood with one foot raised to step into the dark mouth of Death, she savored the sensation while likewise fearing it would recede. Thankfully the vigor remained and she gained hope. Besides, the weather was too sweet for bleak imaginings.

As she walked through the cloister garth after Chapter, she had lifted her gaze to the blue sky and expressed gratitude to God for the warmth of this day so near to Saint Melor's feast. Despite Death's recent dance for her soul, as he pleaded to win it before her hair turned white, Sister Anne had dropped a portcullis on his grim supplication, and Eleanor had no wish to raise the gate.

Lest the clattering creature hold onto any illusion that Eleanor might still be his, the prioress of Tyndal had sipped with determination her dark, meaty broth at dinner and even found appetite for the eel with herbs and onions. The religious in charge of Amesbury's kitchens had done well with the dish, she had thought with appreciation, although she did prefer the defter hand of Sister Matilda at Tyndal.

It was afterward she told Anne and her aunt of her plans to visit Alys' mother. She should offer that family comfort considering their kinsman's horrible death, she said. It was her duty, and, if she happened to find out anything about the ghost, Brother Thomas could pursue the details.

The distance to the house of Mistress Jhone was not far, the novice mistress reluctantly confirmed, and Eleanor promised to stay only as long as her strength allowed. Needless to say, she would take two religious with her as proper attendants, but they could be from the priory. After all, the Prioress of Tyndal said with a playful smile, hadn't her aunt just expressed concern about cankerworm in the fruit trees and wasn't Anne planning to teach Brother Infirmarian how to make some of her most effective potions?

As she kissed her aunt and hugged her dear friend, Eleanor felt a deep joy as if she had just been freed from some dark prison. Eternity in the embrace of God is a thing for which we all long, she thought, but surely it is not a sin to look upon the earth He made so sweet with particular delight after hearing the hushed and seductive voice of Death.

Now outside the parish church, she turned to her attendants and asked to be given a moment alone. Bowing her head in reverence, she continued on a few steps and looked up at the ancient Saxon Cross, the wheelhead shape embracing the symbol of her faith like the arms of a mother about her child.

She rested the tips of her fingers against the weathered sandstone, closed her eyes, and imagined the countless monks or nuns that must have done the same, even before Queen Elfrida had founded Amesbury Priory. Had Edgar's queen also touched this stone, her soul raw with guilt and grief? Or had Guinevere, weary with age and ancient lust, before she begged entrance to a religious house nearby?

Eleanor's fingers tingled. Was it a coincidence that each story involved a woman burdened by violence and passion? Might there be a message for her in their stories? Was she herself not a woman guilty of lust and sick of bloodshed. Did she not long for God's peace too? A sense of comfort and understanding slowly filled her, and Eleanor began to believe that the invisible spirits of these two, long-dead women might be beside her. For just one moment, she wondered if her aunt could be wrong about ghosts.

"I, too, have done this, my lady, but not since I was a lad. Do you think the cross was here when King Arthur rode to his death on the plain?"

Eleanor swung around to face a well-favored man, well into his third decade of life, with eyes so brown they reminded her of good English earth. A merchant of some wealth, she decided after a brief inspection of the fur trimming on his very soft robe. Nor is he too modest to flaunt it, she concluded wryly.

"You have the advantage of me, sir."

He bowed with grace. "Herbert of Amesbury, my lady, a wine merchant by trade."

Alys' suitor? How providential, Eleanor thought. "I am…"

"Prioress Eleanor of Tyndal." His smile conveyed pleasant warmth. "News of your arrival has spread, my lady. Your reputation as prioress of a Fontevraudine daughter house is well-known in Amesbury. We are proud of you in the village as well as at the priory that nurtured you."

"Proud?" Eleanor raised her eyebrows with mock dismay.

Herbert bent his head in courteous concession. "A sin and not a sentiment that your fellow religious would express, but we secular creatures, with more errant souls, indulge in it with frequency. Pride we may feel, but the priory gains greater honor as more tales of your competence reach us." He noted her attendants with some curiosity. "You have business outside the walls, my lady?"

"Sister Beatrice bade me visit the sister-in-law and niece of one Wulfstan, a laborer in this priory's fields." She gestured toward a house but a short distance away.

"Ah! The young woman is my affianced."

Not as *affianced* as you would like to assume, Eleanor said to herself. Careful to conceal her thoughts, she quickly changed the subject. "You are a purveyor of wine, Master Herbert. Does your family supply the priory with its most excellent vintages?"

He closed his eyes. "Nay, another has always had that honor. I pray that God has given my father's soul peace, but I fear that he was not as clever at worldly business as he might have been while he lived. There were markets he failed to capture."

"I see that you have improved on the family fortunes, however." The prioress inclined her head to indicate his fine attire.

"Indeed." Master Herbert bestowed on her a most dazzling smile.

A man who does not wish to hide the light of his talents beneath any bushel, Eleanor thought. Alys had also been correct. The man did have a full complement of teeth.

"Nonetheless, wine is a business that requires travel to my vineyards in Gascony, and I had hoped to settle more permanently in Amesbury once my dear Alys and I were married. Before her father's death, he and I had agreed that some of my many contacts, acquired over the years outside of England, might be useful in improving his wool profits as well, but he knew men in London who could act on my behalf in those places."

Eleanor nodded. When she and her new prior had agreed to increase the number of sheep owned by Tyndal, he, too, had acquired such agents for the foreign trade.

"After the marriage, I had planned to find another to run the vintner trade, perhaps a man without family, and spend more of my time closer to home and devoted to wool. After the sad death of Alys' father, I feel compelled to avoid dangerous sea travel and remain in Amesbury, for he not only left my affianced but a widow as well. Both women need the security of my presence."

He might be a tradesman over fond of his success, Eleanor thought, but she liked his show of consideration for the needs of his new family. A man not without compassion, she decided, glancing up at him.

"Were you coming to see Mistress Jhone and her daughter as well, Master Vintner?"

"It would be wiser if I came later," he replied, his lips twitching with presumed humor. "My purpose was to woo, but I fear that might not be seemly when the Prioress of Tyndal visits. Would you not agree?"

With grace, Eleanor laughed.

Herbert bowed, accepted the blessing of the young monk in attendance, and dropped something into his hand. A moment and he was gone.

Eleanor slid her hands into the sleeves of her robe and watched him walk away. Their meeting had been too brief for more than a hasty assessment, although she acknowledged that she had enjoyed the man's clever and blunt speech. What she found troubling was his attire: a soft woolen robe, with nap so new it was still long and had never been brushed; fur-trimmed, and decorated with gold pins. All this suggested vanity and excessive pride in worldly gain.

She was a nun, of course. Having rejected even the simplest feminine ornament, she knew that she might be disposed to see sin in any blatant display of wealth; but she had also learned to distrust men, when it came to business matters, who preened like peacocks. Unlike Tostig, her direct-dealing partner in the ale trade and a man who cared more for the beasts he also bred than any personal adornment, these well-clad merchants often tried to hide less than honorable practices behind the blinding light of their gold jewelry.

Nevertheless, there were always exceptions to any rule amongst mortal men, and Master Herbert had jested about pride himself, a quality she found refreshing. There was something else she liked about the vintner: his desire to care for what was left of a sadly bereaved family. That had touched her heart. Maybe the man truly was just a new widower, awkward in his courting of a girl not much more than half his age who he must know was in love with another man.

To Eleanor, albeit an old woman of twenty-two summers and not of the merchant class, Master Herbert was agreeable in appearance, with a head full of dark hair and lean enough in body to suggest he did not spend too long at table. Besides excellent teeth, he had taut, clear skin on his face that argued against a greater fondness for his wares than was wise. Eleanor realized with mild surprise that she might not have minded giving her troth to such a man had she been the affianced.

The image of a certain red-haired monk now flooded the prioress' heart with dulled but still palpable pain. Nun she might be, she said to herself, but she was a daughter of Eve and knew how reason melted in the flames of a woman's passion. Nay, had she been told to marry this vintner when her heart and body longed for another, she would be as distraught as Alys. A more rational man might find it easy to view this situation with cool logic, but Eleanor of Tyndal understood all too well how the young woman felt in this matter.

The prioress leaned against the house and vigorously shook the image of the handsome monk from her head.

"Are you ill, Sister?"

Eleanor jumped away from the wall and quickly turned to face the speaker.

Standing in the doorway was a gray-fleshed woman, dressed in robes of equal drabness, who looked much as Alys might when she had reached near two score years.

Chapter Fifteen

Thomas strode to the library, his expression cheerless, his gaze determined, and his tongue thick as if wrapped in rough cloth. Not only did his head hurt but he ached all over after spending the night on the other side of the priory walls, passed out on the damp ground with only a grass nest for bedding.

Upon first awakening, he had kept his eyes tightly shut while images from the previous evening danced through his mind with the mocking gracelessness of gangly imps. When he dared to squint at the sky, the sun's angle confirmed his suspicion that he had missed several of the Offices. Briefly he considered whether he might still join the other monastics for Sext if he hurried, but the contents of his stomach pitched into his throat when he rose. Easing back down on his hard bed, he closed his eyes and decided a quiet musing on his transgressions might be wiser than running off to prayer. He would fast today in expiation for his wrongdoings.

The wine drunk last night was a small enough sin. When he had shed his monastic robes and grown a beard to solve a problem in York last year, his thin-lipped spy master had ordered but one full day of prayer for any sins he might have committed on God's behalf. His cause last night was a godly one as well, and he might even claim that visiting a place so full of tempting worldly pleasures was a worthy test for his soul. Robert of Arbrissel, Fontevraud's founder, would surely have approved the attempt.

Nor had he merely indulged frail mortal curiosity when he listened to Master Bernard's tales of Amesbury and the people who lived there. Fortunately, he had remained sober enough in Bernard's company to remember the details of what he was told. If nothing suggested anything of true merit now, it might later as he thought more on the stories with a sober mind. One conclusion had become apparent. If there were no strangers who had spent any time here or shown any specific interest in the priory, the source of the proposed theft must be local.

And what of the ghost? He could be truthful enough about his failure to find Queen Elfrida's spirit innocent of this most recent murder, but Prioress Eleanor might see something of note in the villagers' belief that demons hid amongst the stones on Salisbury Plain. She often saw things he could not, although time and again she generously asked for his observations.

Thomas rubbed at the grit in his eyes. His prioress was a rarity amongst women, a sex many claimed was plagued by illogic and uncontrolled lust, yet the power of her reason was surpassed by few, in his opinion, and only when she was angry had he seen her gray eyes turn hot like glowing ash.

"In this last, she is a better man than I," he muttered. He envied her ability to stand apart from the sins common to most of Adam's progeny and maintain the masculine balance in her humors while others suffered from their frailties, joyfully selling their souls in exchange for relief from the relentless agony of such weaknesses as lust. "I have not yet made a bargain with the Devil, but I understand why some do," he groaned.

This morning, when Thomas had risen from his grass bed, he had gone to the river and washed himself. Had he not rinsed away the sweat of the night, he could not have faced either Sister Anne or Sister Beatrice, both of whom had bedded men often enough in their youth. He might explain the sourness of wine on his breath, but he could not so easily dismiss the unchaste smell of sex. Therein lay his greatest sin, the least forgivable one, from his evening at the inn.

While the other monks of Amesbury had been singing the Morning Office, Thomas had been deep in dreams. In the past, when Satan's incubus came to seduce him in his sleep, it had always donned the shape of Giles. The caresses Thomas exchanged with that image of his boyhood friend were founded in honorable love, so when his flesh hardened, Thomas cursed the Lord of Fiends and did not condemn himself in the morning for any greater wickedness than a common failing of a man's sex.

Last night, however, the Devil had introduced a disquieting variation in his cruel sport. The incubus who drew the monk into his arms may have worn the body of Giles, but the face was that of Sayer. When Thomas awakened, bursting out of this dream with a rare orgasmic joy, he had lain on the ground, grateful for the physical release of dammed-up seed but terrified by feelings he did not understand.

Why had he been cursed with this strange new affliction? Were his lonely walks through the dark silence of the monk's cloister, when his sleepless nights gave fetid birth to his black humors, not penance enough for the one act of sodomy he had committed with Giles?

Other monks, when they suffered similar dark longings, took the flail to their backs to keep their souls from falling into Hell. That he knew. Some fasted until their manhood was too weak to sin. Nothing, however, had ever spared Thomas from his dreams, even when he was in prison, after he was raped, and when he once beat his back bloody.

He stopped, uncomfortably aware that he stood near the library walls. Cautiously he looked up. Sayer was not there. At least God had been kind enough to grant him that reprieve. The roofer was one he did not want to see again for a very long time.

He slammed his fist against his chest.

The smaller limbs of the tree above him moved gently in the breeze.

"If You scorn me, why give me any peace? If You do not, why scourge me with this new and fiendish apparition?"

Thomas leaned his head against the bark, but the only thing he heard was the pounding in his head. "Very well," he said, pushing away from the tree, "since God deigns no answer now, but I feel no hot breath of Hell on my cheek, I shall see to the Amesbury Psalter."

⟨ೲഗ ೲഗ ೲഗ⟩

The library was tiny and combined with the scriptorium. Although there were books stacked neatly in a wood-lined recess near the door, and others presumably stored in the wooden chest nearby, Thomas saw only two tonsured heads bent over their work, their left hands holding the parchment flat while they labored to create the text with their right.

Amesbury Priory was not renowned for illuminated work, but the monastery had wealthy patrons whose educated daughters, and sometimes widows, came here as nuns. These were women who prayed with more piety in the presence of God-inspired beauty, and the priory would set any talented monk to the task of filling such a need. It was a pity, he thought, that there were only two.

As he wandered over to look at the books in the recess, he recognized some that Sister Beatrice had loaned Prioress Eleanor, works that Sister Anne had described to him in detail. Both of them had been amazed at what their prioress read. After meeting the formidable Sister Beatrice, they wondered no longer where their leader had gotten her taste in everything from the works of the sainted Augustine to *La Mort le Roi Artu*.

Here was an herbal he had seen, a work not elaborately illustrated but done adequately enough. When their prioress had loaned it to them, he and Sister Anne had soon memorized the details but nonetheless regretted returning the book itself to Amesbury.

Thomas walked back and stopped to look over the shoulder of one monk. The man was so deep in prayerful concentration on his illuminated letter that he was unaware anyone stood so close. His work was not skillful, but the robes of the archangel were folded with a certain grace even if the colors were muddy.

"May I help you, Brother?"

Thomas turned to see an elderly monk standing next to him.

"I am called Brother Baeda, the librarian. By your garb I know you belong to this Order, yet I do not know your name. You are from…?"

"Tyndal, Brother. My prioress has traveled here to see her aunt, Sister Beatrice, and I accompanied her. My name is Thomas."

The man's toothless grin was warm. "You came with Prioress Eleanor? I knew her when she was just a novice. A thoughtful, devout, and clever girl, she was. Surely our noble King Henry was inspired by God when he sent her to your priory."

Thomas bowed his concurrence. "I have heard about your famous Psalter and was told that Prioress Ida sent it here for repair."

The monk studied Thomas with interest. "Then you are the one to do the work? I thought it would be done by an older man who was not of this Order…"

"Nay, I am not skilled in such artistry. I came only to look at it."

"It is a fine manuscript, but how did you learn of it?"

"Prioress Eleanor suggested I take the opportunity to see it while I was here."

"Ah, she would remember the Psalter, wouldn't she? Come," Brother Baeda said and gestured for Thomas to follow him.

⁂

Thomas' eyes opened in awe when he saw the beauty of the Psalter. Although the book looked too heavy to hold comfortably in two hands, it had obviously been much used, most probably by the prioresses of Amesbury as it rested on the prie-dieu in their chamber. One corner on the right side of a page was smudged, and the edges were wearing thin. The tear in the upper left was the object of the intended repair.

What troubled him was the placement of the book on a table where anyone could quickly grab it. Other prized works had been stored carefully away. Why was this one left out?

"Forgive me, Brother," he said at last. "I have been rendered speechless by the beauty of this work. The blue of the Virgin's robe is as bright as a jewel, and the angels above her head show a divine grace." The fact that the nursing baby at Mary's breast was red-haired had much caught Thomas' attention and he did wonder at the illuminator's intent. Would Jesus have had such coloring? He looked closer. Maybe the tint was more of a brown.

"Let me show you other examples of its wonders." The monk turned over another page and pointed out a mermaid playing a stringed instrument, carefully incorporated into the "U" in Psalm 94.

Thomas raised an appreciative eyebrow. Now that was a figure Brother John at Tyndal might enjoy as much as he since they both loved music.

"And this! It is very different from anything else you will see." The librarian's face glowed with enthusiasm.

The figure was a birdlike human, but unlike most sirens, it bore a man's head, covered by a round and spiked Jewish cap.

The creature strangely reminded Thomas of Sayer. He cleared his throat.

"You are familiar with the work of the Sarum Master?"

"Nay, Brother Baeda."

The man's face brightened at the prospect of telling a new-comer what others here had most probably been told all too often. "Look at the folds in the robes, how graceful and soft. He was known for this in all his works and was the envy of other illuminators in England and elsewhere."

"He is a local man?'

"Salisbury. This work was done about twenty ago and was the prized possession of a nun in our Order. See here how he portrayed her."

Thomas studied the small figure of a woman in plain robes kneeling at a gold lectern on which a book rested, open to a page inscribed with a red "B" for *Beatus*.

"Forgive me if I misunderstood, but I thought this treasure was here for repair and that few visitors came to see it. I do wonder why the Psalter is left exposed where it might suffer more damage."

The monk shook his head. "You did not misinterpret my words, Brother, but I have chosen not to move the manuscript more than need be, and, over the last few days, the work has drawn interest. You are the second who has asked to see it."

"Second?" Thomas' heart beat faster.

"Aye, young Sayer has visited twice and begged to view it. At first, I thought it odd that Wulfstan's son should care so much about religious works like this, but he had many good questions about it. I was pleased to answer them."

Thomas might not have been so well pleased, but he was also not quite as surprised as Brother Baeda.

Chapter Sixteen

Mistress Jhone poured a dark red wine into a plain pewter cup and handed it to the Prioress of Tyndal.

On the nearby table a servant had placed a generously filled plate of thickly cut apples, so carefully preserved that their skins were still brightly splashed with red and green; a huge wedge of green-veined orange cheese; and a large loaf of grainy bread, hot from the baking. In a tone suggesting that the welfare of her soul depended upon the nun's assent, the widow begged the prioress to sample everything.

Eleanor voiced courteous appreciation for the bounty presented to her, then carefully selected a slice of cheese, one of apple, and positioned each on top of the fragrant bread according to some obscure plan. In this manner, she disguised her scrutiny of the woman before her.

Jhone's face and hands were as devoid of color as her robe. A narrow scar, shining white, sliced through the woman's upper lip; another cut through her left eyebrow. Tiny wrinkles crossed her forehead, and the looseness around her neck suggested that she should be two decades older than her undimmed brown hair and her daughter's sixteen years would support. Only the corners of her eyes and the skin around her mouth lacked any mark, an absence Eleanor found distressing. Had the woman never laughed?

Alys may not have exaggerated in the tale about her father, Eleanor concluded. The signs of grief gouged into the face of this widow might well be explained by the death of a husband, but she saw no evidence that any joy for his life had preceded it. As the prioress glanced at the widow's pale eyes, she wondered how Mistress Jhone could lament the death of such a spouse. Newly freed of a brutish mate, the widow remained subdued as if afraid any speech might still invite pain.

The law permitted a man to strike his wife, for cert, but there were limits. Although some secular and religious men suggested there was merit in these beatings, Eleanor knew of no rule requiring such cruel treatment. In any case, she had known few men who did not honor their wives, even those they no longer loved or perhaps never had. Compared to this woolmonger, godless beasts showed more tenderness in their mating than he had to his wife.

Eleanor suddenly realized that she had let the silence linger too long. "Your generosity in sharing this gift from God is praiseworthy," she said, looking up at the widow with a smile.

"You are kind to grace us with a visit, my lady," Jhone whispered.

"I could do no less. Your sister's husband was foully murdered outside the priory. We all grieved to hear of this worthy man's death."

Jhone's eyes shifted nervously from left to right. Her face flushed in uneven splotches of pink. Clearing her throat, she raised her mazer of wine and drank deeply.

"Sister Beatrice knew that the discovery of his body made the horrible blow twice as painful to you. I have come to offer God's comfort and soothing prayer."

The widow set her cup down on the table with excessive care but remained silent.

Eleanor shook her head. "No one at the priory could imagine who could have hated him so much, for the act was not one of common violence."

"The ghost."

Eleanor blinked at the hushed accusation. "Forgive me, but I do not understand."

Her color now a mottled crimson, the woman jumped up, grabbed the plate of food from the table, and thrust it at the prioress. "Please have more!"

Eleanor rescued the plate from the widow's shaking hands. "Surely his death was caused by a mortal creature. Although I have heard of this spirit, I cannot imagine what quarrel Queen Elfrida might have with Wulfstan."

"Master Herbert believes the ghost is not the ancient queen but the wronged soul of his dead wife, Eda. As evidence, he says witnesses claim the specter's crown is made of glowing spikes, not gems or gold." The widow's usual pallor returned. "He must be right."

Eleanor raised her eyebrows with encouraging curiosity. "Did Mistress Eda have reason to harm Wulfstan?"

"He died for his sin in begetting such an evil son as Sayer, a man whom Satan most surely favors."

Eleanor noted that moisture now glistened on the woman's forehead. "Is this the same man who repairs the priory roofs?"

Jhone's eyes flashed with reflective anger. "The very one, my lady. As we all know in Amesbury village, he is a rogue."

Eleanor looked down at her hands. She was still holding the plate. "Wherein lies his sin? If he is so evil, I must wonder why he is allowed to work within the monastery walls," she asked, setting the serving dish back on the table.

The widow licked her lips. "I believe my husband asked the same question, my lady. He considered Sayer a worthless fellow in all respects, although one deemed uncommon handsome. When my nephew was hired by the priory, my husband joked that the nuns must have enjoyed seeing him up on the rooftops, near naked..." The woman covered her mouth, her eyes widening with fearful distress.

That gesture must be an habitual one after many years of marriage to such an evil-minded man, Eleanor concluded. What right did the woolmonger have to cast any stones? Some nuns most certainly did sin in the heart but rarely willingly and almost never with any joy. With difficulty she managed not to counter a dead man's lewd accusation with the outrage she felt. It would serve no purpose.

"Forgive me, my lady, he said that only for my ears. I should not have repeated it." She extended her hands as if begging for mercy. "My heart knew differently."

"What did Prioress Ida say when he spoke to her about this threat to religious chastity?" Eleanor took care to ban indignation from her tone.

"He did not do so, believing there was no purpose." Jhone quickly lowered her head. "Women's minds are incapable of reason, he said, because their bodies itch constantly for coupling."

Eleanor shut her eyes as she felt her face grow hot. This woman did not deserve her wrath for repeating what a husband had said, and those cast down eyes spoke eloquently enough of the widow's own shame at his words. Women sin, Eleanor thought. We are mortal, but neither my aunt nor Prioress Ida is a fool. They would not allow any man to behave in such a bawdy manner around the religious of the priory. She took a deep breath. It calmed her.

"Queen Elfrida's spirit might be angry with the roofer if Sayer tempted the religious with unchaste imaginings. Of that, I can conceive. Why she would extend her quarrel to the man who sired him is less clear to me." Eleanor's lips turned up with a thin smile. "But perhaps a queen may have reasons we cannot comprehend. Yet you say that the ghost is that of Mistress Eda. Why would she murder Wulfstan for fathering a rogue?"

"For the same reason King Edgar's spouse might have. You see, my husband told me that Sayer had seduced Master Herbert's wife." A spasm began to throb in Jhone's cheek. "I never accepted that Eda would have sinned with him, but my husband believed she did. Thus he added his voice to those who said she must have committed suicide from the pain of her tumor, although he thought she had done so out of adulterous shame."

"He proclaimed her adultery at the crowner's inquest?" Eleanor asked, noting this one difference of opinion between the woolmonger and his meek spouse. She wondered at what price Jhone had held it or if she had even voiced the thought until now.

"Nay. He said self-murder was a sin, whatever the reason for it, and refused to put public horns on Master Herbert, a man he called *friend*."

"Was your husband a witness to the adultery?" As soon as the words were out of her mouth, Eleanor knew she had erred. Lulled by the widow's brief show of independence over Eda's virtue, she had forgotten how effectively this husband had used terror to rule Jhone for so many years. The widow had been well-trained to defend him. Casting doubt on his word so soon after his death was most ill-advised.

As expected, Mistress Jhone's back straightened like a stone pillar. "I would never have questioned him on such a matter. I was ever a dutiful wife, my lady." Her voice snapped with outrage.

Scornful laughter shattered the brief silence between prioress and widow.

Startled, Eleanor turned around.

Alys stood in the doorway.

"How dare you repeat such a loathsome tale, Mother? Have you forgotten how Mistress Eda bathed your wounds after my father beat you until you almost died and the babe you carried did? You may choose to set aside her benevolent acts, but I will not forget the food she brought for me or the broth she helped you sip when my father disappeared for days, drinking himself senseless at the inn. As for my cousin Sayer, he would never have touched her any more than she would have bedded with him!"

"Unnatural child!" Jhone shouted at her. "Satan has bought your tongue and put lies in your mouth about your dear father."

The two women stared at each other with such great anger that they lost all power of speech. Then Mistress Jhone wilted like a flower deprived of water and turned away.

Alys stepped back, shaking from the war of words with her mother. "I beg forgiveness, my lady," she said to Eleanor. "After suffering the shock of finding my uncle's body, I was blinded by my grief and failed to recognize or honor you as the Prioress of Tyndal."

"There is never disrespect in calling me *sister*, a title all women share in God's world."

"Even if this holy lady forgives you for that rudeness, Alys, you have more wickedness to repent. No child has the right to speak as you have just done either to or about a parent." Jhone's words hissed like flames struck with water.

Alys slipped to her knees. "I have sinned, Mother. Strike me but forgive as well. My heart honors you despite my harsh speech."

Jhone raised her hand. The first slap snapped her daughter's head to the right, the second to the left.

Eleanor winced with each blow but dared not intervene.

Turning from the sight of the red marks she had left on her daughter's cheeks, Jhone grabbed the plate abandoned on the table and waved it around at arm's length as if the offering would keep some malevolence at bay.

Eleanor accepted a slice of fruit she did not want.

Alys bent her head and said nothing.

"I forgive you, daughter," Jhone whispered, now pulling the plate to her breast as if it were a babe. The food fell to the floor. A small dog leapt up from one corner of the room and chased after a rolling bit of cheese.

Alys remained on her knees. "My lady, I beg admission to the priory as a novice in your Order."

Jhone slammed the plate down on the table with such force that it might have cracked had it not been pewter. "You most certainly do not!"

"I do!"

"And you will fall into mortal sin just like your aunt after she claimed she had a true and holy vocation!" Jhone's voice rose with contempt. "That randy youth you want in your bed is no different from Wulfstan. Bernard will mount you in the shadow of those holy walls and, like Drifa, you will lose all calling to chastity..."

"That is not true!"

"Did Wulfstan not get my sister with child? Ask her, if you refuse to believe your own mother. Only one full moon shone between the time they came to the church door and the day she bore Sayer in much pain, a most worthy reminder of her carnal sin." Jhone reached out to grasp her daughter's hand. "Listen to me, child, please!"

Alys rose and turned her back on the two women. "Bernard is not like my uncle and would marry me first," she muttered, "although I see less sin in conceiving a child in joy than out of loveless duty."

"Had your aunt married as our parents wished, she would have been the wife of a prosperous man. Instead, look at her! Is her face not lined with cares and have you not seen her fingers bleed from hard work? Now that Wulfstan is dead, who will earn the bread to feed her family? An eldest son, who may one day hang for his evil ways, or the younger ones who have no skills except begging? If your eyes are not blinded by the very Devil, you cannot deny the truth of what I say. Honor the greater wisdom of your parents and you will prosper. Follow your lust and you shall end up like my poor sister."

"My aunt is a good woman," Alys replied. "You have never, until now, said otherwise."

"I love Drifa," Jhone said to Eleanor. "As my daughter says, she has been a faithful wife and a blameless mother. Nonetheless, she went contrary to the wishes of our parents and has paid in suffering for that offense."

Eleanor nodded. "Perhaps your sister did not have a true calling, but your daughter might…" She looked over at Alys with sympathy.

"My lady, I long to keep my only remaining child nearby to comfort me in old age and to close my eyes at death. I want grandchildren, and I want a secure future for my family." Tears blanketed her cheeks as Jhone gestured weakly at Eleanor. "Is that so much to ask of a daughter?"

Alys put her arms around her mother. "Bernard and I would give you such a home and, if God so blessed us, grandchildren enough." Then stubbornness once again set her features, and she stepped back. "I cannot marry Master Herbert."

If I cannot stop this quarrel between these two, Eleanor decided, I might as well attempt to guide it. "And this young man of whom you speak? Is he so unacceptable?" The prioress put a soothing hand on the mother's arm. "I only ask to better understand."

Jhone shook her head. "He is like a fledgling, my lady, with but twenty years on this earth..." She reached out and touched her child's hand.

"Twenty-one, Mother," Alys replied but did not resist the widow's touch.

"And a glover," Jhone sniffed. "He has nothing and will starve if God destroys the crops or sends other plagues for our sins. At such times, men give their spare coin to God, not glovers."

"And Master Herbert?" Eleanor asked, observing that both mother and daughter looked much alike when arguing.

"A vintner, a man successful in his trade, and now a widower with whom my husband became friends."

"At the inn," Alys said in a low voice, "where, it seems, they serve friendship along with ale."

Her mother ignored her daughter's words. "My husband knew his health was failing. You see, the strain of becoming such a successful woolmonger had aged him much." The widow's pride in the achievements of her merchant husband gave brightness to her tone.

Alys rolled her eyes but said nothing.

Jhone glared at the girl before continuing. "Since I failed to give him the son he needed, my husband decided that the vintner should marry our only living child and learn the wool trade from him. After which, Master Herbert could take over the business. That plan suited the interests of them both."

Not an unreasonable proposal, Eleanor decided. Fatigue began to fill her body with heaviness. If she stayed longer, would she have the strength to walk back to the priory? She willed the tiredness away.

"My father had a competent man who could have run the business for him, and the man is still there. He can handle everything for us now. There is no need for me to marry Master Herbert."

"That man is leaving to take on his own apprentices, although he promised that he would find another experienced in wool who can work under Master Herbert's direction. The business is well established but needs the firm hand of a clever merchant, not a mere boy!" Jhone looked at the prioress, her eyes pleading for understanding. "I beg of you, my lady, speak reason to this willful child for it seems she must hear it from someone other than me."

Eleanor nodded.

"Sadly, my mother wishes only to hear her husband's voice," Alys said with more tenderness than her words would suggest.

"How dare you speak as if he were not your sire?"

Alys shrugged. "My father thought only of earthly profits. He would never have seen more gain in a heavenly marriage than in an earthly one, but I shall not make the same mistake—if I am forced to choose only between a vintner and God."

Although Alys' argument reminded Eleanor somewhat of her own when faced with a similar choice some years ago, the prioress knew this girl would prefer a secular life as long as she could marry Master Glover.

"Your father was a true Christian! How dare you suggest otherwise?"

Alys threw her hands up in disgust.

Jhone twisted a handful of her robe. "You should be grateful that he chose Master Herbert, a most kind and charitable man, for you to wed. How many would be willing to marry into a family whose reputation has been soiled as ours has been by your uncle's past and your cousin's present sins?"

"Bernard does not care about old or unfounded rumors! Why will you not see this same quality in him?"

"Your glover is an impractical youth, someone who would rather ride out to that pile of pagan rocks and imagine things that never happened. Master Herbert is a sensible man, one who knows the importance of profit and will provide well for you and your children."

"Bernard has virtues!"

"You see," Jhone said with a conspiratorial glance at the prioress, "she cannot deny that her boy is a dreamer."

Eleanor's head was starting to spin.

"His gloves are finely made, and he has a craftsman's eye! Have you not seen the beautiful objects he has given his mother?"

"Pretty baubles, things she cannot use like we do our pewter and plate. He should be investing in items of worth, not buying useless trifles."

Mistress Jhone might have won that argument, Eleanor thought.

"He is moderate in his ways, has never raised a hand in anger, and…"

"…is easily led by others, especially women."

"He listens to my ideas and believes I would be a valuable partner in his trade. Where is the sin in that, if we prosper? As to the rest, dare you say I speak falsely?"

The mother snorted her contempt.

To my mind, at least, Alys won that point, Eleanor decided.

The church bells began to ring the hour.

Eleanor brightened. Now she had reason to leave before she fainted with weariness. Slowly she rose. "I fear it is close to None, and I must return to the priory."

"My lady, will you return and give my daughter the benefit of your wise advice? Surely you can see that she has no calling to become a nun?"

Delighted at the invitation, Eleanor nodded. If God grants me wisdom, she thought, I might bring the balm of peace to this mother and daughter. If He is willing, I may also find out what sins Wulfstan committed long ago and why a vintner's dead wife would wish to kill the father instead of the son, a man who may have helped send her soul to Hell.

"We will speak together soon," Eleanor said, looking at Alys with a reassuring smile. "Sister Beatrice would wish it."

Or will after I tell her what I have heard, the prioress said to herself, then left to collect her obedient escorts from the kitchen.

Chapter Seventeen

Eleanor walked slowly back to the priory. At this sluggish pace, she would miss the Office, but surely God would understand and accept her humble, silent repetition of prayers. Had she not been kept in the village by the need to restore peace to His house?

The meeting with Jhone and Alys had brought many interesting things to light about both ghost and murder, troublesome questions that hung like broken threads from a tapestry. They must fit somewhere, but she could not see how they should be placed to make the pattern clear. Perhaps Brother Thomas had some enlightening news and was waiting for her to return.

As the image of the monk occupied her mind, she was surprised that her thoughts of him were unaccompanied this time by the usual pang of guilt. The cooling of her flesh, temporary though that might be, had most certainly been a welcome respite from her relentless and gnawing hunger to bed the man. By pushing back the fiend who tormented her so, God had brought a gentle shower of hope to her scorched soul.

Wasn't there a treatise that dealt with love between monastics and spiritual friendship? Her aunt had mentioned it years ago when Eleanor was ready to take final vows, but she had never read it. Now she remembered: it was written by Aelred of Rievaulx. Might his words help her cope when the Prince of Darkness sent his imps once again to set fire to her loins? Although the great Cistercian abbot would not have discussed the possibility of such a thing between men and women, Eleanor wondered if his principles could apply in an Order where the two sexes must interact in holy purpose.

Her step lightened. When she finally had time alone with her aunt to seek advice on her sinful longings, Eleanor would ask her opinion on whether the abbot's treatise had insights to help both a prioress and a frail woman.

Meanwhile, what sin could there be in appreciating a man who had proven his worth as an instrument of God's justice? Without question she liked his courtly wit, but she also respected his gentleness as he consoled those in Tyndal's hospital, in particular the suffering children. She doubted he had come to the priory with a strong vocation, but she found him diligent in his duties and wise as a confessor to her nuns.

All told, he had proven himself to be a good man, and she had grieved when his black humors recaptured his spirit on his father's death. Even Sister Anne had failed to comfort him as he fell into a silence darkened with sorrow. She prayed he broke it with his confessor.

At least he had cheered when her aunt had given him the task of discovering what lay behind this ghost, she thought, then frowned. Was it the chance to serve God that refreshed his soul, or had he simply enjoyed escaping from walls he never wanted to surround him in the first place? The thought troubled her. How strongly did the world pull at her monk?

Eleanor glanced back at her two attendants. Although they had remained meekly quiet during this trip into the village, she noted the eagerness with which they now looked around, as if storing rare glimpses of the secular world to savor once they were back within priory confines. Were either truly suited to the contemplative life, she wondered, or were all mortals so joined to the dust from which they came that no one could truly leave the world? Maybe Brother Thomas was no different from any other.

Neither, perhaps, was she. She stopped to take delight in the sight of her beloved Avon. On the path along the river, she noticed a plump young merchant in close conversation with one of his men. The laborer gestured toward the priory walls. The merchant laughed, a sound that seemed both hearty and full of joy to Eleanor's ears. As she smiled at their merriment, she decided that Man might be weak to find pleasure in the earth, but surely God found little sin in this appreciation of His wondrous creation.

She nodded in sympathy at her two attendants, now pink-faced with embarrassment from their not-so-secret thoughts, and resumed her walk to the priory gate. There were less innocent enjoyments here than the sight of a river, however. Had it been too cruel to send Brother Thomas to the inn, a place full of worldly temptations? She had good reason to be confident that he was true to his vows, but she knew from her own experience how quickly flesh joined Satan's games. If she, a woman who had no doubt about her vocation, had suffered lust, how much harder would it be for one who had less of a calling? She closed her eyes and prayed the monk had sinned little beyond taking more drink than might be wise.

The issue of religious vows turned Eleanor's mind back to the contentious debate within the woolmonger's family. Alys had no true calling to become a nun in any Order. That was quite clear. She was most suited to becoming a wife, and her mother had good reason for choosing a successful merchant as the girl's husband.

Although Eleanor had never met the glover, she had not found Master Herbert either ill-favored or insensitive. The match between the pair might not start out with mutual love, but that could grow if each treated the other with thoughtful respect. The marriage between her own father and mother had been arranged as a union of property, not hearts, yet Baron Adam still grieved over his wife's death some sixteen years later. Despite her sympathy for Alys, Eleanor knew it would be best if she found some way of getting the girl to make peace with her parents' choice of spouse.

That aside, what had she learned about this ghost? According to Jhone, there was a connection between Wulfstan's death and the vintner's dead wife, but Eleanor could see no logic in the supposition. Even assuming the soul of Eda was seeking vengeance for her place in the Devil's kingdom, why kill the father and not the son who led her there? And who, besides the vintner himself, would have reason to seek revenge?

She shook her head. That last thought was ridiculous. Why would Master Herbert kill the adulterer's father but pursue marriage with the cousin of the seducer? And why would any killer pointedly bring attention to a tie between his adulterous wife's death and Wulfstan's murder, a link that could well point back at him?

Stopping at the gate, Eleanor closed her eyes and forced her tired mind to see reason in any of this. Nay, the laborer must have been killed by someone who had a quarrel with him, not with Sayer.

"My lady!" The porter's tremulous voice broke through her jumbled thoughts. Although bowing out of respect for her rank, his expression resembled that of a loving father.

She greeted him with affection.

"Brother Thomas has begged an audience when you return."

"Please send him to Prioress Ida's lodging," she replied.

As she started to walk in that direction herself, she stopped, her mouth open in wondrous amazement. Had she not returned from the house of Mistress Jhone filled with deep weariness? Yet now her body had lost that exhaustion. God was most kind!

◌────◌ ◌────◌ ◌────◌

Brother Thomas accepted a mazer of wine and watered it well. "I fear I bring little news."

"May I ask if you slept well, Brother?" Anne teased.

The monk's face flushed. "I did oversleep all the Offices until now. For that, I will do penance…"

"And drank more than you are accustomed to do?" The prioress' voice suggested no reproach.

He nodded. "Far more than any man ought, my lady. Brother Porter must have long been in his bed when I returned. I slept in the grass, quite near the priory walls. Today, I swear Satan has taken over Hell's smithy and is pounding an anvil in my head."

"That is penance enough," Eleanor replied. "You were toiling at God's work, and if that is the worst of your sinning..." His admission of drunkenness was frank enough. Surely he had committed no greater error than this one touch on Satan's hand. She exhaled with relief and quickly nodded for him to continue.

"There are no recent strangers in Amesbury, except ourselves, according to a young merchant I met at the inn. He knew of no one who might have a grudge against this priory." He hesitated.

The pause was not lost on the prioress. "No one?"

"The merchant said he was the only one who might, then swore he was jesting."

"Did he explain what he meant?"

"He is unmarried and grieved that the priory was able to win so many pretty girls to God's service when he could not gain the hand of any. Perhaps he feared he would be forced to marry some elderly widow."

"You spoke only to this merchant?" Anne offered more wine to Thomas.

He refused with an amiable wince. "He had much to say, including that many in the village believe demons have lurked for years near the mammoth stones that lie not far from here." He hesitated, as if waiting for his prioress to ask a question.

Imps so long in residence did not interest her. She gestured for him to go on.

"Some lawless men as well, he said, but they rarely trouble local folk and may be from the village itself. As for the priory, he told me it brought so much custom to the town that anyone would be hard-pressed to find any enemy. Standing as high as it does in the king's favor brings honor to Amesbury as well as coin."

"What had he to say about the ghost?" Eleanor asked.

Thomas lowered his eyes to a silent study of his mazer. "The merchant discounted the rumor that our ghost was Queen Elfrida since the priory has disciplined the wayward monks."

Eleanor saw his face turn red. Surely, she thought, he was not embarrassed by their particular sins. After all, he could not have come as a virgin to the tonsure. "Did he mention the other possible wandering spirit?"

"He denied that tale as well. According to him, Mistress Eda, the vintner's wife, was too charitable a soul on earth to be so cruel in death, even if she was in Hell for her sins. *Sweet Eda*, he called her."

"Was he kin to this woman?"

"I fear I did not think of that question, my lady."

"His words indicate some devotion. Perhaps he was in love with her before she married?"

"I do not know the lady's age, but the merchant is younger than I while the vintner is much older."

Eleanor turned pensive. "Disparate age does not always repel passion, even if the woman is the elder."

Thomas blinked.

"It is a question worth answering, I think. From what you have reported, your merchant seems doubtful that either alleged ghost truly drifts in the river fog. Did he suggest any source or basis for these rumors?"

"Nay."

"Did he mention the murder? In particular, was there any hint of rancor between Wulfstan and a family here? Perhaps Mistress Eda's?"

"He said that Wulfstan had no enemies and had had no part in the verdict condemning the woman's body to burial in unholy earth." A look of confusion spread over his face. "Forgive me, my lady, but I thought you did not want me to ask anything about the man's death."

"Nor did I, when I sent you out to seek gossip about phantoms, but now I have reason to be curious about any tales that are abroad. Did you not tell me that Mistress Jhone is related by marriage to Wulfstan?"

Thomas nodded.

"I had a most noteworthy conversation today with the woolmonger's widow and learned that the vintner's wife was her close friend. Although she seemed quite distressed by the idea, Mistress Jhone claims Mistress Eda was seduced by Wulfstan's son. As a consequence, she believes that the woman's damned soul must have murdered the father in revenge for her adultery with the son. Not a logical conclusion, I freely admit, but an interesting accusation."

"The son who works at the priory?" Anne asked as she passed a well-watered mazer of wine to the prioress.

"Sayer," she replied. "Did you see him last night, Brother?"

Thomas studied the rushes under his feet for a long moment. "Aye, but I could not discuss anything with him. When he joined me, he was drunk and soon passed out."

"I wonder if he is working today, Brother. You would know best about this, but do you think the effects of last night's bright joys might make him eager to speak to a tonsured man on this day after?"

Anne laughed. "Surely he would welcome any excuse to avoid hammering."

"I doubt he will admit adultery with the vintner's wife, or perhaps he might, but this story from Mistress Jhone is the only hint so far that there was some possible quarrel connected with Wulfstan," Eleanor said. "Sayer might say something that casts light on this matter."

"The man was not on the library roof when I passed by earlier." Thomas took some time replacing his untouched wine cup back on the table. "Shall I return to seek him there?"

"I think it is safe enough. It is daytime, and there should be monks enough around. Do not press too hard for information, however, but, if you learn anything of note, we can pass it on to the sheriff when he sees fit to return from his hunt." Eleanor shifted in her chair. "One other question. Your merchant. What was his name?"

"Master Bernard. He is a glover."

Eleanor's eyes widened. "Indeed! You thought him an honest man?"

"No less than most in trade."

Eleanor glanced over at Anne to see her reaction to this remark. Before the nun had taken vows, she and her husband had owned an apothecary. Her expression was benign.

"He was very generous in sharing his wine and giving me coin for prayer..." Thomas stopped and put his hand to his mouth. "Forgive me, my lady, but I failed to mention one thing I did notice about the merchant. When he jested about his grudge against the priory, I sensed no true rancor but did hear some grief in his words. Perhaps I was mistaken..."

"You are quite right in your observation, Brother. Young Alys, although she is to be Master Herbert's wife, wants to marry this glover and has said she will take vows rather than go against her heart. According to her, Master Bernard loves her well in return, but Mistress Jhone claims he is both improvident and greedy."

Thomas snorted. "Both men may be beset with the sin of greed, my lady, but, of the two, I did not like what I saw in Master Herbert. He may be well-favored, but he struck me as a cunning man. The glover?" The monk shrugged. "He is a dreamer, for cert, but I might pick Master Glover to be the more trustworthy."

"I have not met Master Bernard but did meet Master Herbert on my way to the woolmonger's house. My own impression of the vintner is quite different from yours, but I did not speak with him long."

"My encounter was brief as well," Thomas conceded. "There was something else that I may not have mentioned before. When I asked Mistress Jhone and the vintner if Wulfstan had enemies, the widow suggested there might be something relevant that had happened of late. Master Herbert quickly hushed her and refused to let me speak further with her."

"A kindness, I think, to a woman who was among those who discovered Wulfstan's headless corpse and is a widow recently bereaved of her husband."

"Shall I pursue the reason with her now, my lady?"

"I will do that for I have cause to return to her house. I suspect that she may have meant the seduction of Mistress Eda by Sayer. That would explain why the vintner did not want her to speak of it. Surely he would not wish the story repeated in public."

Thomas did not look pleased.

"You do not like the wine merchant, Brother. Surely the reason is founded in more than his trade?"

"I cannot say for sure, my lady. There are some that do good amongst their fellows." He smiled at Anne. "Others reek of avarice. There is a sour smell about this vintner."

"I would never disregard your opinion and will think more on it. Nor have I met the glover so cannot judge whether Mistress Jhone is correct in her judgement of him. Should I meet Master Herbert again, I will keep your words in mind."

"I see one more troubling aspect to this murder," Anne said. "The phantom remains accused of the act, and all witnesses have claimed the apparition is one of two women: Queen Elfrida or Mistress Eda. Few women have the strength to do what was done to that corpse. Yet how could a man be mistaken as a woman's ghost?"

"An excellent question and one to which I have no answer," Eleanor replied. "Even though I dismiss the idea of ghosts, something has been troubling the priory. Might a human murderer hide his deed behind the form of a damned soul, casting all suspicion on a creature which cannot be brought to mortal judgement, and thus escape justice?"

"Master Herbert," Thomas said, almost under his breath.

"I doubt it. Would you not agree that he would be more likely to kill Sayer, not the father, if the son had seduced his wife? And why would he eagerly arrange a marriage with the cousin? When he spoke of Alys and her mother, he expressed great devotion. That is not the way of a man who has been wronged by a family."

"I agree, my lady." Thomas' voice suggested regret.

"We need so much more information. I shall return to talk with Mistress Jhone and her daughter. The house is near enough not to tax my strength. In the meantime, I think you should seek out our lusty roofer."

Thomas flushed. "If he is not to be found, do you have another task?"

"A visit to Wulfstan's widow, Mistress Drifa. As a member of this Order, if not of this community, Sister Beatrice would want you to bring her comfort. Perhaps this widow will be the one to help untangle the dark knot."

"And what of Master Bernard?" Anne asked.

"Brother Thomas might have reason to meet with him again, although another visit to the inn is not wise, especially at night." Eleanor smiled at the monk with sympathy. "My aunt can find reason to send you out on market day."

"I will do as you ask most willingly," Thomas said.

"And I pray we learn the truth soon." Eleanor shivered as if some unseen thing had just stroked an icy finger on the back of her neck. "I fear that Satan is not yet done here."

Chapter Eighteen

Thomas chose to visit Wulfstan's widow first. He was purposely delaying any further contact with the son but, with God's grace, hoped he might learn enough without having to talk to Sayer at all. At the priory gate, he asked the porter for directions to Drifa's dwelling, explaining that he had been sent by Sister Beatrice to offer comfort.

The place was easy enough to find. Thomas knew what to expect of a home where a husband had been a laborer in the priory fields and one son a bit more skilled. As a consequence, he was surprised to see a house larger than he imagined with a flock of many healthy chickens, watched over by a large and bright-eyed cock with his leg tethered to a stake, in the front of a round poultry hut.

A woman's voice, raised with mild maternal irritation, caught his attention, and he followed the sound around a corner to a freshly tilled garden. It was with much relief that he did not see Sayer amongst the busily working brood, whom he assumed must be the younger siblings.

"Mistress?" Thomas asked with gentle courtesy. "I pray I have not come at a time inconvenient for you."

The woman he addressed was jabbing a sharpened stick into the ground while a lad of about thirteen summers followed, carefully dropping and covering seeds.

A spring crop of peas, Thomas concluded.

She turned around and smiled. Lean, with nut-brown hair and an impish tilt to her head, she much resembled the elder son she had borne. Although her skin was roughened from exposure to sun, wind, and most likely her years in this world, the widow's hazel eyes were bright with affable curiosity.

"You are most welcome, Brother. A visit from the priory is never amiss." She cast an affectionate look on the lad beside her. "Finish this work. You know how well enough if you set your mind to it. And keep your sisters at their tasks while I offer this holy monk some ale."

From the expression on the boy's face, Thomas had no doubt that she would be obeyed—and out of love, not fear.

As the monk followed her through the open door into the dim and smoky house, he noted how alike, yet how dissimilar, Mistress Jhone and her sister were. Their height, coloring, and head shape might be the same, but there all resemblance ceased. Jhone's eyes were dull. Wulfstan's widow had a sparkle yet in hers. Both may have lost the support of husbands, he thought, but Drifa lacked the scars that marked the face of the woolmonger's widow. Hard though this woman's life may have been, Thomas doubted she would have thought her sister's possessions worth the price.

"I come to offer consolation on the death of your husband."

She nodded, pulled a rough bench from against the wall, and gestured for the monk to sit. A mottled cat yowled protest at the disruption in his nap and skittered across the floor to the door, scattering straw as he ran.

"I am called Drifa," she said, disappearing behind a partition.

Thomas looked around him. The three small windows and open door let in little light, but the footed pot over the fire, bubbling with a bean pottage, and lack of animal stench suggested a well-run household. Bastard son of an earl though he was, he had grown up with women of peasant birth. He was not surprised at what a woman could do with little enough to aid her.

Hearing the clunk of an earthen jug as Drifa poured ale, he also realized that he expected her to cope with the death of her husband. Not all women of poor families faced these things with grim determination any more than did all widows of noblemen when their lords were killed and the enemy was at the gates, but this place showed the touch of one who, no matter what her sorrow, believed in the importance of feeding children, planting a garden, and milking that nearby lowing cow. Mistress Drifa was not one who would fall into a whining grief.

Unlike her sister with her quivering meekness in the presence of the wine merchant? Maybe he was being unfair to Mistress Jhone. She might have deeply loved her husband and had worries enough to add lines to her face: a business to keep prosperous and a strong-willed daughter to marry off. Perhaps Mistress Drifa found more strength because she did not grieve as profoundly for her dead Wulfstan.

The widow was standing in front of him, a wooden cup filled with cool ale. Her hand trembled briefly. When he accepted the drink with courteous thanks, she abruptly turned away and went to stir the pottage.

"When you return to the priory, would you please tell Sister Beatrice that I am grateful for her kindness. She sent word that my husband may now be buried in sanctified ground and that she will pray for his soul."

"She wished to know if there was anything you might need…"

"My eldest has employment there. A cooper has taken on my next, and the lad you saw outside has his father's capable hand with the earth. As for my little girls, I may have a mother's blindness, but I think they will be pretty enough to win the hearts of worthy men." She gestured around the house. "As you see, I have sufficient land for a garden, keep chickens for eggs, and I own both a young cow and two goats for those who find their milk easier to digest. God has been merciful to me, Brother. My living children have health. My sons have wit enough to earn their own bread, and my daughters already show the cleverness needed to make excellent wives. When I am old, one of them will care for me."

"Yet the death of your husband…"

"Shall I weep until blind, Brother, or curse God because Wulfstan died, a fate that must come to us all?" She stood and faced him, hands on hips.

"Surely you grieve?"

"Aye. I shall miss his snoring at night and his grumpiness in the morning." Her lips curled into a trembling smile.

Thomas remained silent.

"Forgive me, Brother. I did not mean to speak with such discourtesy to one of your chaste vocation." Drifa tapped one breast. "Seeing these sagging paps and his headless body, you may not understand how Wulfstan and I did burn for each other in our youth. I had almost carried Sayer to term when we married, and I suffered the agonies of Mother Eve on his birth. Yet we continued to couple without moderation, until lust burned out as must any raging fire. If a couple is fortunate, the ash remains warm. If they are not, it turns bitter as well as cold. My husband had his mortal failings, as do I, but we knew comfort in each other beyond the payment of the marriage debt. He will always have the heart he won when he was a smooth-skinned, handsome lad. I miss him and am grateful that I need not marry another to feed my family."

Thomas listened to the laughter and voices of the children outside. Considering the range of their ages, he concluded that the ashes in her marriage must have remained quite warm for some time.

He looked back at the widow. Her blunt tongue was comforting. After all, his own mother had been a serving woman. When she had died, women like this had raised him. As a girl, Drifa may have longed for pretty speeches and love songs, as young women do, but there was little time for softness when babes came. Then work was hard, and earthly grief built a permanent hovel in the heart.

"As you say, death must come to us all," he said, proceeding with the same frankness she had shown, "but your husband's soul was sent to God by some mortal hand. I cannot help but wonder what man could have hated him so much…"

Her eyes narrowed. "Do not take common gossip to heart, Brother."

"I would never do so, mistress," Thomas carefully replied. "Yet might there not be some truth in the tales?"

"The ghost has been blamed." Her tone was artificially light as if she hoped he might believe this. Her look said that she herself most definitely did not.

"A ghost with a man's hand, I fear." The ghost was clearly not the gossip he was supposed to have heard. Thomas prayed he would not have to ask what the stories were, for he suspected she might not tell him if he revealed his ignorance.

Drifa's shoulders sagged. "For all their differences, Sayer would never slay his father. Nor is my son capable of beheading any man in that heinous fashion."

Thomas felt his stomach clench. He controlled his voice with care as he continued. "I did not think the rumors true, yet I could only wonder why anyone would suggest he had."

Drifa waved one hand as if swatting a fly. Color returned to her face. "You were once a lad yourself, Brother. Do not all sons fight with their fathers when they reach a certain age? Sayer is a reliable lad and a hard worker, but he has his ways and Wulfstan had some quarrel with them. They cannot see how alike they are, equally stubborn and wild in their youth. Nonetheless, both are good men in their hearts."

Thomas blinked at her poignant use of the present tense but continued. "Their differences were well-known, of course." A safe enough observation, he thought.

The widow threw her hands up in a gesture of disgust. "Both had had more drink than was right for any man, and they were fools to fight at the inn. When I heard each one pissing outside the door that night as if he had hail in his bladder, I knew Satan had had his fun with them even before they staggered inside and passed out alongside the cow." A flash of loving amusement passed over her face. "The next day, the innkeeper told me what had occurred. I was horrified and begged Sayer to make peace with his father, and a public one at that, for no son should ever threaten to kill his sire."

"Surely your son was right to be angry," he continued, hoping his voice did not betray either his ignorance of what had happened or his discomfort with what she had just told him about the argument.

Drifa offered the monk more ale. This time her hand was steady as she gave him the filled cup. "He is a boy still and unsettled in his ways. I reminded my husband that he had been engaged in enough questionable things himself as a youth, situations that put his life in danger although they brought enough coin to pay for this plot of land. Nor, I told him, had he changed until our third child was born. Only then had he seen that working on priory land was a wiser way to earn the bread we ate and a path less likely to lead him to a hanging. He must show patience with Sayer, I said, since he himself had come so late to manhood."

Thomas decided he did not want to learn what Wulfstan had done since it was obviously against the king's law. "Surely your husband must have seen that your son had done nothing that different from what he had in his own time." Perhaps this question would lead her into further explanations?

Drifa's eyes widened and she exhaled, the act evoking relief rather than resignation.

What had he said that was amiss? Silently, Thomas chastised himself. Hadn't he but rephrased her own words?

"You have the right of that," she said quickly. "My greatest grief is that Sayer and his father did not make peace before my Wulfstan died. They would have, you know, but there was not enough time for two such stiff necks to bend. Not knowing what was to come, I laughed at how alike they were in that. Now I weep, for they did most truly love each other."

From the easy manner of Drifa's last words, Thomas knew she was either lying or hiding some dark truth, but it mattered not which. The expression on the widow's face told him that he would learn nothing more no matter what or how he asked.

Chapter Nineteen

With two silent monastics trailing a respectful distance behind them, Sister Beatrice and Prioress Eleanor walked along the path by the Avon.

The novice mistress stopped, put her hand on her niece's shoulder, and bent her head toward the opposite bank of the river.

Following the direction of the gesture, Eleanor saw Mistress Jhone approach that muddy and weed-infested burial ground reserved for corpses whose souls had been damned by God.

"She visits every day," Beatrice said to her niece.

The widow walked to the far edge of the graveyard, fell to her knees, and covered her eyes.

"Why?"

"That is where Eda is buried. It matters not that some believe she is the ghost that haunts this byway. The two were childhood friends and loved each other like sisters."

"When she spoke of her to me, she did not mention that she came to visit her grave."

"Her husband disapproved."

Eleanor raised an eyebrow. "I did not think she ever dared to go against his wishes."

"She has not always been as compliant as she would have others believe."

"How so?"

"She may bewail her sister's marriage to the base-born Wulfstan, reproaching Drifa for her itching lust and opposition to their parents' wiser choice of spouse, yet Jhone herself married after her maidenhead was breached and to a man her parents did not like. As many do, she forgets her own sins and condemns others for a like foolishness, while claiming a virtue she does not have."

"The woolmonger got her with child?"

"She bore a daughter, one that died at birth. Her new husband fell into a rage, claiming the child's sex was God's punishment for their sins. He longed for a son, but she only gave him girls. All but Alys failed to thrive. I do think he had always been a wrathful man, but his beatings grew more numerous after each failure to prove his seed strong enough for boys. One night he struck her until she miscarried the very lad he wanted. After that, she could not conceive. He lost himself in drink."

"I now understand why the mother refuses to let her daughter marry the man she wants. The widow's own choice was a tragic one, and she must fear that the girl will make the same mistake."

"She does. Yet she adores her Alys and, for all her faults, Mistress Jhone is not a cruel woman. I think her heart wishes she could let her daughter marry the glover."

Eleanor looked back across the Avon. The woolmonger's widow still knelt in the grass near her friend's unclean grave.

Falling into quiet thought, she and her aunt continued on their way down the path that now twisted away from the river and nearer to the priory walls.

"What do you know of this Sayer?" Eleanor asked, breaking the silence.

"A scamp like his father was in his youth, but I find no real evil in him." Beatrice's smile was affectionate.

"Mistress Jhone says her husband believed Wulfstan's son may have seduced the vintner's wife. Out of guilt for the sin committed and not from the pain of her illness, she killed herself."

Beatrice raised one eyebrow. "I would not put much credence in the word of a man who was often so drunk he could not walk the short distance home and passed out where the night soil was tossed."

"Moreover, she said her husband thought the roofer deliberately displayed his nakedness to foster carnal longings in the loins of chaste nuns."

"My dear, I was too long in the world to pretend I do not notice a handsome man, but, if Sayer strips for his work, he does so only on the monks' side of the priory. On the rare occasions that anything needs repair in the nuns' cloister, he willingly bundles himself so modestly that I fear he will sweat himself sick on summer days."

Eleanor laughed.

"As for seeing Eda with Sayer, I wonder who told Master Woolmonger that tale? I myself do not believe it."

"Alys hotly denies that her cousin would do such a thing and says her mother's friend was an honest woman. Maybe she knows the source of the story. I shall ask."

"Do not think I am easily deceived about Sayer. He is no innocent. After Prioress Ida hired him, a monk admitted that the roofer had arranged a tryst for him with the local whore at the village inn."

"I thought Prioress Ida had put a stop to this?"

"She told Sayer that she would not allow him to continue working for us if he abused her kindness by leading our monks into sin. She said he was shamed by her discovery and even willingly told her where the breach in the wall was, although Brother Jerome had already taken her to the place."

"A break which she caused to be repaired. Do you believe he was truly repentant or has he continued this wicked business?"

"The vow of chastity is renewed in our priory, but I would not swear to that of others. Our innkeeper claims he himself has never bothered with the morals of monks. Those who travel and come to his establishment have dry throats, he says, and he serves them ale or sells them meat for their stomachs. What other needs they might fulfill is none of his affair, although he claims he does not sell women. I have reason to know he lies." Beatrice shook her head. "Did the lad not suggest to Brother Thomas that pleasures could be found at the inn for monks who were but visiting? Fortunately, I gather your monk succumbed only to wine and not to the women who served it."

Eleanor's face grew hot with color. "Sister Anne gave him some remedy for his head, I believe. He slept in the grass not far from the priory gate," she said, looking over her shoulder. "Yet you tolerate Sayer despite all of this?"

"I am fond of young men, having married one many years ago and borne him two sons. Aye, despite his rakish ways, I like Sayer. Although Satan holds his soul in his hand at times, he is a caring man who longs to do the virtuous thing but does not always succeed. In many ways, he is still a boy, unmarried and unsettled in his life. His father may have been querulous on occasion but he was a good man in sum, and I see much of Wulfstan in his son. A worthy wife will do much to take Sayer from his wayward path. "

"If Satan does control him, why do you not believe he might have seduced the vintner's wife?"

"Although he leads others into carnal sins, I have never heard any rumor that Sayer himself is unchaste with women." Beatrice chuckled. "I know his mother. No son of hers would dare take a girl's maidenhead unless he brought her to the church steps as Wulfstan did with Drifa."

"Perhaps Brother Thomas will hear more about this tale of adultery and ask Sayer about it when he sees him." She looked up at her aunt and grinned. "Or his mother, whom he may also visit this day."

Unable to resist, Beatrice reached for her niece's hand and squeezed it gently. "I am so glad you came back to us, my child. I have missed your company so very much!"

In happy silence, the two women continued to stroll along the river bank.

Suddenly, Eleanor pointed to a spot at the edge of the Avon. "Was it here that Wulfstan's body was found?"

Beatrice shaded her eyes against the strengthening sun and looked around. "I think this is the place, although my aged memory may be failing me. Brother Infirmarian described the place so."

"*Aged* indeed!" Eleanor's expression glowed with both love and humor as she bent over and parted the weeds with one hand. "Ah, here are marks in the mud. Someone slid just there and here they trampled the reeds. Unless Wulfstan was killed by several men, this must have been where his body was found." She looked up and followed her aunt's gaze. "Is that where the wall was broken?" Eleanor wended her way through the knee-high weeds in the direction of the stone fence.

"Aye," the novice mistress replied, following along.

The Prioress of Tyndal folded her arms as she studied the masonry. The silence was broken only by the harsh cry of a nearby crow.

"Did Prioress Ida have this done by the monks or did she hire the work done?" Eleanor ran her fingers over the mortar.

"She hired a villager, fearing that another weak monk might wish to preserve some way over the wall."

"Who was it?"

"Wulfstan, although he must have had help. The task was too quickly done to be finished by one man."

Eleanor frowned and turned to her aunt. "Please tell me what you think this is and if there are more like it. I cannot reach but believe there might be some..." She pointed toward two places higher up.

Beatrice ran her hand over the mortar, looked up, and touched another place, then another. "Were I younger and more agile, I might easily climb to the top here for these indentations in the mortar are sufficiently deep while the stones protrude enough for toeholds, methinks."

"I feared as much." The prioress walked slowly along the wall for several yards as she studied the mortar for like flaws.

Her aunt did the same in the opposite direction.

At last they turned to face each other, their expressions somber with growing uneasiness.

"We will check the other side of the wall as well," Beatrice said, "but I suspect I know what we will find."

Eleanor looked back to the spot where Wulfstan had died. "Might Wulfstan or one of the men working with him have been paid to leave this path into the priory?"

"I hope I have not been fooled by a fair pretense of honesty, yet I feel certain that Wulfstan was innocent of this."

"We must ask who worked on the repair with him." She touched the wall again. "I dread even to say this, but might he have seen someone who came over this wall, a man who so feared discovery that he killed Wulfstan?"

Beatrice looked back at the rising stonework. "Who in the priory could possibly have been that crazed with fear? The errant monks have been punished, but not cruelly. Their own souls suffered more than their bodies. Even if one monk had a mistress in the village…nay, the prior knew well enough to ask and none of the men confessed to that."

"Or else someone was in the priory who should not have been and did not wish to be seen coming from it. As you taught me, walls were never intended to keep us encloistered but to keep the world from disturbing our prayers. This wall may have failed in its purpose and, worse, Wulfstan might have been the unwitting instrument of his own death."

Chapter Twenty

"Brother Thomas! What a pleasant surprise to see you again. Did you find lodging at the priory?" Bernard clapped his well-clad hands together in apparent pleasure at such an unexpected meeting.

In the brightness of day, the merchant appeared younger than he had in the dimmer light of an inn at eventide. The man's round cheeks wore the pink of youth, and his blond beard looked as soft as a lady's gloves. Although the expression in his eyes still had that sharp watchfulness of an older man, the sparkle of boyish enthusiasm was well mixed in. No wrinkles yet bothered his brow, and he had very white teeth. Thomas probed one of his own that felt a bit uncomfortable.

"I did," the monk replied, "and they have found use for me already. I have just returned from the house of Wulfstan's widow."

Bernard bowed his head with respectful solemnity.

"She is much grieved that her son and husband failed to make peace after their quarrel. It was a most troubling thing between the two." If Drifa would not tell him the details, perhaps this glover would. Thomas felt the bite of hope.

"Sons and fathers do argue," Bernard acknowledged. "Even my honored sire lost his temper with me from time to time, and he was slow to wrath." He hesitated as if considering his next words. "Nonetheless, I never said I wanted to kill him. My heart always knew he was right, and my mother, God bless her sweet soul, would have roasted me before the Devil got me if I had not obeyed him." A grin caught him up. "I think I feared her anger more than my father's!"

Even without wine, the fellow was talkative, Thomas noted happily. He continued. "I was dismayed to hear that Sayer had done so. Do you know the man? I wondered if he was a rebellious son or simply an imprudent one."

Bernard's smile faded quickly. "This is a small village, Brother. We all *know* each other, but I would not claim that Sayer and I are well acquainted. I cannot give you an answer to that question."

Thomas hoped his expression did not betray his surprise. Not only was he sure that Sayer and this man had been in close conversation at the inn door, but he wondered how the glover could not know the cousin of his beloved Alys. "Did you perchance overhear the argument at the inn?" he asked. "If I knew more about the quarrel, I might give greater comfort to Mistress Drifa, or even offer soothing counsel to her son."

Bernard frowned in thought.

Is he trying to remember the night, Thomas wondered, or is he making up some lie?

"I had just walked in. It would have been difficult not to hear the fight between the men. They bellowed like bulls and swung fists at each other like drunken bears."

"Over what?"

A shadow passed over the young man's face. "Wulfstan's widow is a good woman, and I would not spread stories to add to her sorrow."

"I do not seek gossip for idle reason. Mistress Drifa feared many heard the nature of their hot words and she is shamed. Of course, her son's arrangement with the innkeeper..."

The glover looked around to make sure no one stood close by, then bent to speak more privately into the monk's ear. "If you know that, I will not offend by confirming that Wulfstan liked not some of the things his son did to gain coin. Sayer was paid fairly by the priory for his work there, but many in the village knew that he had, at one time, arranged worldly pleasures for monks who climbed the priory walls." He straightened. "I repeat that only to point out the merit of Sayer's repentance. The man had not led monks into sin of late, and we all believed that he had reformed. His father might not have been so convinced."

That easy reply was but a simple rephrasing of the knowledge I suggested I have, Thomas thought. The man does not evade direct answers with much skill, but how am I failing to get the information I need? "Surely the father was not so virtuous himself?" he said, trying another path.

"I see the old tales are still about! My father claimed that Wulfstan was well rewarded for letting certain local men know when a fat mercantile purse would be riding through Amesbury, the owner of which he also made sure enjoyed much ale before departing the inn."

"How dare Wulfstan condemn his son so cruelly then when he had committed crimes himself? Sayer might have laughed at him for his belated discovery of virtue, but I find it hard to imagine he would have threatened to kill him for it."

"Sadly, I cannot give details of their quarrel. I came too late, and the insults they were throwing at each other might be said by any two men in a heated argument."

"Have you heard from anyone else…?"

Bernard stiffened. "I did not listen to idle talk, nor did I ask questions. As I told you last night, Brother, I am a man without a wife who goes to the inn, not to trade tales of others, but for a decent meal, enjoyed in some solitude, at reasonable cost."

"I did not mean to suggest otherwise, but I am a stranger here in Amesbury and long to bring peace to both Mistress Drifa and her son. For that reason, I hoped you could educate me on the character of both father and son. For instance, if I knew that Sayer was just a foolish youth who would never actually kill his father…" Thomas looked at the glover with an expression he hoped brought meek supplication to mind.

Bernard's eyes still expressed wariness. "Murderer? That is a harsh accusation. Sayer is a maker of mischief and has played boy's games too long, but I do not think his failure to take on a man's duties and estate proves him to be a brutal creature."

Thomas said nothing, praying his silence would encourage the glover to say more. For once, the garrulous merchant was thrifty in speech. "I thank you for telling me what you have, Master Bernard," he said at last.

The two bowed in courtesy, and, as Thomas watched the glover walk away, he groaned in frustration. He was still failing to discover the identity of the ghost, and he was getting nowhere in his mission of finding a manuscript thief.

Or was he? Questions buzzed in his mind like irritating flies, but his attempts to capture their significance failed. Why would a roofer want to learn so much about the Psalter? Was the argument between Wulfstan and his son just a drunken quarrel? Why did he sense that Drifa was lying, and what lay behind the meeting he had witnessed between Bernard and Sayer?

Thomas rubbed at his temples and wondered if his blindness was caused more by his lack of wit or by his contradictory feelings about the man around whom all these questions seemed to revolve.

Chapter Twenty-One

Surely he had seen a light in that window, Brother Baeda thought as he hurried up the stone stairs to the library. Even though the light had now vanished, he felt obliged to make sure nothing untoward had occurred. He would not have bothered to check, but two nights ago some young novices had slipped in and poured ink on one of Brother Jerome's parchments.

"The brother is such a querulous fellow and so sensitive about his talent with color and design," he muttered. No doubt of that. Jerome did rank his own work more highly than was warranted, his efforts falling far from noteworthy quality, but that did not excuse the lads for what they had done. Just because the monk had unfairly accused them of impure thoughts, after they joked about his drawing of Eve entwined with the snake in Eden, was no reason for them to damage any work done for a holy purpose.

An irreverent chuckle escaped the brother's lips, and he immediately prayed to be forgiven. The snake's tail was most unfortunately placed as he remembered it, and he should have said something to Jerome at the time. Knowing that the monk would roar in fury at the very suggestion of creative incompetence had stopped him, however, so perhaps he ought to have taken some blame for what had happened the other night.

The boys had been quite properly reprimanded for the damage and assigned the penance of scrubbing the stones in the warming room, but might that have been mitigated if he had come to their defense? Now he wondered if they had resented the duty and returned to tweak Jerome's rather pointed nose one more time.

He swung open the library door. His eyes were accustomed to the dark, and he saw no boyish shadows in the room.

Quickly, he walked over to where Jerome worked. All tools had been put away and no undone manuscript left out. Apparently, the monk had not yet started anything after the novices had ruined what he had been toiling over for days. He raised a hand to his mouth, suppressing another laugh. That tail!

Some movement or shifting shadow caught the corner of his eye and he turned toward it. Must have been his imagination, he thought. If the boys had returned, surely they would have betrayed themselves by now with the uncontrollable laughter of mischievous youth.

"Come forth!" he ordered nonetheless, hoping his voice expressed admonition mixed with just the right amount of forgiveness.

Nothing.

"It will be better for you if you come now. No damage has been done and thus no sin committed!"

Nothing.

The hairs on the back of his neck rose. Could the ghost of Queen Elfrida have entered the room? Nonsense, he thought. He had only felt a chill draught from the open door. Spring may have come, but didn't that night air still nip at aged spines?

He shook off the feeling and glanced around the area near Jerome's work place. Something was different, he realized, and then he gasped.

The Amesbury Psalter was lying on the floor.

Surely he had not left this precious work out! He rushed to pick it up, praying that no damage had been done, begging God's forgiveness for being so forgetful, so careless.

As the monk bent to retrieve the Psalter, he heard a sound and raised his head.

He screamed only once.

Chapter Twenty-Two

The young novice, who had brought the news of Brother Baeda's death, trembled as if facing God Himself. Those who knew Sister Beatrice understood why.

"No ghost could have done this deed. How dare anyone suggest that conclusion to me?"

"He is just a boy," Eleanor whispered to her aunt. "Let him tell his tale."

Beatrice sighed. "Forgive me, lad." She closed her eyes and muttered a calming prayer. "Repeat your story, and I shall not interrupt again. Truly, you need not fear my anger nor shall I blame you for the thoughts and words of others. Be assured that I do know the difference between the message and a messenger's belief."

The lad swallowed. "Brother Jerome heard the scream and rushed to the library." His adolescent voice rose to boyish soprano, then cracked into a baritone before falling into nervous silence.

"And did he say why he was so near?" Eleanor's tone was gentle, not only for the sake of the boy but her aunt as well. Sister Beatrice might be silent, but the prioress knew from experience that the novice mistress was probably grinding her teeth.

"My lady, I should not…" The novice was sweating.

"Sister Beatrice has promised that you will not be blamed for anything you say." Eleanor gestured toward the novice mistress. "This murder is a grave matter, and it is a man's duty to tell what he knows of such a vile deed, even if the facts reek with the terrifying stink of the Devil's work." The sharp odor drifting from the quivering novice enhanced the image. "I can see a man's courage in your eyes so do not let your fear of frightening us keep you from frank speech. We may be women but, as leaders in this Order, God graces us with the strength of the Queen of Heaven herself."

"Well said, my lady," Beatrice said, her eyes shining with delight. Pride may harden most hearts into insensate things, but a woman's sin, looking at her child, is a softer one.

The novice straightened his back and pulled in his chin. "Brother Jerome said he was on his way to the library after prayer because..." His face turned scarlet with embarrassment but he went on with only a brief hesitation. "...because he was afraid one of us would return to eke out more vengeance on his work after he revealed we had cast ink on his image of Eden."

Beatrice's lips twitched as she glanced at her niece. The story had given the two a merry moment.

"Continue," Eleanor said, hoping her expression suggested encouragement, not the amusement she felt.

"Brother Jerome thought someone had been injured when he heard the cry so he shouted that help was coming. As he approached the building, he saw a monstrous black shape hovering about the door. The creature had no face, only eyes licked by flames." The boy gulped. "Then the stench of Hell struck his nostrils, and he felt his soul grow weak. Quickly he prayed for God's protection from the great Fiend. It was this timely plea, he says, that must have saved him from Brother Baeda's fate. Although he immediately lost all consciousness, he soon awoke, still in this world and lying on the ground. The damned soul was gone. My lady, I beg pardon for saying so, but Brother Jerome claims the creature matched all descriptions of the ghost. Although he had never seen any mortal man quite so huge, he believed it wore a woman's robes. I only repeat..." The boy fell to his knees, shaking like a lone leaf in winter's first storm.

Beatrice spread her arms as if to hug the boy. "Like a man, you have bravely reported the events, and I thank you for that. Fear not. I do bark but rarely bite—or at least rarely bite the innocent. Go to the kitchen and ask for ale and cheese on my orders." She shook her head. "You need filling out, lad. You could pass for a ghost yourself."

The boy stumbled to his feet and ran as if afraid the novice mistress might change her mind and chew on him despite her words to the contrary. He was in such a rush that he would have knocked over Sister Anne as she entered the room if Brother Thomas had not been immediately behind her.

"Two people of calm and reason," Beatrice sighed to her niece. "Are we not grateful after the tales we have just heard?"

"Did the poor corpse provide any hints to the cause of his death?" Eleanor asked.

"A sad sight," Anne replied. "He was choked with such strength that the cord was still embedded in his neck. We left the body in the infirmary where Brother Jerome is now praying for his soul."

"Our librarian was a modest man in life." Beatrice's voice was edged with weariness. "God will surely keep his spirit but little time in Purgatory."

"This second murder should not have happened." Eleanor's grey eyes turned to an ashen dark as she looked at her aunt. "I have failed you."

"Cast those thoughts from your mind now."

"But I…"

"Hear me out on this. Our priory has only the wits God gave us to bring the vile murderer of these men to justice. As I did after Wulfstan's death, I will send word to the sheriff. As he did then, he will insist that ghosts are outside his authority, especially one that kills within a priory, and his hunting companions will hear much about our presumption in troubling him with this matter!"

"But I am doing…"

"…more than he. At least you and Brother Thomas are asking questions while Sister Anne brings her knowledge and acute observations to our aid." She glanced at Thomas. "Now is the time to tell us what more you have discovered."

The monk repeated the gist of his conversations with Mistress Drifa and Master Bernard, although he continued to omit what he had heard from the dead librarian about the roofer's interest in the Psalter.

"So it would seem that Sayer, our man of many talents, is a possible suspect?" Beatrice raised a cautioning finger. "I am not condemning Wulfstan's son on such weak evidence, but that is more than the representative of King Henry's justice would have discovered even if he had bothered to try. Let us see where our combined knowledge might lead us."

"Did you find anything else of note when you examined the librarian's body?" Eleanor asked Anne.

"Nothing on the body itself, my lady, but the position of the corpse might be of interest. The body was lying on top of a Psalter, a most magnificent work if I can judge from the depiction of Jacob's dream that lay open."

"That could only be the one sent by Prioress Ida for repair," Beatrice suggested. "We have no others with such remarkable images."

"That was what Brother Jerome said. He was quite distraught when he saw it under the corpse but waited until I was done to see if the work had suffered damage."

"Brother Jerome waited? A minor miracle," Beatrice muttered.

"From the way his body lay, the librarian was kneeling or bending over when he died. I could not tell if he had been holding the Psalter, and then dropped it, or was retrieving it from the floor when the killer struck."

Thomas' eyes narrowed. "Was the Psalter damaged?"

"Apparently not. When he examined it, Brother Jerome expressed relief that there were no bloodstains."

"I find it odd that the Psalter was not stored safely away until the monk came to do repairs," Beatrice said.

Thomas cleared his throat. "I might be at fault for that, Sister. When I came to give an account of my evening at the inn, Brother Porter told me that Prioress Eleanor had left the priory. Since I had heard your monks speak of this wondrous Psalter, I went to the library to see it. Brother Baeda was kind enough to show me the work."

Eleanor frowned. "Yet you and I met together later in the afternoon. There was time to put the Psalter in the manuscript chest afterward. Had Brother Baeda grown so careless about the works under his care? I remember him as a most meticulous man."

"He had not changed. Our brother loved the books like a father might his children." Beatrice turned with a wry smile to Thomas. "He must have been pleased at your unexpected interest."

Thomas met her gaze. For a moment they studied each other, and then he nodded as if conceding some private debate. "The Psalter was open on the table when I entered the library. Brother Baeda mentioned that word of its presence there must have spread, for I was the second to beg leave to see the book of late. Perhaps a third came later, and the brother did not have time to return the treasure to a less public place."

"Or else the first returned?" Eleanor suggested. "Who was this person?"

Thomas looked down at the floor and worried the rushes with his foot. "Sayer."

"Did Brother Baeda say what sort of interest our roofer showed?" Beatrice asked.

"Sayer expressed delight with the work itself and asked how such a valuable item was stored to protect it from accidental damage."

"Wulfstan's son showed a most commendable concern for the safety of our holy works." Beatrice's eyes revealed no shaded meaning in that simple statement.

"A worry that I share," Eleanor cried out. "Dearest Aunt, I know you believe Sayer to be a harmless rogue, but the direction of all we have learned deeply troubles me. May I have permission to present my concerns?"

"I wish to hear them."

"We know that man led weak-fleshed monks into sin for coin. His own father had ties to lawless men when he himself was younger." She turned toward Thomas and Anne. "Today, my aunt and I saw toeholds in the wall Prioress Ida had asked Wulfstan to repair, gouges in the mortar that would allow someone to enter and exit this priory. Even if he was innocent of that foul treachery, someone who helped him was not. I must ask if Sayer was his assistant."

"A question easily and soon answered. Please continue, my child."

"A moment ago, we learned that this son, who has followed his father's example of dishonest behavior, asked pointed questions about this priory's treasured Psalter. Soon after, an unknown is seen escaping from the library after slaying a monk, the body found lying on this same book. Why was the killer there? Might these violent deeds be related in some way to the Psalter? Theft of relics and fine works done in God's name is not unusual. Maybe Sayer and his father found a way to benefit from the theft of this manuscript, quarreled over some detail, and the son killed his father as he publicly threatened he would? Now he has killed Brother Baeda who happened upon him while he was attempting to take the Psalter."

Thomas' face turned a dark red. "You have observed well, my lady, and I cannot dispute your conclusion that Sayer might have killed the monk in a botched attempt to steal the Psalter. Yet I cannot believe he killed his own father, despite the argument at the inn and his drunken threats."

"Sayer may have had minor differences with his father, but that quarrel is the first I have heard that the two might have had a serious disagreement." Beatrice glanced at Thomas before turning again to her niece. "The idea about a planned theft of our manuscript is most interesting, however."

"You know more of both men than I, Aunt, and understand the world far better. I beg you to show me where I have erred."

"In nothing, I fear. Yet neither Wulfstan nor Sayer has ever been a brutish maen. The father was not alone in hungering after another man's fat purse, then joining with friends to equally distribute such wealth." No mirth lightened the novice mistress' laugh. "Do not mistake my meaning in this. A crime was committed, but merchants lost money, not their lives. And, aye, Sayer took advantage of men's weaknesses for his own profit. Both father and son were disgraceful in their wickedness; nonetheless, neither ever added murder to his wrongdoing. Man may be an evil creature by nature, but each mortal has his special vice. Sayer's has never been bloodshed, although theft of a Psalter might not be beyond him."

"Sayer's mother speaks well of him," Thomas said softly.

"As did his cousin, Alys," Eleanor conceded.

"Although many might argue against me on this, I am not so sure we ought to ignore the faith of an innocent girl or the testimony of a mother." Beatrice turned to Anne. "I say this as a woman beyond the age when illusions are common."

Anne chuckled. "I might have said a woman who had not yet reached those years when she is like to paint the past with the softer colors of delusion."

"You flatter me, Sister. Yet I fear Sayer is involved in this matter even if I question his role as a killer."

"If Sayer and his father plotted the theft of the Psalter and argued about it for some reason, the killing might have come about by accident," Eleanor suggested.

Thomas turned to Beatrice, his hands extended as if pleading with her to agree. "I found Mistress Drifa creditable when she said the quarrel would have been of little consequence had Wulfstan lived. She is not ignorant of her loved ones' wrongdoings, no matter how much she might despise the deeds. Could such a crime as this theft have seemed a petty thing to an honest woman? That said, I suspected that she was hiding something, something she avoided telling me. Whatever that might be, however, I cannot believe it was murder."

The novice mistress agreed. "Rogue the lad may be, a corruptor of those who long to be seduced and mayhap a thief, but he has always been a gentle man, willing to help the sad recover laughter with merry jests. That is not a man who kills with the cruelty we have seen here."

Thomas bent his head in concurrence.

"Do we agree that Sayer is most likely implicated in some way, even if we hold doubt that he slew Wulfstan or Brother Baeda?" Eleanor looked around at her companions.

They all nodded.

She went on. "Unless we give credence to ghosts or believe that chance murder has suddenly become the custom here, we must recognize that the killings share a common element. That is the roofer."

"My lady…"

Eleanor held up her hand at Thomas' mild protest. "Do not misunderstand me. I am not condemning, but I would be remiss if I did not note the connections. Sayer's father was in charge of repairing the wall, a flawed mending that allowed continued access to the priory. Wulfstan is stabbed and beheaded near the very place. Sayer asks questions about the Psalter. Soon after, Brother Baeda is throttled with a cord in the library."

"When we met at the inn, Sayer was surprised that I had found a way out of the priory. His reaction may prove he was not the one who left the toeholds in the wall," Thomas said.

"Or else he was amazed that you discovered his covert path, Brother," Anne replied.

"If that was true, he could have killed me to preserve the secret after I left the inn," Thomas protested. His face fell. "Or might have done so if he had not passed out from drink."

Eleanor leaned toward her aunt. "Is it possible that someone from within the priory is the culprit?"

"Not of our librarian's death at least. Although Brother Jerome is often too full of righteous zeal, I am grateful that he chose this time to note those present at the Evening Office," Beatrice said. "Only Brother Baeda failed to be there and no one could have left the chapel in time to kill the poor man. If the monks are innocent of that, I cannot imagine any were guilty of Wulfstan's killing."

Eleanor looked over at Thomas. "And you believe that Sayer is an unlikely father killer?"

"I do," the monk murmured.

"I find it hard to believe that Wulfstan wanted to steal our Psalter." Beatrice shook her head. "He had honored the king's law for so many years."

"Since the birth of his third child." Thomas spoke so softly he might have been talking to himself.

"Unless he learned of his son's plot and wanted to share some of the profit," Anne suggested.

"There is something else to consider." Eleanor reached out and touched her aunt's sleeve. "I do not believe in ghosts any more than you, but we cannot deny that Wulfstan saw something before his death and was most frightened of it. Might this alleged ghost have been Sayer playing a prank?"

"A man in a woman's dress? That is most unusual." Beatrice glanced at the faces around her. "Very well, it is possible and has been done, but surely the father would have recognized his oldest son. The man was shaking when he told me about the sighting that morning. His rank sweat is not easily faked."

"Unless he was so convinced because of the tales that it was the ghost he failed to see a familiar face," Anne added. "Fear plays an imp's tricks with mortal eyes."

"We are circling problems but finding no solutions." Eleanor turned to her aunt. "I beg approval…"

"Do what is needed," the novice mistress replied. "We will get no assistance from the secular world."

"Brother Thomas, you are the best one to find Sayer and question him. If the man has not fled, he may be innocent, yet have something to tell us about the wall, the manuscript, and his father that will bring clarity to everything. For your own safety, do this only in a public place and with much caution. If he is not a killer but is guilty of some other crime, we can offer mercy…"

"Our faith demands it," Beatrice said.

Thomas agreed. In the weak light, his face was white.

Chapter Twenty-Three

Eleanor hoped the tranquility of the priory gardens would ease the pain this violence had brought to her soul. On those occasions when she was able to fill her spirit with silence, she knew that her position as prioress forced her into the brutality of a secular world far more than was good for any one who had sworn to serve God alone. But He demanded special sacrifices from each follower, and her particular oblation allowed many others the encloistered peace required for concentrated prayer. "We may not quarrel with the road we are set upon," she reminded herself. "We must only pray that God grace us with compassion and understanding."

If there was ever a time when she needed both, it was now. Eleanor had left the chambers with a mind aching for answers. Never before had she felt so confused by events, by contradictory perceptions, and by the number of people who might be involved.

What questions would bring truth to the fore in this most complex maze of ghosts, murder, Psalters, and intentions? There was some connection she was failing to see and almost nothing she could dismiss.

Wulfstan seemed to have no enemies, despite his lawless years, and she could not set aside his equally long record of reliable, honest labor. His son may have led others to sin, but her aunt, who surely knew him best and agreed he might be a thief, thought murder beyond him. Were father and son involved in a plot to steal the Psalter, as she suspected? Was the quarrel but a drunken spat?

Who was the ghost? Was it a boy playing the fool or a killer in disguise? Mayhap Sayer? Was the spirit a woman or a man dressed up to look like one? Perchance Jhone, seeking to frighten both village and priory into reconsidering the condemnation of her childhood friend? As unlikely as that seemed, it was not something Eleanor could set aside either. And did it matter whether the shape was judged to be a queen or a local spirit back from Hell?

And what of this Bernard, a man in need of money to win the woolmonger's daughter and a profitable business? His name had not even been mentioned as a suspect, but she wondered if it should be. Was he a dreaming boy who truly loved his Alys, or a scheming thief who sought to sell a stolen manuscript and thus gain what he could not earn as a merchant of gloves? Even if Sayer and his father had planned the theft of the Psalter, they needed someone to sell it for them, a man who could travel with ease.

The prioress pressed her fingers against her brow. Her courses may have ceased, but a familiar dull ache was now starting over one eye. She must ask Anne to prepare that feverfew potion which helped with the blinding headaches she often suffered.

Suddenly, she heard a noise and looked up.

A crow hopped to a landing on the path in front of her.

If this was the bird nesting near the library, the creature must feel more certain of her brood to leave it unguarded. Or was it stealing just a few minutes away from the high-pitched chirping of demanding and featherless infants? Eleanor chuckled at the thought. The bird was no different from any other mother.

She stood very still, finding delight in watching the bird totter along the path as if seeking the quiet to be found between rows of flowering bushes and budding plants. Most called crows ungainly things, their rolling gait like that of drunken men, their feathers askew as if they cared naught for appearances, but Eleanor did not agree. This creature did not remind her of a drunkard or some slovenly woman. Instead, it was like any young mother, stiff and pained from birthing, with little time now for the preening of her maiden days.

Many also hated these birds for their sooty color, calling them Death's servants or Satan's fowl, but Eleanor had always liked their clownish ways, wondering if God had made them dark of hue to remind mortals that laughter must be found in sadness. Or else, she suddenly thought with some irreverence, they contained the souls of jesters condemned to Hell for telling bad jokes in the king's court. She raised a hand to cover her laugh. The thought was impudent, but she knew her aunt would enjoy the image as much as she.

Her gesture caught the bird's attention. The crow turned and studied the Prioress of Tyndal, its bright black eyes gleaming like tiny polished pebbles. With a raucous and annoyed caw, it spread its wings and flapped back in the direction of the tree.

Eleanor sighed with regret, raising a hand in apologetic farewell as if the bird had been an acquaintance with whom she had shared a few pleasant words before innocently saying something to offend. "At least it succeeded in turning my thoughts from murder," she said, bending over a prickly evergreen shrub with fragrant yellow blossoms.

How delicate the petals, she noted, yet how fiercely protected by the sharpness of the bush. She laid two fingertips on a flower with caution. Even soulless plants defend their delicate offspring, she realized. What a miracle motherhood was, turning simple shrubs and weak women into creatures capable of the most remarkable feats.

Hadn't Sister Beatrice just wrought a maternal miracle? Were it not for her aunt's loving cleverness, Eleanor knew she might have succumbed to Death's charms out of indifferent weariness. Yet she had gained strength in the last few days, no longer falling asleep after dinner and requiring someone to wake her for prayer. Look at how much she had walked today without losing breath or growing numb with fatigue.

As she continued along the path, listening to the soft whoosh of green leaves rising and falling against each other in the sweet-smelling breeze, she remembered thinking, after her fever broke, that those who approach death begin to long for it even though they will leave loved ones. Eleanor had looked forward to dying, deciding that Tyndal could do just as well under Sister Ruth and grateful that she would be freed from the lust she suffered for Brother Thomas. Yet Sister Beatrice had teased her spirit back to the earthly life with ferocious determination. Like any good mother, her aunt knew well how to save a child from danger.

In the distance, the crow cawed loudly from her nest.

Eleanor raised her hands to her mouth. "O slow-witted woman," she gasped. "Surely God sent that crow as messenger, yet I have been standing here, so absorbed by selfish thoughts of my wretched self that I was blind to the insight He granted me."

Picking up the hem of her robe, she ran from the cloister gardens.

The priory bells rang out with joy for prayer.

Chapter Twenty-Four

"Come join me, monk!" Sayer sat on the library roof and waved his hammer. "You will feel closer to God."

"Come down to earth," Thomas countered, unable to hold back a grin. Then a heavy darkness settled around his heart. "I want to talk to you."

"I have work to do and what light remains is precious." He gestured for Thomas to go inside. "There is a way to the roof up some stairs. At the top you will find an opening that leads onto the scaffolding. Once there, I will help you climb to a seat, and we can talk while I continue at my task."

"I have not your firm footing."

"Afraid of dying, monk? What sins do you fear might send you to Hell if you fall unshriven?" Sayer's smile suggested he was jesting, but his tone did not match the look.

Thomas recoiled from the blow to his honor. If the man was suggesting he was a coward, he would prove otherwise. "Which stairs am I to climb?"

The steps were steep, and the window through which he edged was small. Now as he balanced himself on the narrow scaffolding and stared at the sharp angle of the roof, Thomas asked himself whether a true monk would have surrendered his pride and turned down Sayer's implied dare. How often did he betray his insincere calling in just such ways?

Whatever the roofer's intent, he showed gentle courtesy by helping the monk climb the steep pitch to a safe place. Once settled in, Thomas gazed at the view and understood why some envied soaring birds. From here he could see beyond the walls and across the river to the strange mounds the monks mentioned only in hushed tones. The village was also on the other side, quite tiny from this great height and filled with bustling miniature people. Do we look that small to God, he asked himself.

"You have fallen silent, monk. I thought you wanted to talk with me." Sayer raised his hammer with a flourish and whacked a new nail into the slate patch.

"I wonder at what a man can observe when raised higher than he might otherwise be. Now I see why angels have a far greater understanding of the earth from their vantage point in Paradise." Or so Thomas decided he might have been thinking if his eyes had not slipped from contemplating the heavens to Sayer's muscular stomach. He looked away.

"A most philosophical monk. Surely you did not wish to talk of angels with me, for I shall confess I much prefer the feel of the earth than any angel's breath." Sayer studied Thomas with mock gravity.

"Where were you last night?" The monk cursed himself for such an unsubtle question. He should tease the truth from this man, not bludgeon it.

"Surely anything you might need me to do for you can be done tonight."

"I am afraid to come to the inn. The ghost has struck again. We had a murder here."

Sayer froze, then dropped his hammer.

In silence, the two men watched the tool tumble to the ground.

"Who died?"

"Brother Baeda."

"I grieve." Sayer swiftly rubbed at his eyes. "He was a virtuous man."

"You knew him well, did you not? So well, in fact, that he told me with what delight he had answered your many questions about the Psalter belonging to Prioress Ida."

Shifting his crouch, Sayer stared down at the distant ground.

"Your interest both amazed and pleased him."

"I may be unlettered, Brother, but I am not stupid."

"I do not understand what you mean." Thomas cursed himself again. The tips of his fingers burned to touch the man. He hid them in his sleeves.

"I shall rephrase: I am no fool. Do you wish to cast suspicion on me?"

"I meant no such thing! Surely you were elsewhere last night. At the inn? With many witnesses?"

Sayer rose and balanced himself with care. His face reddened. "I was enjoying what you have foresworn, Thomas of Tyndal, and that is more than you need to know."

"A witness!"

"None that I will name." He turned away and eased himself from the roof to the scaffolding.

"Wait!" Thomas called out. "I cannot get down from here."

"Find your own way out of your predicament, monk. I shall not help you." The man stood on the scaffolding and glared at Thomas, but his expression soon softened. "Although I believe you have some reason for wanting to call me Cain and mark me for his deed, I would not have you die here from your woman-ish fears." He gestured with a mocking toss of his hand. "Slide on your belly like a snake, and you will slip into the scaffolding like a birthing babe."

Thomas reached out his hand, but Sayer had already left.

Chapter Twenty-Five

Eleanor sped through Amesbury at such a determined pace that her two attendants were left some distance behind. In a dutifully courteous but clearly anguished tone, one cried out a plea for her to wait. She stopped and, turning, saw a plump young merchant emerge from a path between two houses.

"I am Bernard the glover, my lady," he said in warm greeting. "Mistress Alys told me what comfort you have been to her family after this tragic murder of her uncle."

"Grief is part of the human condition, good sir, but God never intended it to come without His comfort." Eleanor's suspicion of the man was briefly tempered with sympathy for young lovers. If he knew of that very recent visit, he and Alys had managed to keep in contact despite Mistress Woolmonger's probable and disapproving watchfulness.

"Are you returning to visit Mistress Jhone?" he asked, folding one hand over the other before resting both on his heart.

"Today I go to Mistress Drifa's house." With some amusement, Eleanor noticed that his gesture succeeded in showing off, to much advantage, the hand-stitching on the back of his glove.

"Alas, poor Wulfstan!"

His words might have been spoken in a tone more appropriate to a monk in a holy day pageant, but Eleanor sensed no hypocrisy. "Did you know him well?" she asked, uncomfortably aware that something insistent had just bitten her memory like a hungry flea.

"Since he was Alys' uncle..." The man's concentration wavered. His eyes stared into the distance.

Eleanor suspected that distraction was caused only by the word *Alys*. "Thus dear to her, I am sure, and a man quite without enemies?" To her dismay, whatever the gnawing thing was, it had vanished like the ghosts haunting Amesbury Priory.

Bernard blinked. "I believe he had none." His eyes focused again on the prioress.

"Although I had understood he was a poor man who labored in the priory fields, I have learned that his widow and children were left some land. What noteworthy good fortune! Or was he possessed of a hidden but remarkable prudence?"

"Everything he gained went to benefit his family, my lady. Whatever tales you may hear, let me assure you that I believe, along with most in our village, that he repented any sins long ago."

"No ancient quarrels with former companions who might have held a grudge when Wulfstan chose a different tune for his dance?"

Bernard laughed. "Or else his sinful ways caused little harm to those in Amesbury, as he himself claimed."

"And does the village consider what his son has been doing harmless as well?"

The glover's expression faded to one more vacant of meaning.

"I ask only to understand what danger Wulfstan might have courted that could have led to his death."

"I am not sure of your meaning, my lady."

"Come, Master Glover, I cannot imagine you have not heard that Sayer arranged for agreeable women and strong drink for any monk who leapt the priory walls. This is no boyish prank. It is against God's commandments. I must ask if Wulfstan joined with his son in this particular and recent disregard for the law."

"God is a far sterner sheriff than the man sent by the king, I fear. King Henry may turn his thoughts from the demands of secular rule whenever the bells ring for prayer, but our sheriff finds the cry of his hunting dogs more compelling. Wulfstan feared God's justice more than the king's law and with good reason."

"So Wulfstan's sins were counter only to the king's edicts while his son's offended only God?"

"Please, my lady, I am a glover, not a man learned in the art of debate! All I can tell you is that Wulfstan tried to honor the lords of both earth and heaven in his last years. He may have associated with robbers, but, after his wife persuaded him to reform, he lived within secular law. As for details of his past, the village chose to know as little as possible should anyone ever be called to testify. The merchants affected, you see, were never local men."

"If Wulfstan's past sins have been cleansed and he has not fouled his soul with new ones, I have no desire to delve into any links to lawless men. I do, however, have both the right and duty to inquire into ghosts, creatures that plague monastic peace for supposed sins against God and which may have turned to killing. The priory has suffered two deaths. Wulfstan was a laborer on monastic lands. Brother Baeda was a monk."

"Brother Baeda?"

"Last night he was found murdered in the library."

"God forgive us all!" Bernard's cheeks blanched to a wan pink, and he staggered back a step. "Disinclined to action or not, the sheriff must be summoned. We have no other choice."

"He has been delayed."

The glover grimaced with apparent frustration. "This news does not surprise me, but what else can we do?"

"You may have answers to my concerns." She waited for a response, debating how frank she should be in her questions. If he were involved, the direct approach would gain her naught. The indirect, on the other hand…

Silently, he nodded.

"Since his father is innocent of offending God's law, I thought Sayer might have followed his sire's example and longed to atone for his own evil ways. What might you know of this?"

Bernard's eyes narrowed. "Again I fail to understand your question, my lady."

"If the spirits have turned murderous because of some offense committed against God, the son's especial sinning may be connected to these deaths. If Sayer is truly repentant, he might provide information that will protect the priory from further violence."

"I am not the one to ask about his thoughts, actions, or ability to do what you seem to wish." He looked up at the sky, his expression a study in reluctance. "You had best ask his mother or else Sayer himself, for I do not know the man well."

"I shall," she replied.

"I fear I am late back to my shop."

"It would be discourteous to detain you further."

Bernard bowed abruptly and, without further word, quickly walked away.

The man lies, Eleanor decided, *although he may have fair reason.* Her mind insisted that his motive was malicious, but her heart was not as sure. Was he protecting someone? If he loved Alys, he would wish to shift all suspicion from her family, including Cousin Roofer. On the other hand, Bernard had not actually defended Sayer as he had Wulfstan. He had claimed ignorance of Alys' cousin and avoided direct response to any questions about the man.

Eleanor frowned, as her mind chased itself in circles, but suddenly brightened as she grasped the thing nibbling at her memory. Was it not yesterday, crossing the Avon after visiting Mistress Jhone, that she had seen the glover in merry conversation with another man?

Treading on the heels of that recognition was a chilling thought. Unless Bernard had inherited a more profitable trade than would seem to be the case, he would not have many apprentices and certainly not one of such long standing that he would be of much the same age.

The man walking beside Bernard was no fellow merchant, rather a laborer of some ilk by his dress. Was he one of the glover's workmen? Nay, their easy manner with each other made her doubt that. Could it have been Sayer, cousin to his beloved Alys? If the latter, why did the glover deny knowing the man, and had the reason anything to do with murder?

Chapter Twenty-Six

Thomas winced as Brother Infirmarian cleaned his bleeding hand with some stinging liquid.

"I won't ask why you were on the library roof, Brother, but I suggest that there are easier places to talk to God."

Despite the throbbing in his wound, the monk chuckled. "Sayer was showing me some of the skills needed to repair the slate."

The infirmarian raised an eyebrow. "Indeed," he said, resuming with an application of salve. "Is your priory at Tyndal so poor that monks must be trained to do such work?"

"We have lay brothers enough, but, since Sayer is only rarely on the ground at this priory, I had to climb closer to Paradise to offer consolation for his father's death. He continued his labors while I did."

Brother Infirmarian reached for a binding. "His grief must be sharp. A sad thing to quarrel with your father and have him die before you can settle the matter."

"Had it caused so deep a rift between them?"

The monk shrugged. "Sayer is a bit of a rogue, much like his father when he was younger, but I think Mistress Drifa would have forced them to make peace."

"Then the dispute involved nothing that would cause either to harm the other?"

"Oh, you heard that Sayer swore he would kill Wulfstan?" The infirmarian laughed as he finished the binding and sat down beside Thomas. "I wouldn't put much credence in that,

Brother. I once told my father I would kill him and he survived four score!"

"And what was your disagreement about?"

The man's eyes twinkled. "There was a girl I wanted to marry. My father was opposed. It was then I threatened him."

"How did you resolve the matter?"

"My beloved died before we could wed, and I took the cowl. With a repentant heart, my father cursed his obstinacy and begged forgiveness. I promised him daily prayers, and we wept together in each other's arms. Fathers and sons have ways of making peace. Had Wulfstan lived, I have no doubt that he and Sayer would have done the same."

"Do you know the cause of their quarrel? If so, I could use that knowledge to bring a more effective comfort to the son."

"Although I listen to gossip like any other wicked mortal, I put little faith in it. True or not, the stories are often entertaining, but I do not repeat what I hear. The Fiend loves those who spread scandal."

Thomas hoped he hid his regret at the infirmarian's admirable restraint. "You are wise not to repeat it," he said. "I grieve that many are not so hesitant about telling tales and pray that no one has spread damaging lies about Sayer and his father."

The monk looked away.

The gesture told Thomas that some story must be abroad. All he had to do was find a man willing to tell him what it was.

⟶ ⟶ ⟶

As he walked through the garden of the monks' cloister garth, despondency dropped over Thomas like a sodden cloak even as questions raced through his mind. A cawing distracted him. Looking up, he saw the dark shape of a crow. It circled overhead before flying off, perhaps to the nest near the library.

Had Sayer returned to his work? Even if he had, Thomas knew he would not seek him out there. He could not. His face turned hot with an emotion he did not want to name, and he forced his thoughts back to the recent discussion with his prioress and Sister Beatrice.

He hoped he had not betrayed his shock when Prioress Eleanor suggested that someone might be trying to steal the Amesbury Psalter, yet he had also felt relief at her joining the pieces in that way. Even though he could not speak of his own commission from the Church in this matter, he could now count on her cleverness and support as he had longed to do. Of course, he was pleased that he had won this small victory over his spy master. He might owe the man gratitude for saving his life, but he did not always respect his judgement and resented the power the man wielded over him.

His small pleasure quickly soured. Was Sayer the thief Thomas had been sent to catch? Was Drifa's deft-witted son a brutal killer? His heart still rebelled against any conclusion that Sayer might be involved, even though he knew there was cause enough to believe it. A man's reason ordered him to acknowledge that the roofer was implicated in the crime. In this they had all agreed, but another emotion, devoid of logic, shouted otherwise to him.

For Thomas, the world had turned upside down since that night at the inn. Sister Beatrice and Prioress Eleanor bore women's bodies, but their souls housed a man's solid reason. He was afflicted with a woman's perceptions. That these had served him well in the past did not soothe him now. Indeed, he cursed them. When had the Prince of Darkness stolen his manhood and given him a woman's soul? If men became women and women men, he snarled, the end of the world must be close to hand.

Nay, it was his soul that was in disarray, not the world. The novice mistress and her niece were holy women, given strengths beyond their sex by their vocations. On the other hand, God had surely given him to Satan for his plaything.

Even Sayer had taunted him about suffering womanly fear when he sat on the roof. Womanly, was he? The monk uttered an oath. Yet he had reached out for the roofer's hand like some maiden begging a knight to save her from distress. Thomas' stomach roiled with disgust at himself.

That his logic was weak and he had shown cowardice at that great height were less terrifying than the betrayal of his body. He could argue that an incubus had put on Sayer's features when he had swyved the roofer in his dream, but Thomas could not ignore how he trembled on the roof like a virgin on her wedding night, longing for the embrace while fearing the loss of her maidenhead.

"I am no man at all," he cried out. "I am a creature made in the image of Satan with a man's sex and a woman's breasts!"

Amidst the bursting buds and flowering shrubs of that silent monastic garden, he fell to his knees, bent his forehead to the earth, and wept. His howls of pain were as sharp as the wailings of one damned beyond any hope of forgiveness, and he beat his head against the ground as if one torment could numb the other.

At last the roaring in his soul diminished and his sobbing subsided. Gulping air like a man who has almost drowned, he sat back on his heels and swiped angrily at his damp cheeks. "Why have You done this to me?" Thomas raised his eyes heavenward.

The light became too bright for his reddened eyes. He covered them.

"You cannot deny it," he whispered angrily into his hands. "The Prince of Darkness may have sent this cruel affliction, but You allowed it. Did You not let Satan plague Job, jesting that he would never turn his face from You no matter what he suffered? Perhaps Job did not do so, but I am not he. I curse You for this!"

Thomas uncovered his eyes and bent down to touch the uneven particles of earth while he waited for God's hot wrath to destroy him. Terror of eternal torture for his blasphemy numbed him, but he could not retract his words.

A hush in the gentle wind and a silence that held neither condemnation nor peace were all that greeted him.

Thomas looked up. He was alone in the gardens.

"Torment me as You will then," he said in soft voice, "but surely You cannot hate me more than the one who murdered two innocent men, two unshriven souls howling for justice."

That said, Thomas rose unsteadily to his feet and set off in the direction of the village.

Chapter Twenty-Seven

A small shadow edged across the garden to the place where Drifa knelt, pulling young weeds from the dark earth. She jumped to her feet.

"My lady!"

"I did not mean to frighten you," Eleanor replied. Was the pallor of the widow's face the result of grief, or was another visit from the priory cause for fear?

Drifa rubbed the soil from her fingers as color returned to her cheeks. "Forgive me, but my thoughts had fled elsewhere. Your visit is most welcome."

There was gratitude in her tone. Looking around and seeing no one else about, Eleanor guessed the reason. Solitude was often a traitorous fellow, eager enough to open Heart's gate to the cruel assault of Sorrow.

"Please come away from the sun. The season may be spring, but the light can be harsh." The woman gestured toward the door of the house. "I have but modest fare to offer you…"

"Brother Thomas praised your ale, mistress," the prioress replied.

"Your monk is kind and a man of austere tastes, my lady."

The two women studied each other for a moment, and when their expressions had shown satisfaction in what each had concluded about the other, they turned toward the dwelling.

At least Bernard had told the truth about one thing, Eleanor concluded as she stepped over the threshold. Wulfstan had spent whatever coin he might have earned from lawless men on items that would benefit his family, not on luxuries. Many squawking chickens were outside, and a hairy goat had greeted her with impudent gaze, one green weed drooping from the side of its mouth. The house was quite large, with three windows, but inside she saw little difference between this place and the home of any other poor man.

As Drifa poured amber liquid into a crudely carved wooden cup, Eleanor noted the freshly laid rushes on the earthen floor as well as the absence of clutter. Whatever his faults, Wulfstan had won himself a diligent wife and one who seemed to have loved him.

"You have been blessed with a large family," Eleanor said conversationally after expressing appreciation for the sharp-tasting but refreshing ale.

"Most of our children have lived and flourished." The widow fell silent.

"Your eldest works most diligently at whatever the priory requires."

"When my husband told Prioress Ida that Sayer could offer many skills for the wages of one man, she was pleased to hire him."

A woman of modest speech and much caution, Eleanor noted. Like many wives who have little time for chatter, Drifa's restraint was sired by thrift, not fear as had been true of her sister, Jhone.

"To have such a talented son must have given you and your husband much joy."

The widow nodded.

"I have heard that the son resembled his father in many ways." Eleanor laughed to give her words a lighter meaning. "The two must have been very close."

The widow leaned back against a pillar.

"Yet I believe they quarreled just before your husband died?"

"The whole village seems to have heard the story, my lady."

"What heavy grief that must bring you."

The sharp intake of breath might have been a sigh or a sob.

Eleanor reached out a comforting hand. "Each of us has sons, mistress. Although you got yours from your husband, God gave me mine. In our Order, a prioress may suffer as the Virgin did when she saw her child dying on the cross, yet strive to see the purpose beyond the misery of mortal flesh. Although I endured no physical pain in the bearing, God commands me to love all men under my rule as if they were truly sons of my body. With that love, I suffer as much as any mother when they fall ill or sin. You and I have some sorrows in common."

Sayer's mother said nothing.

"Please sit beside me," Eleanor said, her voice dropping into a soothing tone, "and let me offer solace as one woman to another. Are men and boys not foolish in their heated words over things that are fleeting? I, too, have grieved deeply when my monks rage on and on about some petty matter. As you yourself have done, I bear the blame when they strive one against another until their humors cool, and peace comes slowly. Thus I understand how deeply you mourn over this bitter quarrel."

Hot tears burst from Drifa's eyes and rolled down her cheeks in a flood. As she slid down onto the bench, Eleanor gently embraced her. The woman's sobs could have not been more despairing if she had just seen her child tumble into Hell's flaming maw. Stirred by the bleakness of Drifa's suffering, Eleanor herself began to weep. For an unmeasured time in that smoke-stained room, the two women clung together, finding a small amount of succor from worldly pain.

At last Eleanor whispered: "Take comfort. In death our souls lose mortal blindness and learn a more godly compassion. Your husband is wiser now and has surely pardoned your son's errors."

Drifa drew back, her red-rimmed eyes still haunted with inconsolable despair. "I pray that he has, my lady, for he claimed the lad was the Devil's spawn."

"Surely not for leading willing monks into the arms of tavern wenches? Your son repented of that, and Prioress Ida had punished the men who strayed. The wall was repaired. All that was in the past."

"Wicked though that had been, it was not the reason my husband said our son was cursed." The widow rubbed the corners of her eyes dry with the tips of two fingers. Her cheeks still shone with dampness.

"What was the cause?"

Drifa covered her face.

The prioress' touch on the widow's arm was gentle. "There is no sin Sayer could have committed that God would not wash clean. We mortals are so quick to condemn, but God is perfect love." Eleanor chanced a smile. "And I do think He grants the Queen of Heaven, a mother herself, the right to bless other mothers with some of that perfection, don't you?"

Drifa dropped her hands and looked at Eleanor in amazement, before her eyes softened with hope. "My son may have seen twenty summers, but he is still a boy, my lady. Satan has made merry with him for cert, but he is not wicked. I told Wulfstan that Sayer need only marry and earn a man's status to return to more godly ways. I thought my husband had agreed but he only hid his anger!"

"Boys do foolish things…"

The mother began to cough, her face turning scarlet as she tried to catch her breath. "Wulfstan came home in a rage one night," she gasped. "He had seen Sayer near the river. Another man was swyving him like a whore."

Speechless with shock, Eleanor could only nod.

"That night I calmed him, but soon after he and Sayer got drunk at the inn. The following morning, my husband confessed that he had told our son he would geld him if he ever did such a thing again. My son had shouted that he would kill him first."

As the prioress prayed for words to soothe this woman, she begged God for an understanding she herself lacked. She was not so unworldly as to think some young monk at Tyndal might not suffer the same weakness, but she knew of none. If presented with such a man, would she face him with a mother's love like Drifa, or would she curse him as Wulfstan had Sayer?

Her thoughts raced on. Sodomy was a most unnatural vice, one akin to murder, or so the Church taught. If Sayer was guilty of this sin, might he be equally capable of killing his own father?

Eleanor took a deep breath. There was one powerful argument against this conclusion. Sister Beatrice was not a woman to suffer evil, or be deceived by it, and she had shown much tolerance for the man. Did she not know that Sayer was a sodomite? What if she did? Her head spun with bewilderment.

God must have given her tongue comforting words despite her own swirling confusion. Eleanor could not remember what she had said to Drifa, but the widow's gaze had shone with weary peace when they parted.

As she turned her steps back to the priory, Eleanor knew she would spend much time tonight on her knees, begging for understanding from the Queen of Heaven.

Chapter Twenty-Eight

The smell of sizzling fat made Thomas' stomach growl. As his growing hunger began to temper the anguish he had felt in the garden, he found himself amazed at the resilience of a man's belly. God would surely punish him for his blasphemous insolence in time. Of that, he had no doubts. Meanwhile, he accepted the gift of a hot, dripping pastry from a tradesman. The first bite of that pie was a joy.

The weather for this market day was fine, a balm to the spirit, and the bounty in the stalls was a miracle to behold. To his left was a mound of purple and white carrots just picked from the garden. Fresh yellow onions, causing less torture to sensitive stomachs than those stored over winter, lay next to cream-colored turnips. Although the steam of hot fruit tarts spread a most appealing scent of spice mixed with sweet, Thomas' hunger was now satisfied.

Something brushed by his leg, and he glanced down to see a lean, red cat in pursuit of something small and gray. The sight reminded Thomas that he had his own prey to hunt, a man who had sent two souls to earlier deaths and greater torture than they deserved. Even though he did not have the slightest idea where to start looking, he felt spurred to the task. If he resolved these murders with speed, God might even grant him a little mercy for his own wickedness.

As he pushed his way through the crowd, a thought burst into his mind, the memory of something he had ignored at the time and since forgotten. When his spy master told him of his assignment regarding the Psalter theft, the man mentioned that the Church had received warning about the danger to the manuscript. Now Thomas asked himself who had raised this hue and cry. Was the detail significant?

"I should have had the wits to inquire," the monk muttered, stepping back to avoid a rumbling cart filled with precariously stacked barrels. "But I would have been told if the fact mattered to the quest." Men might be fair sport for the priest, but surely that thin-lipped creature considered the Psalter too valuable to deliberately hide crucial information. In any case, Thomas had not asked, numbed as he was by grief over the news of his father's death.

Important or not to this undertaking, the identity of the informant was provoking his curiosity. Might it be Sister Beatrice? That would not surprise him, and, considering her inquisitive study of him earlier, he thought she suspected more about him than she chose to reveal.

He waited until a woman with two overfilled baskets passed by, several children with lesser burdens in tow.

Since the spy master seemed to view women as beings formed from a mere rib only to serve Adam's sons, the priest might have judged her involvement not worth the noting. A poor decision, Thomas thought. With pleasure he imagined the expression on the man's face should he ever try matching wits with the formidable novice mistress.

"Watch your step!" a voice cried out.

Thomas looked down.

A legless man sat on a cart just in front of him. The man's hollow cheeks spoke eloquently of starvation.

Thomas found a coin meant for tongue-loosening ale, dropped it into the man's hand, and walked on, forcing his thoughts back to the question. If Sister Beatrice had been the one to alert some bishop that the Amesbury Psalter might be stolen, would she not assume that someone would be sent to investigate? But if she knew that, why had she not said anything?

Perhaps she had been ordered to remain silent to prevent alerting the thief. He, too, had been forbidden to speak to anyone about his role here. Nonetheless, she might well have guessed that he was the one. Why else would she have set him on this task of finding the ghost, allowing a monk she did not know to visit the inn and wander about the town like some clerk?

A loud crash made him jump. To his right, a butcher was cutting meat while a spotted bitch with engorged teats danced and whined at his feet. The fellow tossed the creature a bloody bit, and she raced away with her treasure.

Thomas shook his head. Had the novice mistress said anything about her suspicions to Prioress Eleanor? Although he might have preferred that, he doubted Sister Beatrice would have broken a vowed silence even to a loved relative. She seemed as much a woman of strong principles as her niece.

If Sister Beatrice knew about the threat to the Psalter, then someone must have told her. Was the source a man or woman, religious or townsman? How did this person find out? Thomas cursed that his bound silence prevented him from asking her the identity and that her own vow would stop her from answering even if he did.

As he paused to let men driving sheep go by, he looked over the passing flock and discovered that his wanderings had led him back to the inn. He gritted his teeth, trying to banish his dismay.

The source of the tale was most likely a secular man, seated inside that inn and listening to gossip and plots. Both women and monastics were less likely to hear rumors about thievery. As he had already confirmed, men interrupted their conversations to jest at monks in an inn. Serving wenches were an equal distraction and cause for lewd remarks. Only a secular man, and a local one at that, could remain unnoticed while men spoke together of secret things. Although he was unsure how he would find the man out, he knew he had little choice but to try.

Thomas crossed the road to the inn door.

Chapter Twenty-Nine

Eleanor halted. As they walked through the market stalls, she had glanced behind and caught the wistful expressions on the faces of her two young attendants. How thoughtless she had been! They were probably hungry.

"Oh, I do remember the delicious fish taken from the river while I was growing up at this priory," she said. "That man over there has pies made from them. Shall we honor God's bounty and eat one?"

When the eyes of her attendants brightened, Prioress Eleanor gestured to the merchant, who brought them a sampling of his wares. He might have given the food as a gift to the benefit of his soul, but Tyndal's leader gave him both blessing and coin.

While her youthful religious chewed with undisguised pleasure, Eleanor turned her attention to the surrounding crowds. Not far to her right, she recognized Bernard and Alys, standing in front of his display of gloves. They were holding hands and gazing at each other with undisguised rapture.

Hearing a shout redolent with outrage, the prioress turned to see a scarlet-faced Jhone elbowing a path through to the pair, their moment of delight now ended.

"How dare you, sir?" the mother exclaimed. "And you, strumpet! Did I not forbid you to come near this man?"

"I wanted to look at his gloves, Mother. That is guiltless enough. Even you admit that his work is of the best quality."

"He had no need to fondle your hand. He had no reason to look upon you with such undisguised lust…"

"Mistress, I was but taking her hand to measure it for a glove. As for any intent to dishonor, I am blameless!"

Eleanor noticed the slight bulge in the man's robe. Innocence may have dwelt in the glover's gaze, but elsewhere the virtue had departed.

The spell cast by romantic imaginings shattered, Alys tossed her head in fury at the slur on her virtue. In doing so, she caught sight of the prioress standing near. "My lady!" she cried out.

Bernard and Jhone spun around.

"I did not see you," the widow said, covering her eyes as if hiding what a prioress might read in them. "I beg pardon for any offense!"

"As there was none, there is no need."

"Then please excuse us, my lady," she mumbled, her face a mix of conflicting hues. "I have errands to attend with this daughter of mine."

Eleanor nodded and gave her blessing.

Jhone grasped her daughter's arm with a firmness that demanded obedience and aimed her child away from the booth. Although Alys might have been reluctant to obey and surely felt the defiance of thwarted passion, she wisely did not cast even one backward glance at her beloved.

"A tryst?" Eleanor asked, turning to Bernard.

Embarrassment colored the glover's cheeks. "Alys and I try to meet whenever possible, but her mother is so clever at discovering our evasions that we rarely have more than a moment together. How she is able to read our thoughts remains a wonder to us."

"You both know that Alys is to marry Master Herbert." Although she had her suspicions about the glover, Eleanor found herself in sympathy with the young lovers. Whatever the truth about Bernard, she still did not want to encourage behavior that could easily lead to less chaste conduct than holding hands.

"Alys has not given her consent, although I fear she must do so soon."

"Can you refute the reasons behind her mother's choice?"

"My heart denies her logic, my lady. If her mother only knew what Alys and I feel for each other…" His eyes filled with tears. "My dearest one and I could do so much together to gain the wealth the vintner now has. Mistress Jhone claims I am nothing more than an impractical boy with no prospects, but my glove designs are gaining favor amongst those who can pay for carefully crafted work. Alys has an eye for what her mother should recognize as the more practical elements of business. We know our union would be blessed."

"If Alys does not marry as her mother wishes, has she not expressed a desire for the cloistered life?"

Bernard shook his head angrily. "In truth she told me that she would take holy vows only to avoid wedding a man she does not love." As soon as he had said the words, the glover realized he had just denied his beloved one escape from a hateful marriage by admitting she had no calling to the religious life. He groaned and slapped his hand against his forehead.

As the young man slumped against the table of his stall, his eyes turning dark with despair, Eleanor's heart softened. "Are you able to prove that your profits have increased, that your reasonable prospects make you a match equal to the vintner even if your current state does not?"

Bernard's expression conveyed utter defeat. "I cannot easily counter the wish of a dead husband, my lady."

If that was true, then this man had no pressing reason to chance the theft and sale of the Psalter, unless he had pressing bills. "Is it that," she asked, her voice gentle, "or hold you such debt…"

"All merchants owe something, but my father taught me prudence in business and thrift in habits."

He has not taken offense at my prying, Eleanor noted, then changed the direction of her questions. "I cannot understand why Alys' father and the vintner were so eager for this marriage," she said. "Although Master Woolmonger would have wanted a wealthy tradesman for Alys, I do not see the gain for Master Vintner. He has wealth enough, and wool would be a new trade for him. Wasn't he deeply wronged by Mistress Jhone's kin? I am as surprised that the woolmonger dared to suggest the union as I am by the vintner's willingness to accept it."

"Like a foul odor, that tale drifts through the village!" The glover frowned. "I myself overheard Master Herbert tell the story to Alys' father one night at the inn. Others must have as well for I would never have repeated something like that. Mistress Eda was an honorable woman and her husband most assuredly mistaken. I never gave credence to the accusation."

"Did Master Woolmonger perhaps deny that his nephew was the seducer?"

Bernard shook his head.

How very odd this matter is, Eleanor thought. "Were you well-acquainted with Mistress Eda?"

"As well as I knew most of my mother's friends, although the vintner's wife was younger by some years. My mother praised her faith and sweet temper, saying she wished her own daughters would follow Mistress Eda's example. All who knew the lady respected her charity and honesty."

Eleanor had listened to his words most carefully. They did not suggest any untoward passion between the glover and Eda. "Perhaps she was innocent of adultery, but what of Sayer? Might he have tried to bed her and been refused?"

Bernard opened his mouth.

"Do not claim improbable ignorance of the man as you did before." The prioress lowered her voice. "Is he not Alys' cousin?"

The glover coughed as if he had swallowed wrong. "Did I say I knew him not? Although I am not well acquainted with her cousin, Alys has vouched for his gentle and honorable treatment of women. I myself have no direct knowledge that would contradict her opinion," he added quickly.

"A man who treats women with honor—except tavern wenches. Those he sends to tempt weak-fleshed monks," Eleanor countered.

"Of these rumors I should not speak, my lady," he stammered, "but I shall confirm that Mistress Eda was not capable of being a faithless wife. She was most devout."

"A pious woman who committed self-murder?"

"I may be one of the few who disbelieved that tale, but I am not alone. Even those who said she must have committed the sin were sympathetic and believed the agony of her illness brought such deep despair that her many hours of prayer could not daunt it. Despite his story of adultery, her husband defended his dead wife, claiming she had fallen into the river and died by accident. He was quite distraught when her body was condemned to burial in unsanctified ground."

"How could he have grieved so if he thought she had crowned his head with a cuckold's horns?"

"Maybe he was a most forgiving spouse."

"Was the woolmonger such a close friend that Master Herbert might confess this humiliation to him?"

"My lady, I know not all that transpired between the two men. I have often seen them together, and did overhear that one discussion, but it is not my custom to listen to private talks." The glover was showing signs of an uneasy impatience.

"Forgive my curiosity, Master Glover. I shall ask no more about that." Indeed, she added to herself, I doubt you will tell me more anyway.

The color in the young merchant's face quickly faded to a more natural pink.

"More to your concerns, I fear you have little hope of gaining Alys' hand if you have neither coin nor the blessing of a dead husband."

Bernard sighed. "I do not mean to wrong Mistress Jhone. She most truly loves her daughter and only wants the best for her as is right. Had my father died, leaving me more wealth than hope, I might still be able to persuade her to grant our wish for marriage, despite her dead husband's plan. Master Herbert demonstrates his prosperity daily by his dress and most public generosity in alms. In comparison, I am a poor man. My brother and I support our mother, and I confess we both do what we can to help her recover some joy in life. To that purpose, we spend our spare coin on things to delight her heart, for her grief at my father's death has been most profound."

Eleanor's heart sank. She had hoped to dismiss the possibility that the theft and sale of a manuscript might be this young man's way of finding the coin to buy his love. Reluctantly, she put Bernard Glover back on her list of suspects.

Chapter Thirty

A man flew backward through the inn door, hitting Thomas with such force that he landed on his back in the dust of the road.

"Satan's black balls!" the stranger roared. Struggling to his knees, he gagged and spat out teeth.

Thomas grabbed at the man's arm. "Are you not injured enough? Go home," he urged.

"Nay, monk, he must stay. He is still alive," a familiar voice scoffed.

Thomas looked up at Sayer. From the high color of the roofer's face, he guessed the fellow was drunk.

With another oath, the unknown man rose and took to his heels down the street. When he was a safe distance away, he stopped to yell further abuse before quickly disappearing around a cart.

The roofer helped the monk up. "Are you hurt, Brother?"

As he grasped Sayer's proffered hand, Thomas felt a dampness and saw a rivulet of blood trickling over the man's fingers. "You are bleeding," he said. "Was the fight worth that?"

"Spoken like a monk," the man replied, but his tone was gentle.

"I will buy you a drink. There are some questions I have for you."

Sayer stiffened and dropped Thomas' hand. "Like a dog you are, sniffing about so eagerly." Then his mouth twitched into a lopsided grin. "But I would be foolish to turn down the offer of ale from a monk with coin to buy it. That is such a rare wonder I will save the story to amaze my grandchildren when I am too old to keep their respect otherwise!"

Directing Sayer to a quiet table, Thomas gently shoved the roofer onto the bench and slid in so close to him that the man was pushed against the wall where he could not escape. The monk gestured for a serving wench to bring ale.

"Why did you and your father quarrel?" he asked when it arrived.

"That was between my father and me."

"There are those who say you, not some ghost, killed your father."

Sayer pointed to the inn door. "You saw the last man who suggested that to me, but I would not strike a monk. I earn bread for my mother and kin from the priory."

"I did not say you had done the deed, only that others have claimed it. My curiosity is not idle, nor do I accuse. I ask only for the truth. Do you not think the priory that gives you work has the right to know? If you do not answer me, another may well demand it and with less kindness."

"Two pitchers are on your bill." The young man tossed back his ale and poured again. For a moment, he said nothing, then looked at Thomas with unfocused eyes. "My father did not approve of some of my ways," he slurred. "Is that enough for you?"

"Was that disapproval reason enough for you to threaten murder?"

"Ask yourself why I would kill him. Might I not prefer to find a wife and start my own family rather than support my mother and my siblings?"

"Yet you were heard to say…"

Sayer shrugged with evident annoyance. "I no longer recall the exact cause of our fight. He was drunk as was I, a condition that offers sweet forgetfulness after days filled with the questionable joys of unrelenting soberness."

"Had he enemies?"

"All men do."

"I grow impatient with evasion. You know well enough what I mean, and, if you are innocent, you would serve your cause better by speaking the truth."

Sayer rubbed at his eyes. "Although I accused the ghost after seeing my father's corpse, no such creature had any cause to harm him. Queen Elfrida would not have cared what my father did as long as his labor provided her monks with enough food to sustain their prayers on her behalf. At that he worked hard, although he sometimes spoke ill of the priory's religious when his back ached."

Thomas nodded.

"As for Mistress Eda's spirit, my father agreed with my mother that she was wrongly accused, thus her phantom had no reason to harm him. The vintner's wife was honest and caring in life. Even after suffering the agonies of the damned, her soul would be incapable of murdering anyone so foully."

"You loved her?"

"Even rogues may honor goodness."

"There are tales abroad that you bedded her."

"You say such a story is about?" Sayer's face darkened with anger. "A fool told that lie, Brother, and a greater one believes it."

"Then I must ask again about old enemies. Did your father have them, perhaps from the days when he performed service to men who broke the king's law?"

Sayer gave the monk a meaningful look as he poured the remaining ale into his mug.

Thomas waved for more drink.

With a thud, the serving wench set another jug down on the table.

"There is no truth…"

Thomas growled a warning.

Sayer drank deeply, poured, and drank again. "I knew the stories well enough from others, but my father never spoke of those times. Most of the men either died long ago or else returned to more lawful pursuits, as did he." The roofer fell silent.

Compassion battled against suspicion inside Thomas' heart as he watched Sayer clutching his cup like a shipwrecked sailor holding onto a floating spar. "Why did you two fight?" he asked at last, his voice soft. "You remember well enough. Do not feign addled wits with me and claim your reason has grown rotten with ale. Your words have been too quick."

Sayer looked up at the ceiling, his mouth quivering with barely controlled grief. "Brother, ask not why we fought." His voice hoarsened with tears. "This I do swear to you on any holy relic: I did not kill my father. My soul may be so black that even God in His mercy would turn His countenance away, but I loved the man who sired me!" With that, Sayer began to weep.

Thomas reached out to touch the man with a gesture of sympathy but his hand froze. Instead, he quickly slid from the bench and found a serving wench. "Here is coin," he said, gesturing back at the roofer. "Make sure he has what he wants to drink, plus food and a bed for the night, should he need either."

The agony he had seen in Sayer's eyes was an emotion he himself had hoped to set aside one day. Now he doubted he ever could. Filled with his own confused fears and sorrows, Thomas hurried from the inn.

Chapter Thirty-One

"Prioress Eleanor! What a pleasant surprise to chance upon you here." Master Herbert bowed with grace. "Are you on your way to visit Mistress Jhone and her daughter?"

"I am returning to the priory," she replied, praying that her tone concealed the dismay she felt at this meeting. After the recent discussion with Wulfstan's widow, then Master Bernard, she longed to return in time for the soothing prayers of the next Office.

"I fear that you think ill of me," the vintner said, blocking her path.

Eleanor cast a covert glance at the sun and then heard the bells. Even if she left now, she would be late for prayer. Maybe God had sent the vintner to speak with her and He would bring her that understanding later when she knelt alone in her chambers. With a quiet sigh, she surrendered to the circumstances and inclined her head with an encouraging gesture toward the merchant.

He smiled. "I do understand why Alys might prefer a tender boy to this man with hints of hoarfrost on his brow..."

Silver-headed was not a word anyone would use to describe this still dark-haired and well-favored merchant, Eleanor thought, and she found that unsubtle plea to affirm his manhood mildly offensive. Swallowing her irritation, she gestured sympathetically.

"...but I had hoped to win her over in time. Such a union is in both our interests, and I am not so aged that she would have any reason to complain of me."

"You do not long for the lady herself?" The prioress shaded her question with the tone of one who understands the merits of mutually profitable marriages.

"It would be rude of me to suggest I fancied only her dead father's business." He stroked the thick nap on his robe. "A business I need not, but one I am most willing to take on for a wife able to bear sons. Of course, I do find her most comely."

Eleanor looked at him askance. "A woman worth bedding, but will you treat her kindly even if she does not bear those sons?"

To his credit, the vintner looked abashed. "My lady, I would never treat her ill."

"Would your first wife have agreed?"

Herbert's brow furrowed deeply. "Who has accused me of cruelty?"

Eleanor shook her head. Although the vintner clearly expected her to continue, Eleanor remained silent, hoping he would feel obliged to say more himself.

"I am confused by your question, my lady. My wife was a most pious woman, and we bedded only for sons. It was our share of earthly grief that none lived, but I treated her with respect as a man should his wife and did my best to persuade the crowner that she died by accidental drowning. No woman who spent so many hours in prayer would have killed herself." He shrugged. "Do these actions point to a thoughtless husband?"

How very strange, Eleanor thought. Once again she was faced with a man who tells another that his wife cuckolded him, then shows forgiveness by arguing against any verdict of self-murder. Although she should have respected him for his Christian charity, she felt oddly uncomfortable with it.

"You testified at the hearing?" she asked.

"Grief tried to keep me away, but I spoke on her behalf most passionately."

Herbert's story of Eda's piety and his defense of her manner of dying certainly matched that of the glover. Even if she heard a hint in the vintner's words that he might have preferred a more eager bed partner than he found in Eda, she detected nothing that fostered suspicion that he had been harsh to her. Alys' fears seemed to have less and less basis.

Herbert suddenly looked over Eleanor's head, his widening smile one of peculiar delight. "Is that not your monk, my lady?"

Eleanor spun around. Rushing toward them, from the direction of the inn, was Brother Thomas.

⟡ ⟡ ⟡

When Eleanor greeted him, Thomas did not know whether he should feel gratitude for the interruption to his grim mood or dismay at the sight of the fine-looking merchant standing so close to his prioress. He quickly dismissed both thoughts and replaced them with concern for Tyndal's honor. His prioress might know he had reason to be outside monastic walls, but her companion did not.

"My lady," he said. "I am most pleased to see you. I have just returned from offering solace to Sayer as you requested."

"At the inn?" The vintner's tone dripped with contempt.

Thomas felt his body grow rigid with anger at the disapproval he saw in Herbert's eyes. He swallowed his sharp reply, but his throat burned with the effort. "I saw Sayer enter the inn and followed him there," Thomas said, folding his arms. "The son laments the death of his father."

"And uses his sorrow as an excuse to grow into a sot from drink," Herbert snorted. "Yet I am sure the boy must grieve for a father who was murdered just after they quarreled. It would be an unnatural son who did not, although Sayer has always been a strange one." He shook his head. "Do not accuse me of being uncharitable, Brother, for I am not the only one in the village who thinks his soul does not praise God."

"For what reason is he so maligned?" Thomas continued, his tone as icy as a northern wind.

"Surely you would not ask me to repeat cruel gossip? If you spoke with him for any time, you must have seen the color of his soul for yourself." He bent his head toward the inn. "Satan finds joy in those who choose worldly indulgence over godly acts."

Thomas clenched his hand into a fist, then pressed it behind his back to keep from striking the man down.

Herbert smiled without humor. "Yet he may well have made peace with Wulfstan before the killing." He shrugged. "I would not know that."

Eleanor, who had remained quite silent throughout, now turned to Thomas. "I am grateful you have performed the mercy I requested, but I believe Sister Beatrice has another service for you."

The monk bowed. "I was just returning to the priory to seek her out, my lady." He suspected there was nothing the novice mistress wished him to do, but he guessed that his prioress had read his anger well. In any event, he was grateful to escape this offensive vintner.

As he walked away, and Eleanor resumed her conversation with Herbert, Thomas heard an uncharacteristic animation in her voice. The thought that his iron-willed and most virtuous prioress might be attracted to the dark-eyed merchant flitted briefly through his mind. The very idea made him uncomfortable, and he quickly turned his thoughts elsewhere.

Perhaps he should visit Brother Jerome? Now that Brother Baeda was dead, the irascible monk had taken on the librarian's duties, including care of the Amesbury Psalter. Time having somewhat faded the horror of murder, the witness might remember more about the killer he had seen.

Chapter Thirty-Two

Had Eleanor known about Thomas' momentary displeasure and the cause, her reaction might have been guilty delight mixed with surprised amusement. Herbert was an attractive man, even clever were she to be fair in judgement, but no imp would ever take on his form to torment her in dreams. Whatever charms this vintner might possess, they were not unflawed. He was an easy temptation to set aside.

"Your words have touched this heart, my lady, and I have found merit in them," the vintner said as he shifted his gaze from the departing monk back to the prioress.

"What frail logic have you transformed into something of value, Master Herbert?"

"God has surely sent you to bend me to His will. You see, I have suddenly lost all desire to go abroad and think I would find comfort in remaining near my first wife's lonely grave. I would never step on cursed soil, but might not my presence and daily prayers give her tortured spirit some comfort even in Hell?"

Souls in Hell were not granted ease, but Eleanor did not want to discourage the man from an act that might bring him respite from grief. "Yet you still wish to remarry?" she asked.

"Aye, I do, weak of flesh that I am. I would surely die of burning if I did not find a wife." He flicked his hand toward the priory. "Unlike your young monk, I have no religious calling, and sons are needed if any business is to continue and prosper."

"Have you new hope that Alys will accept you as husband?"

He shook his head. "You spoke of kindness and thus persuaded me that further delay in this marriage is hurtful to all concerned. Until Alys is firmly pledged to me, she will persist with her dream that she may yet wed the glover. While I have tolerated a young girl's itch for a boy, I now understand that there is great danger in continuing to do so." His gaze was almost caressing as he looked down at Eleanor. "Women who stay in the world have led men to their damnation since Eve gave Adam the apple. Master Bernard would have to be a saint not to bed Alys if she continues to give him encouragement. No matter how much patience and compassion I might wish to show in this matter, I do require that my first born be of my seed. Is that not reasonable?"

"You should expect it," Eleanor replied truthfully, yet she was unsettled by his mocking tone.

"Thus all sweet courting must end. Although I am loath to do so, I have no choice but to make one final trip to Gascony, and so I go to Mistress Jhone to insist that the marriage be arranged before I leave."

"You know that any woman may refuse a marriage..."

"Alys might have that legal right, but surely she understands both the profit in our union and her moral obligation. The marriage was her dead father's wish. It is her mother's. It is mine. How can she refuse?"

Eleanor nodded with barely concealed reluctance.

"Once Alys and I are vowed to each other, I can take this last journey without fear that the mother will weaken and let the girl marry Master Bernard." Herbert folded his hands. "The boy is only interested in the wool business and would cast the widow from their hearth as soon as he had the daughter. I would not be so cruel."

Why fear that Mistress Jhone would suddenly change, a woman who had shown no bending at all in this matter heretofore? Eleanor frowned, yet she could not quarrel with the vintner's fears regarding Alys and Bernard. Their meetings might seem too brief to the pair, but the prioress knew how quickly lust flamed and how little time it took to find a mutual quenching. "When do you leave?"

"Within the next few days." He gestured with frustration. "You see why I need an immediate answer. My courting skills are indeed rough, but I *like* Alys. She may be young, but she is not a child and has a quick wit. She is like a bright fire, and I am a cold man without a wife. My heart finds warmth in her light spirit. In time, we could surely learn to love each other…" He fell silent.

"I will pray for good fortune in this matter," Eleanor said, carefully choosing her words. The vintner might have won her compassion with these latest arguments, and she feared that Bernard had an interest in stolen manuscripts, but her woman's heart still sided with the younger couple.

Ignoring any ambivalence in Eleanor's fair wishes, the merchant smiled as if God Himself had approved his venture. He quickly asked a blessing, then hurried off to the woolmonger's family.

Eleanor longed to follow but knew she had no cause to interfere.

Chapter Thirty-Three

"Had this manuscript been stored properly, Brother Baeda would still be alive!" Brother Jerome might be an elderly man, but his opinions were as firm as his wiry body.

"What mean you?" Thomas asked, peering down at the item in question, now resting securely inside the priory book chest.

"This holy Psalter was handled without due reverence, and God does not forgive those who treat the work of devout monks, created with pious sweat, in such a casual manner." Jerome slammed the wooden lid shut.

Several silverfish skittered out from under one metal-encased corner and disappeared into a crack in the floor.

"Indeed, Brother, indeed." Thomas rubbed his chin thoughtfully. Considering the fate of Jerome's depiction of Eve with Eden's snake, he suspected the monk's present outburst had more to do with the deeds of unruly young novices than any failure committed by the murdered librarian. "Yet I am at a loss to understand why a ghost would choose to visit it."

Brother Jerome opened his gap-toothed mouth, looked puzzled, and shut it.

"You were about to say…?"

Jerome blinked rapidly. "I was? Aye, I was!" He struck his chest. "My spirit trembles at the thought, but I believe that Satan was at work here. Brother Baeda was an honorable man, and I shall pray for his early release to Heaven, but I fear he suffered from the sin of pride just before his death."

"Ah, pride!" Thomas nodded grave agreement. "Tell me the tale, for we learn most about the Devil's subtleties from the failings of honest men."

Jerome exhaled through his mouth with virtuous disgust.

Thomas was reminded of a horse.

"The Psalter is a most prized possession. When I saw the tear, I told Brother Baeda that I could mend it. My talents in manuscript work may be modest, but they are a God-inspired skill." He bent his head with due humility. "Nonetheless, Prioress Ida decided that no one here was worthy of touching it. Our dear brother informed me that some monk with special expertise had been summoned. Until this *expert* came, the Psalter should have been stored safely away. I think any reasonable man would agree?" He sniffed.

Thomas inclined his head with the anticipated concurrence.

"Bound as I am to obey, I did not argue with our leader's decision, but I was struck with wonder at the careless manner in which the manuscript was treated. Brother Baeda was so willing to show it to anyone at all—even that young rogue Sayer—and thus I saw how Satan had filled our brother's heart with pride. Of all the monks in the priory, he had been found worthy enough to care for the Psalter, and he wanted all to see the treasure he was given to protect."

"I concur. When I asked to see it, he let me view any page I wished."

Brother Jerome turned red, a color that gave bright contrast to the sparse white bristle on his cheeks. "I have no quarrel with a noble and godly interest such as yours. Sayer, on the other hand, is of base birth and the son of a thief. Our librarian should not have allowed a man like that to sully the holy work with his profane gaze."

"Of course."

"Besides being proud, Brother Baeda was too tolerant of young men's sinful ways and often turned a blind eye on their wicked follies. In the afternoon, before the sad evening of his death, he told me that Sayer had come to talk with him yet again about the Psalter." The monk pursed his lips with disgust. "How he could have ignored that youth's wickedness is beyond my comprehension."

"Did Brother Baeda say why Wulfstan's son was so interested in the holy work?"

Jerome winced as if he had just bitten into a bitter fruit. "I am sure Sayer gave him some plausible reason. Our dear brother did not tell me what it was, but I made sure he knew of my disapproval."

"And so you believe the ghost came that night for good purpose?"

"There could only be one reason: to bring the message of God's displeasure."

"A phantom you believe might be…?"

"Queen Elfrida, without a doubt." Jerome's eyes glazed with recollection. "The spirit was tall. A noble lady would be of greater height than one of lower birth." He nodded thoughtfully. "I was confused when she struck me down with unwomanly force, but a soul released from Purgatory would be possessed of far greater strength than any mortal."

"Edifying visions are so rare in these wicked times, and you have surely been granted one. Please tell me more."

"The queen's ghost had much reason to be here. Her sins were so heinous, and despite the wealth she gave at our founding, we had grown lax in our prayers for her soul. Prioress Ida punished the monks who…" He swallowed, unwilling to even name the sin, then continued. "Perhaps that problem was solved, but the queen still had cause for outrage when Brother Baeda gave more attention to young men on their way to Hell than he did to the proper care of her priory's most sacred work."

"Did the spirit tell you this?"

"She had no need for speech. By her presence at the library door, she made her message clear, as she did by our brother's death." His expression grew sad. "I grieve that she found it necessary to kill him so cruelly, but might he not have died from the shock of seeing her unearthly face?"

"Mayhap."

"I pray hourly for his soul."

Thomas nodded respectfully. "As a consequence, you have kept the Psalter away from impious eyes. For that zeal, both the ghost and God must praise you."

Jerome slammed his hand on the flat lid of the chest, drew in his ill-defined chin, and straightened his narrow shoulders. "When Sayer came to me, asking to see the Psalter, I vigorously refused, telling him that his filthy hands would never again soil the illuminations on that precious work!"

"And I am sure you showed him the strength of that chest, lest he try to open it when you were away at prayer."

"He was most curious about that, Brother, so I made sure he got a close look at the metal corners and heavy wood." Jerome shook the key that hung from his waist. "He also knows that I keep this with me at all times."

〇∭〇 〇∭〇 〇∭〇

Thomas raced from the library, his heart pounding with fear. Brother Jerome might be the next to die if this mystery was not quickly resolved.

Was Sayer both murderer and thief? Although Thomas' heart shouted that the roofer was incapable of such brutality, his monk's mind argued with equal force that Satan was blinding him to the truth. Hadn't he just seen a man, struck by Sayer in a fight at the inn? Was that not proof enough of the roofer's violence?

"Prioress Eleanor will see everything with the light Satan has chased from my soul," Thomas whispered as he sped through the priory. Indeed she must.

Chapter Thirty-Four

Silence fell while the servant laid refreshments on a table.

Sister Anne followed the woman from the chambers, paused to make sure no one was outside the door, then shut it. "Our brother is right when he says we must delay no longer," she said.

"Sayer's unusual interest in the Psalter suggests he may be the thief," Eleanor said, turning to Thomas.

"I agree, yet..." Thomas looked away. "...yet Wulfstan's son may be innocent or only a pawn in this game, my lady. Are you sure no one from the priory could be involved?"

"It would be difficult for a monk to sell a Psalter, Brother."

Thomas folded his arms. "For cert, but that also applies to Sayer. Where could a mere roofer sell such a manuscript? Someone else must be involved, making Sayer's crime a limited one. He might be acting on behalf of a monk, stealing the Psalter which he would then deliver to a man outside the priory who could sell it. If he did this while all monks were at prayer, no accusing finger could be pointed at any monastic. He may be little more than a courier."

Eleanor nodded for him to continue.

"He may even be innocent. When I first met the man, he showed no distress that this priory's monks had ceased to visit the inn, although he was willing enough to offer a complete stranger, me, a way to break my vows." The monk swallowed audibly. "If

Sayer had some way to sell the Psalter, or else knew someone who could do so, he might have arranged with some monk to deliver the manuscript to him at the inn long before now."

"I understand your argument," Anne said, "but he has not given you a good reason for his current and most unusual interest in this sacred work. Reverence does not appear to be one of his virtues. We must conclude he has another purpose."

"I agree that there is no explanation for his questions about the storage of the work." Thomas took a deep breath. "On the other hand, he is only in the priory during the day. How could he steal the Psalter then? It would have to be done at night. Only a monk would know the habits of the religious best and when it would be safe to remove the work from the library without the chance of witnesses."

"We cannot dismiss the wandering phantom that has been seen both inside and without the priory walls," Eleanor said. "The library is on the monks' side. If the ghost was created to keep formerly lusty monks quivering fearfully in their chaste beds, someone could climb the wall at night and steal the manuscript without fear of detection. Although this could have been a monk, I suspect the spirit has a more secular form. Based on Brother Jerome's statement, all religious were at prayers when Brother Baeda faced his killer. Therefore, no monk is guilty of this deed, an act that must have occurred during one attempt to steal the Psalter." Her expression was grim. "These two murders continue to trouble me. Brother Baeda's death might be easily explained, but I fail to comprehend why Wulfstan should have died. I asked myself if he was involved because he repaired that wall and may have left the toeholds. Nonetheless, all have claimed he was a man who honored the law for so very many years." She stopped. "I need your thoughts, Brother."

"I cannot cast light on your questions, my lady, yet I see no fault with your conclusions," Thomas replied, his tone hesitant.

Eleanor put her hands together and studied the monk over the tips of her fingers. "Although I believe our roofer is the thief, your argument that someone else has to be involved is well-considered." She frowned. "Tell me, Brother, do you think Sayer capable of murder?"

Thomas gazed at the ground. "He fought with his father before Wulfstan died and even threatened to kill him. Although I cannot discover the reason for the argument, we know that father and son have worked outside the law, both the king's and God's, for personal gain. The father may have reformed, but the son has not, if his attempt to draw me into sin is any indication. If a man commits one crime, may he not be suspect for another?" His voice faded on those last words.

Eleanor grew thoughtful as she mulled over her monk's question. "If you mean the corruption of weak-fleshed monks, I agree that was a wicked deed." She knew the reason for the quarrel but would not speak of it. Cold reason might dismiss Drifa's easy forgiveness and her own aunt's fond tolerance of the man, but her mind could not reject one doubt about the accusation of sodomy: Wulfstan might have been mistaken in what he saw. There was no corroborating evidence. She closed her eyes and said, "Man may sin, yet not be guilty of all evil. Nor is he beyond redemption in God's eyes." At least she had faith in that, no matter how confused she was about the rest of this matter.

"And repent he may have done. As you yourself have said, only one religious has visited the inn of late, and that man is you," Anne added.

"Despite your last words, Brother, I have also heard you express doubt about the roofer's guilt. Do you believe Sayer is innocent in the murder of his father and Brother Baeda?"

"He has charmed me, my lady." Thomas' voice broke, his words stumbling out of his mouth as if he hated to say them. "Perhaps Satan has blinded me to his evil, but I do not think he killed his father. I heard love in his voice when he spoke of Wulfstan. Nor can I imagine that Sayer murdered Brother Baeda. The method of killing was a ruthless act, and I have not seen such cruelty in the roofer. Nonetheless, I cannot overlook his unusual interest in the manuscript." Thomas exhaled, the sound akin to a sob. "Nor can I deny that Satan might not have given him a pleasing countenance to hide a dark soul."

Eleanor said nothing for a very long time.

Sister Anne looked from one to the other, then rose and poured a mazer of wine for her prioress and the monk. "If Sayer is working on behalf of someone else, might that person be involved in the murders instead?"

Eleanor nodded in agreement. "Someone who has access to buyers of precious manuscripts, and someone who sells at some distance."

"And that might be who?" Anne asked.

"Merchants travel," Thomas said, looking hopeful.

"Bernard the glover needs money to win the hand of his beloved Alys." Eleanor put her mazer down without tasting the wine. "He himself creates most artful designs and might well know others who appreciate beautiful things. Among such men there may be those who, if their own eyes covet it, choose to ignore that a work was intended to please God. I also saw him walking by the river with another of like enough age who might have been Sayer. Were they plotting?" She looked upward in silence for a moment. "Yet Satan may have blinded me as well, Brother. I cannot believe the glover is a murderer, and my woman's frail heart hopes that he and Alys can wed. I see no great evil in him."

"On the night I went to the inn, I saw Sayer and the glover in close conversation. When I learned that Master Bernard wanted to marry the woolmonger's daughter, I thought that such speech with a cousin would not be unusual and did not consider any other meaning. Yet I, too, doubt..." Thomas suddenly brightened. "What about Master Herbert?"

"Ah, our vintner! You have little liking for the man, do you?"

"I do not trust him, my lady," the monk replied with open disdain.

Eleanor grew pensive, sipped at her wine, and then smiled. "His dress and manner suggest wealth, but his first wife endured a long illness. If he could not travel to his vineyards because of her ill health, or the cost of her sickness was high, I wonder if his income suffered as a consequence. He is very eager, despite his protestations, to take on a woolmonger's business."

Thomas nodded, both surprise and pleasure obvious in his expression.

"I have not met the man," Anne said, "but I must also ask if he is so eager for wealth that he longs only for a new source of it."

"And I should ask if it is logical that a man steal a manuscript from this priory but remain here and sell wool." From the way Thomas clenched his fists, this statement took some effort for him to make.

"Are there any others in the village who might be allied to Sayer in this matter?" Anne asked.

"I do not believe the innkeeper cares to sell anything but ale and whores," Thomas said. "According to the glover, there are still robbers who lurk near that strange pile of pagan stones, but they do not trouble the merchants of Amesbury and thus must be local men. If they do not torment the village, why would they steal the priory's Psalter?"

"Is the thief a man from somewhere else?" Anne continued.

"According to the glover, no strangers have shown any interest in the Psalter," Thomas replied.

"Then he is either lying or the thief is a local man. We have solved nothing here," Anne sighed.

"We have not, nor do we have time for further debate or questions. Brother Jerome is in danger." Eleanor's eyes turned dark with anger. "Now is the time to weave a web like a skillful spider and trap whatever flies we may." She turned to Thomas. "I have a plot in mind, Brother, but it would require that you return to the inn."

"The trap, my lady. How do you propose to set it?"

Chapter Thirty-Five

The crow from the nest near the library soared into the sky when Thomas left the priory. Had he not been told that birds had no souls, he might have concluded that hers felt an especial delight over her young. With the world rejoicing in the renewal of life, he grumbled to himself, why must he deal with death?

Nay, it was neither death nor the suspicion thereof that pricked sharply at his heart. He knew that well enough. It was the knowledge that he must send Sayer into a trap, one that might well lead to the man's hanging. The earth joined his spirit in protest and seemed to snatch at his feet to keep him from his destination.

When Thomas reached the inn, he stopped, willing a firmness of purpose to fill his soul. After all, Prioress Eleanor had ordered him to perform a task, and he owed her obedience. He might be blinded by the wiles of the Prince of Darkness, but she was not. He had no right to whine like some swaddled babe. He must...

"Why such hesitancy, Brother? After two visits, you have second thoughts about entering our inn?"

Thomas spun around.

Sayer stood behind him.

The monk swallowed, the flame of guilt turning his face hot. "I am distressed," he said quickly. "Will you share some ale with me?"

"More questions, monk? I weary of them and even the promise of ale is not tempting enough to make tolerance bloom."

"I am through with that. Amesbury Priory must find someone else to solve their problems."

Sayer's look softened. He stepped in front of the monk and held the door open for him. "The priory coin has come most often from your hand, Brother. Let it now drop from mine. Enter and tell me what troubles you."

Thomas walked inside. Behind him, the door creaked shut. He blinked at the smoky darkness and breathed in the sour reek of old sweat.

Sayer gestured for the monk to follow.

Can I do this? Thomas asked himself as he settled on the bench. But once the drink arrived and they were alone, he willed himself to the game and uttered a painful sigh.

"What causes your brow to furrow so, Brother?"

"My prioress says we must leave on the morrow. Although I have ignored all this until now…" He gestured at the ale, then nodded in the direction of the vanished serving wench. "My heart grieves for I shall have no such joys at Tyndal."

Sayer gazed at him in silence. "Then your last evening must be especially memorable."

Thomas tried to look both sheepish and eager, an effort made more difficult by the new chill in the roofer's voice.

"I could promise you such a time but do ask if you can leave the priory tonight?"

Thomas nodded. "I believe that I can."

"The wall has been repaired, and the ghost lurks."

Was the man trying to dissuade him? Thomas asked himself. Was he ignorant of the toeholds scraped into the repaired wall? Hope warmed his heart. "I have seen no ghost. Since Brother Baeda's death, Sister Beatrice has ordered me to lock the library after Compline. Now I sleep apart from other monks and patrol outside the building with a cross in hand to protect the sacred works therein from any hellish imps."

"How clever of Sister Beatrice."

He shrugged. "None would know if I slipped away as long as I returned by Matins."

"Then come to the inn when darkness falls, Brother."

"After Compline..."

"Nay, before. Pray if you must, but remember that Matins comes early. I would not have you cheated of any joy when none will warm you once you return to your own priory."

"The library..."

"...shall be safe enough for one night. You have seen no ghost. Most likely, the queen's spirit has found whatever she went there to seek. She might well choose to trouble the monks in their dorter next, or else she has gone back to Purgatory." He bent his head to one side and studied the monk. "If you come early enough, I can promise you a private room and an able woman to serve you the inn's best wine."

Thomas put a hand to his heart as if to still its sinful beating. "Barring some demand by my prioress, I will meet you after the evening meal and before Compline."

Sayer nodded, slid from the bench, and left the monk alone.

A black robe of mourning draped over Thomas' heart.

Chapter Thirty-Six

At the appointed time that night, Thomas went to the inn. He sat on a bench, called for ale, and waited for Sayer, but his hand shook when he reached for the tankard soon placed in front of him. Firmly grasping the thing with both hands, he managed to quell the disloyal tremor.

Anyone seeing this sign of apprehension would surely blame it on his great struggle between the demands of frail flesh and his equally great longing for Heaven, or so he told himself. Unfortunately, his flesh showed no evidence of interest in this planned tryst, an observation he hoped no one else made.

Sayer arrived shortly after, and Thomas persuaded him that he longed for the most popular serving wench. Maybe he only imagined the hint of disappointment on the man's face, but once he had given Sayer payment for his night of pleasuring, the man spoke to the innkeeper and disappeared.

The moment Thomas and the woman had closed the door to the private room, he fell to his knees, raised his still trembling hands heavenward, and loudly thanked God for granting him the strength to win his battle over the flesh.

At first the woman expressed indignation, but he assured her that he would slip away unnoticed and the money agreed upon would not be taken back no matter his change of heart. Her weary face brightened and she winked at him, assuring the monk that she would enjoy the wine and an empty bed.

Thomas soon found himself back in the night and hurrying along the path to the priory and the dark library.

That the sheriff was still in distant pursuit of his fowl and boar mattered not. Sister Beatrice had agreed to her niece's plan and promised there would be men in the shadows surrounding the building, robust lay brothers armed with blessed cudgels, most likely under the command of Brother Infirmarian. Thomas would not be alone.

He looked around. At least I trust the men are there, he said to himself. He could see no one but took comfort in the hope that they were ready to come to his rescue with due speed if needed.

In truth, he did not know exactly what to expect inside the library, although he had ardently beseeched to go there alone. Prioress Eleanor had conceded that one man would be less likely to betray the trap, thus increasing the chances of catching the thief in the act, but she did not think his plan quite safe. Only when he promised to cry out for the aid of others once he had caught the man had she agreed. Thomas prayed she was not angry with him, seeing his stubborn insistence as either disrespectful or disobedient.

He had another reason for wanting to be alone. Although he knew that Sayer would be the one most likely caught with his hand on the Psalter, the monk's unruly heart refused to be silenced, arguing with growing persistence that the roofer was more misguided than evil. Might Thomas not reason with him tonight, persuading the man to reveal who was behind the theft and even agree to give witness to the murderer's deeds? If so, the monk could argue for leniency on Sayer's behalf.

If he was wrong and the roofer was a brutal killer, he should be able to detain him for a short time until the others arrived. The other problem lay in the number he might meet in the darkness of the library. If more than one was there, he would be in great danger. In that case, he must count on his own strength, wits, and the element of surprise to get him out of the situation.

The library was as profoundly silent as it was deep in shadow. Although Thomas' eyes were used to the gloom, he felt his way to a hiding place with difficulty. At least anyone else who came through the darkness would be at equal disadvantage, he thought, settling into a crouch behind Brother Jerome's work area. The book chest was directly in front of him.

His ears prickled. Had he heard a sound or was it just a mouse skittering along the floor? The silence now seemed full of tiny noises, but as he strained to hear, he was almost certain that someone was coming.

The door opened.

A man entered. He was holding a flickering light.

Silently Thomas swore at himself for not considering this possibility. Could he be seen by the light of that flame? He bent down as much as he could.

His pounding heart quieted as he realized that the thief would not have brought light if there was anyone outside to see it. That meant he knew the monk was the only one who might be nearby, and he was supposedly across the river, busily swyving a woman. The lay brothers must have seen it as well and known that the thief had arrived. He should take comfort in that, Thomas decided.

The man hesitated, then silently walked to the book chest.

Thomas was sure it was Sayer. So that there would be no doubt about the man's intent, he would wait until the roofer began to leave with the Psalter in his arms.

The figure bent, holding the light close to the storage box. Within the briefest of moments, he had broken the lock, lifted the lid, and grasped the Psalter. The lid dropped with a dull thud. The man turned and walked toward the monk.

Thomas rose to face him, but something to his left caught his attention. He jerked to one side. The blow struck the side of his head. Light flashed before his eyes, and everything went black.

Chapter Thirty-Seven

Thomas blinked. He was lying on his side. His head hurt, and there was something warm trickling down his neck. How long had he been unconscious?

"I said I would bring it to you." The voice was Sayer's.

Thomas shut his eyes and held his breath.

"Stupid pup," a man replied, his hoarse voice barely above a whisper.

Feeling a wave of nausea, Thomas willed himself not to vomit.

"You did not recognize a trap when you saw it." The man kicked at Thomas.

The monk bit his lip but did not groan.

"You are fortunate that foolish women run this place and sent but one monk to stop you."

"Did you kill him?" Sayer asked.

"Bring your light."

As the small flame flickered with weak warmth over his face, Thomas willed himself to look like a man who had just died. He should have seen enough of them, he thought, to feign the expression well. If he failed, he would no longer have to pretend.

"He's bled enough to be a dead man," Sayer said, touching the monk's neck gently with his fingers. The light moved quickly away.

Thomas prayed God would take mercy on his soul.

"I will make sure of it."

"You need not bother. I felt his neck. There is no life in him."
Sayer's voice was angry.

"Fancied him, did we?" the man scoffed.

Sayer did not reply, but Thomas heard a noise as if something
was being shaken.

"Stop that, whelp! Have you no idea what a valuable work
the Psalter is? You'll damage it!"

"Then take the thing if you do not want harm to come to it."

The light went out, and Thomas heard a grunt. As much as
he longed to rise, he knew he might faint from his injury. There
was nothing he could do but lie in his own blood.

Sayer laughed. "A child could have done more harm with
that blow. I think I shall keep this for myself."

"Mock if you will, but the Psalter is worthless without me."

Thomas felt himself drift toward unconsciousness. He willed
himself back.

"I might have another buyer."

"Your lies are as wanting as your manhood."

"You are not the only one in Amesbury who needs money
and knows the worth of this piece of painted sheep skin."

The man hissed. "You could not have found another."

"Can you afford to doubt me? Or consider this: I might
choose to save my soul, rather than take money, and confess
who has led me to this crime."

"You would gain nothing by trying to expose me. Who would
believe you, blasphemous rogue that you are?"

"Dare you chance that? You have now killed three men,
including my own father."

"A robber? Two womanish monks? Killing your father was
but long-delayed justice for ancient sins. As for the monks, I
was kind, sending them to Heaven sooner than either had dared
hope."

"And Eda? Even you dare not claim she killed herself. You
drowned her, did you not? She had overheard us talking about
plans to steal…"

"I'll kill you!" the man roared.

Sayer laughed.

"Give me the manuscript, cokenay."

"Only if you can catch me."

The sound of running feet echoed in the floor under Thomas' ear. He heard the door crash against the wall.

Slowly he opened one eye. Both men must be gone, he decided, but hesitated a moment to make sure. Weak and dizzy, he began struggling to his knees.

A hand came to rest on his shoulder.

"It seems you are still alive, Brother," a man said.

Chapter Thirty-Eight

Brother Infirmarian cursed the clouds that had just covered the moon. His phrasing was most secular.

"Brother Thomas has not called for help, and the light has been extinguished in the library." A lay brother pointed to the now dark window.

"The agreement was to do nothing until our brother gave the signal," the infirmarian whispered back. "We must wait a while longer before going inside." He fell silent and stared with evident unease at the gloomy building. "I dare not spring the trap too soon, but I do not wish harm to come to our brave monk either."

"Wait!" another exclaimed softly. "I heard a man's voice. That must be the sign!"

Brother Infirmarian rose and called for the group of lay brothers to follow him. As he did, the clouds mercifully parted like a fortress gate and the moon shone forth just enough to outline two figures emerging onto the scaffolding high above the band of monastic rescuers.

The first shadow leapt onto the roof, scrambling loudly up the steep incline. The second stumbled, caught himself, and awkwardly crawled after him.

Brother Infirmarian ordered his men to halt.

"Is one Brother Thomas?" a lay brother asked him.

A cloud drifted back across the moon, dimming the light.

"I think not, but I cannot be sure. They could both be the Devil's imps." Brother Infirmarian quickly ordered several of the lay brothers to assail the library but gestured for one to remain behind with him. The two men slipped closer to the walls and stared upward, raising their crosses to frighten any demon that might lurk there.

The grey forms on the roof looked like sooty ghosts against the darker roofing. The apparition higher up laughed with wicked merriment.

The men below clutched their crosses to their hearts. "Has the Devil released his minions to befoul God's priory with obscene antics?" the lay brother whispered.

The moon once again escaped its cloud, and the men on the ground could see one apparent mortal stand and wave something over his head.

"Give me that!" the other shadow shouted.

Brother Infirmarian looked at his companion. "Do you recognize that voice?"

The lay brother said nothing, his eyes wide-open with terror.

"Catch me if you can," the first one sang and climbed farther upward.

"Devil's spawn!"

"How fond you are of slandering others! I may be a rogue, but I would never defame the innocent. Now that you are on God's ground, surely you must confess that you lied about Eda. She never committed adultery, did she? Shout the truth to God, and I may give you this Psalter."

"She never forsook virtue," Herbert roared. "Give me the manuscript!" He pulled himself closer to the desired object.

The leaner shadow waved it over his head once again. "And a woman who so loved God would never have committed self-murder, would she? Even you could not claim otherwise, although you let others condemn her. Come," he said, holding the Psalter just out of reach. "Tell me how she died, and I shall release this."

"I held her head under the water until she drowned." The vintner grabbed at the Psalter, then slipped. As he slid down the roof, he screamed, but he landed safely on the scaffolding.

"On this holy ground, will you not ask His forgiveness?"

"Give me that Psalter! Dare you call me a sinner when you are Satan's own bedmate?"

"Now you have hurt my feelings."

To the right, two more men could be seen pulling themselves through a window onto the narrow wooden walkway.

The figure high on the roof lifted the Psalter over his head. "Beg for this." Suddenly he lost his footing. "Here! Catch it!" the man cried out, tossing the manuscript out into the darkness as he tumbled downward.

Master Herbert bent backwards to seize the manuscript as it flew over his head. The thin railing at his back snapped.

Brother Infirmarian, ignoring the screams above him, raced to the man who had just hit the ground.

"The hangman has been thwarted," he said softly.

The vintner's neck was broken in two.

Chapter Thirty-Nine

Sayer lay in the monks' infirmary, his face pale and one arm bound to his chest.

"Does your shoulder hurt?" Bernard asked with frank concern.

"Brother Infirmarian pushed the bone back in quickly enough." Sayer's expression spoke more of indifference than any relief. "I am weak and may not move this arm. That is all."

"When we pulled you back onto the scaffolding, I wept for your pain." The glover wrung his hands and glanced over at the monk beside him. "Had Brother Thomas not been with me, you would have died. I did not have the strength to save you by myself."

"I should thank you both for that," the roofer said, "but I heal only to face the hangman. You should have let me fall to my death and saved the cost of a rope."

"You have killed no one," Brother Thomas replied.

"If I had not agreed to play a ghost to keep everyone inside at night so the vintner might steal the manuscript, my father would have lived. Although I did not strike the blow, I still murdered my father with my greed and wicked foolishness."

"God wants to forgive, and your actions tonight will do much to assuage the evil you have done in the past," Thomas replied, touching the binding around his head without thinking. He winced. "You did not know that my prioress had a plan to catch the guilty, yet you had already plotted to expose both killer and thief."

"Then only my hand will be cut off for my own part in attempting to steal the Psalter? I would rather kill myself than become a further burden to my mother."

Bernard gasped. "Your mother loves you as does Alys. Why make them suffer by committing that cruel and sinful act?"

"When the sheriff chops off the hand, I may die anyway. Satan will get a fine jester when he receives my soul."

"Justice will not be a secular one," Thomas said. "Your sheriff has proclaimed, in front of witnesses, that Church law rules in the matter of ghosts. Since you were the ghost, the priory will decide your punishment."

"Have I not profited from leading monks to sin? Did I not agree to help steal a holy work? Surely the Church would say that I am to blame for the death of my father and Brother Baeda, a most virtuous monk who joyfully shared the Psalter's sacred beauty with this wicked man." He turned his face away. "The Church will love me even less than King Henry's men."

"You conspired to catch Master Herbert in the theft and arranged for me to witness his confession of murder." Bernard folded his arms. "Does that not show repentance for any past sins?"

"Repentance?" Sayer laughed. "I but wanted you and Alys to marry! Once the vintner's crimes were exposed and your courage in catching him out was told, my aunt would accept your suit."

"More is involved, I think," Thomas added.

"Consider the advantage to me if Bernard heard the vintner's confession. It absolves me of killing my father. When he was murdered on the path outside the priory, I suspected who had done it. Only Master Herbert knew about the toeholds I had gouged into the mortar when I finished repairing the wall for my father. When I confronted the man, he did admit the deed, claiming my sire had to die because he recognized him escaping from the priory after a monk cried out in fear."

"If he confessed, why did you not report it?"

"He reminded me that many had heard how my father and I quarreled and the threat I made in the heat of it to kill him. It would be easy to make sure I was arrested for my father's murder."

"A threat most did not believe you meant," Thomas added.

"Dear cousin, why do you continue to cover your soul with foulness? Admit your honest deeds."

Sayer raised an eyebrow. "Cousin? You should not stain your honor by adding me to your family."

"As Alys' beloved cousin, you are mine as well." Bernard raised his chin. "If you insist on confessing your evil deeds, at least add how you planned to trap the man."

"And failed to do so before a kind monk was killed." The roofer's mouth trembled. "Since the vintner had not asked my help in his first attempt to steal the Psalter, I should have known he did not trust me, or else had grown impatient with greed. Once again and without my knowledge, he climbed the wall and managed to slip into the library. Brother Baeda caught him and died. For that, I grieve."

Thomas shook his head. "Yet you came for the Psalter last night. How did you regain the man's trust?"

"I squirmed on my knees and beseeched him for coin, a longing he well understood. Since he had failed twice, I convinced him to let me try. I knew the building best, having reached the scaffolding to the roof from inside the library." Sayer shrugged, then winced with the pain. "When he agreed, I knew he would probably follow, hoping to kill me as soon as he could get the manuscript in hand."

"Surely the ghost could only be accused of so much violence before someone suspected a human hand. How dare he chance another corpse?"

"Queen Elfrida would be blamed for only two murders. Need I remind you how cleverly he disguised his wife's death, Brother? He was most confident, and, although I think his guilty soul may have really wanted hers to seem an accident, he would have had no scruples about making mine look like suicide."

"From guilt because you sold women's flesh? London would be bereft of whoremongers if men were so conscience-stricken."

"This is Amesbury, Brother. Some here would most certainly conclude I had killed myself over sins of the flesh." Sayer's smile was fleeting.

"Might no one have asked if his travel to Gascony was connected to the disappearance of the Psalter?"

"Why? The man was a respected merchant. Even honest men see only what they are led to believe if the telling is cunning enough. Consider how quickly all decided the verdict on Mistress Eda's death because a few were most persuasive."

Bernard slammed a fist into his other hand. "The theft would have been the perfect crime, had you not arranged for me to witness it." Horror washed over his face. "And you might have died if Brother Thomas had not been there! Surely you realized…"

Sayer winked at the monk. "Mayhap I would not have fallen."

"Mayhap," Thomas replied, doubt coloring his voice.

"I have long wondered why Master Herbert claimed you had bedded his wife," Bernard said softly. "Surely there was no truth to that?"

"Never! I fear the reason for his wife's murder and that accusation are found in the same tale. As our monk here may not know, Alys grieved over Mistress Eda's painful illness. Knowing me to be a merry rogue, she asked that I spend an hour playing the fool to make the lady laugh. Instead, Eda burst into tears when she saw me. When I sought to comfort her, she confessed her sorrow. She had overheard her husband's proposal to me about the theft of the Psalter one night when we thought she was deep in sleep. Although she could not quite believe her husband would plan such a blasphemous act, she feared she was not mistaken. My heart broke, and I confirmed that what she had heard was true."

"Why had he planned the theft? Was he not wealthy enough?" Thomas asked.

"His show of wealth was false. Before her illness, she found proof that he had sold his vineyards. When she questioned him, he insisted she did not understand what she had seen, that he had sold but a portion to pay debts left by his father. Although the vintner could be most persuasive in his lies, she was suspicious and looked further, discovering that he had followed his father's example in acquiring debts beyond his ability to pay. Soon after, she fell ill and began to draw away from any interest in those worldly cares, although the blasphemy in stealing the Psalter deeply troubled her pious soul. Nonetheless, he feared her knowledge. When he overheard us talk about the Psalter, he decided she knew too much and killed her."

"That does not explain how he decided you had cuckolded him," Bernard replied.

Sayer snorted with contempt. "He knew that to be untrue. While I was holding his wife, attempting to stop her tears, the vintner came upon us. He flew into a feigned rage, swearing to expose us as adulterers."

"You could have countered the charge with the tale of the theft and repented of your agreement with him."

"With some, Brother, any accusation has the whiff of truth. Were either of us to speak of her discoveries or the theft, the vintner would have claimed we were trying to hide our sin with lies. Mistress Eda was an honest wife. I did not want her honor soiled on my account."

"Why would any man put horns on his own head? He himself told the tale of adultery to the woolmonger and I overheard it. Others must have as well," Bernard said.

"The sharpness of a cuckold's horns may be dulled by cleverness. First, he made sure my reputation grew darker by suggesting the adultery might have been rape. His pride, therefore, suffered a lesser wound. Next, he showed Christian charity by defending the soul of his dishonorable wife. Can you not hear the crowds exclaiming, 'What a noble man'? You see what a crafty teller of tales he was."

Bernard smiled. "You may paint yourself with the Devil's colors, Sayer, but he does not have your conscience."

"My selfishness has brought about two deaths. I will say nothing in my defense and shall go to my hanging without protest."

"What self-interest was involved in getting the vintner to confess in front of half the priory that Mistress Eda was innocent of both self-murder and adultery?" Thomas asked. "Nor did you have any reason to save my life. When Herbert wanted to finish the task of killing me in the library, you drew him away. You knew I was still alive."

Sayer said nothing.

Bernard sat on a stool next to the bed. "I beg you to admit the good you have done and save yourself. Like many, you have done no more than loan your soul to Satan."

"Let me be."

"Sayer needs the advice of a confessor, Master Bernard. Would you leave us?"

The glover blinked, then quickly rose. "I will be walking in the gardens outside."

Thomas took the vacant seat.

"Leave me in peace, monk. I have no longing for any priest."

"Your guilt over your father's death and that of the librarian troubles you deeply, but you have other reasons for wanting to join Satan in Hell."

Sayer put his uninjured hand lightly on the monk's knee. "Do you blame me?" he asked softly.

"Yes."

"I have no wish to take a vow of celibacy," Sayer replied. "I will continue to dance with the Devil."

"Dance with a wife. Beget children. Bring the joy of grandchildren to your mother."

"And thus God will forgive me?" Sayer's laugh was bitter.

Thomas nodded gravely.

"Yet the Church will surely condemn me for the theft…"

"Bernard will tell Sister Beatrice how you plotted to save the Psalter and expose a killer at the risk of your own life. I will swear that you saved my life and confirm the vintner's confession to the murder of both Brother Baeda and Wulfstan. Brother

Infirmarian and several lay brothers heard Herbert confess to his wife's killing. Prioress Ida may even count it a blessing that you frightened vow-breaking monks back into their solitary beds."

"My father..."

"...was killed because Herbert grew greedy and tried to steal the Psalter without paying for your help."

"The librarian's death..."

"...is on your conscience. His soul needs your prayers. I repeat: those are not your most troubling sins."

"For all my sins, monk, name my punishment."

"Marry, take on a man's responsibilities, and find joy in that."

Sayer drew back his hand. "Did you find your own answer in God's arms, Brother?"

Thomas closed his eyes and turned away.

Chapter Forty

The grave was little marked. The dirt once mounded over the pit had sunk, leaving only a small rise in the earth, but new growth sprouted there with a particular vigor.

In contrast to the lime green of young grass, the dress of the kneeling woolmonger's widow was dark as a night without stars. Her fingers curled like claws as she covered her face. Yet when she uncovered her somber eyes and looked up at the bright heavens, her face was not as aged as it had seemed only a few days ago. Her features now held a hint of youth and even a certain beauty.

Drifa helped her sister rise, but Mistress Jhone gently shook her hand away and stood motionless, quite careless that her robe was stained with sodden earth. A soft cry escaped her lips as she looked down at the little grave, and she stretched forth an open hand as if longing to grasp something only she could see. Weeping, she pulled her arm back against her breast and shuddered. Then she let her sister take her into her arms where she sobbed with all the force of pent-up grief.

"Eda is at peace, mistress. God has rendered justice," Eleanor said, her voice as soft as the breeze against their faces.

"She will be reburied in holy ground?"

"Tomorrow."

"She is no longer in Hell?"

"I doubt she ever was," Eleanor replied. "The Prince of Darkness may have blinded the crowner and his jury with ignorance and hardened hearts, but God would have known the truth."

Drifa wiped Jhone's cheeks with an elder sister's love. A smudge of dirt remained under one eye, but tears quickly washed it away.

"I came here every day to pray," the woolmonger's widow whispered.

Her sister took her hand and pressed it.

"Most would not have done so, mistress. This is the burial ground of condemned souls. Many fear the contagion of their wickedness," the prioress said.

"I knew she was innocent, my lady. We had been like kin from the day we could first walk. I owed her a friend's steadfastness," the woman replied with simple, unwavering belief.

Eleanor glanced at the uneven ground surrounding them and so many graves of the damned. The silence of this unholy place made her shiver, yet she caught herself wondering how many more innocents were buried here, condemned by men but never by God.

Mistress Drifa kissed Jhone on the cheek and once again pulled her sister into the comfort of her arms.

In silence, the prioress watched the two sisters and smiled at the tenderness between such resolute women. Would she herself have been able to show such bravery, kneeling on this cursed earth and persevering in the belief that a friend was innocent when a community might well rebuke her? Would she, like Drifa, continue to see goodness in a son who kissed the Devil's hand? The actions of these two had raised questions that she knew she would ponder long after her return to Tyndal.

"My lady, I have much to thank you for," Jhone suddenly cried out, throwing herself on her knees before the Prioress of Tyndal.

Eleanor gasped. "You have no need…"

"I have another favor to beg."

"Ask it but do not kneel to me." Eleanor raised the woolmonger's widow to her feet.

"My sins have been grievous ones! Like my husband, I was blinded by Master Herbert's well-crafted cloak of wealth, but God has now torn that pall from my eyes. My daughter shall marry her glover, a man I might have found worthy enough had it not been…"

Although Jhone turned her face away, Eleanor saw anger flash in her eyes. Was the cause her husband's inability to see Herbert's true nature or her own unthinking complicity in a decision that would have forced her beloved daughter into the arms of a murderer?

"And you shall have grandchildren to make your life most joyous," the prioress quickly said. The image of plump children racing around their grandmother, graced with Alys' loving determination and Bernard's gentle nature and pink cheeks, was a sweet one.

"I want to end my days in the priory."

"Only Prioress Ida has the authority to grant that plea!"

"But she would listen to you!"

"Seek instead the counsel of Sister Beatrice, a woman far wiser than I and one whose voice the prioress of Amesbury respects."

"As you will, my lady, but there is no reason to doubt my longing to leave the world. I owe God a long penance. I married for lust and fell into a cruel bondage with a husband who had always been an angry man. He beat me when I smiled at the butcher or did not cook his meat the way he liked it. When he struck me so hard that I lost the one son he gave me, he took to drink. As a good wife must, I turned my head away from his growing iniquity and honored my vows of obedience until his death. As a good wife still, I pray daily for his soul, but it will take many years before I can forgive his wickedness toward the innocent even if God does so."

Eleanor looked over at Drifa. Wulfstan's widow was weeping.

"Yet I, too, committed great wickedness when I tried to force Alys into a marriage with a malevolent man. My husband may have been fooled by the vintner's fine show of competence and prosperity, but I bear fault enough myself. In my youth, I failed to heed my parents. When I saw Alys set her heart on the glover, I feared she was as blinded by lust as I had been once. Although she, unlike I, chose a good man, I did not note the differences and was determined that she follow the path I had refused." Jhone's face darkened with grim determination. "Like Moses, I should not cross the Jordan and taint the future of my child and the innocence of her children with my knowledge of wicked ways."

"Mortals do evil things, mistress. It is our nature. Your mistake was born of reasonable fear, but there was no cruelty in your heart. Seek penance and remain in the world where Alys and her babes can bring you joy. Help your sister with her fatherless children. You can bring all these young ones the wisdom learned from your errors so that they may avoid the same faults."

"I fear that the Devil has not let me go," she whispered, "and I would only lead the innocent to calamity as I almost did my daughter. Nor would I burden Bernard with my care. He has proven himself a worthy man, and, despite my cruel words to him, I believe he would be forgiving and generous to me. It would be kinder if I did not accept a place at his table. Nay, after paying my dowry to the Order, the remaining wealth and the business must go to him and my Alys' children."

"There are other good men in the world…"

"I have no wish to remarry. Although the Church says I may without sin, I could not bring myself to bed with another man."

Eleanor glanced at Drifa, asking for confirmation of what she had just heard.

The woman nodded and gazed back at her sister. The tears that flowed down her cheeks glittered with both sadness and love.

"On Judgement Day," Jhone now continued, "I will seek my husband. May God grant that I am able to give him my hand in forgiveness. With God's mercy, I pray he will have learned the horror of his sins. We should stand side by side at God's throne while we wait for His verdict on our various transgressions. For the remainder of my days on this earth, I would find chastity, obedience, and poverty easy vows to take, although I would beg to be granted one wish."

"And that is?"

"Until I die, I would like to come each day and pray beside the new grave of Eda, that her time in Purgatory may be short. She was as virtuous as any mortal can be."

As Eleanor drew Jhone into a comforting embrace, the harsh silence in the lonely graveyard of damned souls softened as if hope had entered the gate.

ᏬᎢᎶ ᏬᎢᎶ ᏬᎢᎶ

On the edge of the graveyard, standing alongside Sister Anne and Brother Thomas, Beatrice watched her niece take the woolmonger's widow into her arms. She might not have heard what each had said to the other, but the novice mistress could read the words writ on faces well enough. After all, she herself had been a wife and mother, then a widow, before she became a nun.

As she watched Eleanor comfort Mistress Jhone, Beatrice pressed a hand to her breast to hold in the joy flooding her heart. Such pride in her niece might be sinful, but she suspected God forgave more quickly in instances like this.

After Eleanor had ridden back to Tyndal, she promised to confess. There would be time enough then to deal with her mortal failings. Beatrice knew she would face the parting with a stern will, after which she would escape to the cloister gardens where she could weep without restraint. Life was such a fragile thing, she said to herself, looking down at the wrinkled skin on the back of her hand. She might never see her beloved Eleanor again.

A few rude tears stung the corners of her eyes, and she angrily wiped them away, willing her mind from such indulgent imaginings. Instead, she concentrated on a butterfly hovering nearby, its delicate wings vibrant with orange, black, and white markings. Quickly it fluttered off, landing on a yellow flower some distance away. In its beauty, Beatrice found comfort. There was, after all, much to be grateful for in this moment.

Master Herbert had been buried in the dark earth, his broken body now food for worms. Few had come to watch as dirt was cast on his bones. No one had grieved. The village and priory were content, believing that justice had been carried out. The vintner's soul, befouled with his murderous and most grievous sins, was facing God's wrath, while the soul of his innocent wife had been snatched from the Devil's claws.

Beatrice knew she would add Eda's soul to her own prayers. After all, the priory had erred along with the crowner in deciding the woman's body must be placed in ground filled with noxious weeds and the rot of unrepentant corpses. We should have known better, she thought, and must bear the greater guilt. After all, such blindness was more heinous when committed by those who had vowed to serve a perfect Lord.

Yet these sad events had brought forth some happiness. Besides the release of Eda's soul to God's hand, Alys and her Bernard would be married with Mistress Jhone's blessing as they had long wished. The bridegroom would surely take over the wool business, promoting one of the more talented workmen to manage it, while he continued to design his beautiful gloves.

Beatrice smiled as she thought about Alys and Bernard. The girl might be willful, but she was possessed of both intelligence and a caring heart. In fact, her spirited insistence that she be allowed to marry a man of her own choice reminded the novice mistress of the days she herself had spent persuading a father that the young knight she had fancied was an acceptable match. Although Master Bernard might not be quite prepared to be ruled by his wife, any more than her own adored husband had been, the novice mistress suspected the glover's love would teach him just as quickly when it was wise to surrender his will. If God granted them no more trials than any other mortal, Beatrice believed the pair would prosper, growing old together in the glow and warmth that love can bring in later years.

Beatrice sighed, a sharp regret stabbing at her heart. Although she rarely looked at her past with remorse, she did grieve over her husband's death. He had left her fine sons, and he had died as he would have wanted in a soldier's armor, but her woman's soul resented that he had gone to God far from her arms and without a last kiss. At least she had had joy of him while he lived, and for that love she would always thank God.

Love? Ah, what a glorious but foolish thing it was, the novice mistress thought, turning her eyes toward a certain young monk nearby. Brother Thomas was a handsome man for cert, and she understood quite well why her niece had fallen in love with him. Were I in the first heat of my youth, she decided, I might well have done so myself.

Not that Eleanor had yet confided this passion to her, but she had seen the blushes, the averted eyes, and the gaze that shone with adoration when the monk's back was turned. It was a fever she had hoped her niece might be spared, but God seemed to give these burdens to those He deemed most precious.

Several in the Church believed that those who did not twist and groan with Job's afflictions could never be found worthy of Heaven. Indeed, suffering did infuse some with God's more absolute understanding. Others, however, it infected with bitterness, jealousy, and the longing to make happier souls suffer as well. She might hate that her niece was enduring this pain, but she knew Eleanor was not one to grow petty with her affliction.

My dear one is no longer a child, she reminded herself, but that cannot stop me from worrying about her. Although she had full confidence that Eleanor was sincere in her vows, she wondered whether this handsome monk felt quite the same about his.

When Sayer had come that night to warn her that the Amesbury Psalter might be stolen, she had alerted Prioress Ida, who relayed the message on to Church authorities. They had promised to protect the holy object and even capture the thief, but no one had come until Brother Thomas arrived with a marked enthusiasm to investigate ghosts. Her niece might have voiced the thought that there could be a link between spirit and theft, but the red-haired monk had concurred with remarkable speed.

She caught herself smiling at this monk who was staring at the earth beneath his feet like a scholar lost in thoughtful debate about the nature of the world. All she had heard from Sister Anne and her own brother suggested he was an honorable man, although one around whom some mystery drifted.

Had his mother been of low birth, seized in the dark staircase of a castle or in the open fields? Or was she a beloved concubine of some rank? In either case, Beatrice knew he must have been sufficiently cherished by a high ranking father, one who could demand placement of an intelligent but bastard son where the boy might rise by the strength of his wits.

Had Thomas come to the cowl with any calling? What ambitions did he now hold, and what would he be willing to do to gain them? To whom might he be bound? Which man's advancement would prove beneficial to his own?

As she looked back across the cemetery of the damned and watched Eleanor walk toward her with Jhone by her side, Beatrice knew she had a duty to perform on behalf of a dead sister-in-law, one who had never seen this beautiful daughter mature into such an incomparable young woman. In addition, she owed it to her own heart that had so joyfully taken on a mother's role.

Thus the novice mistress of Amesbury Priory resolved to learn more about this Thomas of Tyndal, a man with the power to destroy the creature she loved most in the world.

Author's Notes

Amesbury Priory did exist. This prominent daughter house of the French Order of Fontevraud was located within a few miles of Stonehenge and next to Amesbury village itself on the River Avon. Prioress Ida was the actual leader when my fictional Eleanor came to visit her equally fictitious aunt. Almost nothing is known about Ida, especially whether she had a pet of any ilk.

By 1272, the priory was old by all standards, and the land on which it rested was an even more ancient spiritual site. There is some archaeological evidence, based on the discovery of a nearby burial presumed to be Christian, that a religious community might have been there in the fourth century C.E., and some claim that Queen Guinevere retreated to a nunnery of similar name in sorrowful penance for her sins. Whether or not that story, later made famous by Malory, is deemed pure legend, a synod was held in a Saxon church located on the grounds under the auspices of Archbishop Dunstan in the reign of King Edgar the Peaceful.

Edgar's widow, Queen Elfrida, is credited with founding a Benedictine abbey on the site of that church as penance for her suspected role in killing her stepson, Edward the Martyr, in 978 C.E. Although Elfrida was buried (circa 1002 C.E.) at Wherwell Abbey, she made sure that the relics of Saint Melor, a boy allegedly killed under circumstances similar to those of Edward the Martyr, were housed in the new abbey of Amesbury. When those bones actually arrived is unknown. They may have been in the original Saxon church at the time Elfrida founded the abbey, or she herself may have possessed the relics and wished to build them a proper shrine. Along with all other items of value, Saint Melor's bones disappeared many centuries ago, possibly into the hands of either the Seymour family or King Henry VIII.

There is an interesting side note to Elfrida's story. The facts of Edward the Martyr's murder are cloudy, although his successor quickly claimed his half-brother was a saint, thus deflecting any suggestion that he himself was involved in an apparent coup. Indeed, Edward might have been rather a brutish fellow, given to insane rages, whose death brought a great sigh of relief to many. Or else he was a rightful king slaughtered in cold blood. To add to the confusion, some now believe that the queen was innocent of any involvement in the assassination. Whatever the truth, her stepson's death brought her own son, Athelred, to the throne—a monarch now commonly and erroneously nicknamed the Unready.

Up to the reign of King Henry II, Amesbury remained a Benedictine nunnery under the rule of an abbess. Whether or not assertions of monastic irregularities were manufactured by Henry II, who needed to found or re-found three monasteries to fulfill a vow after the murder of Beckett, Pope Alexander III did send two reform-minded bishops, Bartholomew of Exeter and Roger of Worcester, to investigate allegations of immoral behavior there in 1177.

After their visit, Abbess Beatrice was pensioned off (she was rumored to have borne three illegitimate children, although there are allegations that Henry made up that story to get even with her for some act of insubordination many years before), and the other nuns were offered the choice of staying or going to other houses. None stayed.

King Henry soon invited the Order of Fontevraud to formally accept Amesbury as one of their priories, the rededication celebrated in May 1177 when the abbess of Fontevraud Abbey brought twenty-five religious to repopulate the place. Henry paid all travel expenses for the arriving nuns and gave them twenty barrels of wine, a gift that might have helped soothe any lingering effects of their hazardous journey across the Channel from Anjou.

Amesbury Priory quickly became a favorite place with high ranking families and quite wealthy as a consequence. Eleanor, widow of Henry III, retired there in her later years and was buried on the grounds. (The location of her grave has been lost.) A daughter of Henry III (Beatrice), two daughters of Edward I (Mary and Eleanor), a great-granddaughter of Henry III (Isabel of Lancaster), and a daughter of Piers Gaveston (Joan) all lived or took vows there. Catherine of Aragon stayed at Amesbury before her ill-fated marriage to Prince Arthur. Although the fortunes of the house waxed and waned over subsequent centuries, it remained active until December 1539 when Prioress Joan Darrell reluctantly surrendered the priory to Commissioners of King Henry VIII at the Dissolution.

There is little left of the old priory today, although the architecture of the remaining church provides some tantalizing clues to what has vanished. In addition, *The Amesbury Millennium Lectures* (edited by John Chandler and published by the Amesbury Society) as well as *A Short Guide to the Abbey Church of Saint Mary and Saint Melor Amesbury* do much to suggest what a magnificent Fontevraudine monastery this must have been. For those who value history, the disappearance of this historic priory, in all its evolutions from a single gender monastery to double house, is a tragic loss.

Since many details about the priory in 1272 are unknown, I have taken some liberties in describing Amesbury at the time of my Eleanor's visit. Records show that Henry III did donate ten cartloads of lead for roofing, but the tapestries in Prioress Ida's lodgings were woven only in this author's imagination. I do not know if there was a library, and there is no evidence of a scriptorium, but it is reasonable to assume that there must have been at least some place to store books. The religious at Amesbury would have been quite literate, and readings at meals were a standard practice. I decided both sides of the priory deserved a couple of illuminators and at least a small collection of books.

Although some have argued that the extant parish church may not have been part of the priory itself, I have made it so. There is evidence on the outside walls that indicates roofing was attached and could have formed part of a cloister. There is a blocked doorway that is consistent with an entrance to a Chapter House. The church was clearly larger at one time with more chapels, and parts of this building not only date to 1272 but much earlier. Work on the church has revealed a stone column base that may have belonged to Queen Elfrida's original foundation. The Saxon Cross, mentioned in this book, was too wonderful not to place where my Eleanor could enjoy it, and this wheel cross may also belong to Elfrida's time. Fragments are on display at the church and were discovered under the chancel in 1907.

I must confess that I brought a butterfly, the Marsh Fritillary, to Amesbury a few weeks early to distract Sister Beatrice from her sad thoughts. The Chalkland Blue, a butterfly with delicate markings that make the uniquely colored wings look like embroidery, was so tempting, but they are a July and August creature. This book may be fiction, but the wise mortal does not mess too much with Mother Nature even in a novel.

To the best of my knowledge, no one ever tried to steal the Amesbury Psalter, which now rests quite safely in All Souls University Library at Oxford. The work was done about 1250 by the anonymous but famous Sarum Illuminator or Sarum Master, whose Salisbury school also provided Psalters to royalty as well as to Wilton Abbey. His work is evidence of a uniquely and well-regarded English style: elongated bodies, delicate and expressive faces, elaborate and deeply folded garments. For those who want to see a sample of the Psalter itself, the Internet provides a color version of at least one page if one searches under "Amesbury Psalter." Margaret Howell's book *Eleanor of Provence* has a black and white photograph of the same page, and that biography may be available through the public library system.

Although many Psalters were intended for general monastic use, some predated the Book of Hours, common in the later Middle Ages, and were used for personal devotion. In the sample illustration mentioned in the paragraph above, we can see a small figure at the bottom left of the page. We might assume that this woman is a Fontevraudine nun, although her attire is not distinctive and could be either a nun's habit or the simple dress of a widow. (Nuns, then as now, tended to dress in a manner similar to seculars.) In any event, it is believed that the figure was the original owner of the manuscript, since a generic depiction of that person in the work itself was common practice. Her actual identity is unknown, although I have let Brother Baeda believe it to be a nun of Amesbury. Either she or the person who gave her the Psalter must have been quite wealthy, considering the quality of the work. The inclusion of the two feast days of Saint Melor (one of which was May 6) in the Calendar does point to a resident of Amesbury Priory.

Although the manuscript is in reasonably fine condition, I found a description that noted a tear in the corner of one page which shows evidence of an attempted mending. Needless to say, I took advantage of that detail for this story and decided that Prioress Ida would have wanted any damage to such a precious item properly repaired.

I freely admit to a fondness for ghosts, dating back to Grade Three when I wrote my first and last (until now) story about them. I am not alone in this interest. People have been discussing and seeing them for as long as we have records, a fact that suggests the spirits have been of importance, probably from the time we first developed speech and could talk about them. Maybe the desire to keep ghosts at bay was the real reason our ancestors discovered fire with such delight, not some culinary interest or a desire to upgrade the cave with better heating.

In any case, the early Christian church had a major problem with the creatures. They were a pagan thing, always inclined to bother the living if their earthly bodies were not properly buried (Antigone scattered dust on her brother's body at the cost of her own life), or if the living didn't properly pay Charon to ferry souls across the Styx—the latter suggesting that pagans not only thought you could but should take at least some of it with you. Thus Augustine of Hippo insisted, in his *De Cura pro Mortuis Gerenda (On the Care to Be Taken When Dealing with the Dead),* that the dead were not able, by their nature, to involve themselves in the affairs of the living.

Nonetheless, belief in ghosts and the sightings thereof stubbornly persisted with the secular crowd. As the first millennium approached, the Church began to agree there might be some good reasons for ghosts to wander around. After all, the times were troubling, and many believed the end of the world would come on January 1, 1000. The dead could be as restless as the living under the circumstances.

As years went on, there was another reason to support acceptance of uneasy spirits. Although the Christian concept of Purgatory had been around since the beginning of the faith, it became increasingly popular until formally codified in the 15th century. In a society where killing in battle was rather frequent, many died with less than cleansed souls. If nothing much could be done for those in Hell, and those in Heaven didn't need prayers, increasing value was placed on prayer for those in that interim spot for the spotted soul. Without question, the idea that one could do something to help a distressed family ghost move more quickly to Heaven was very appealing and found growing favor in the Church, as did the idea that sightings could prove instructional (saints) or frightening enough to change earthly behavior. Spectral wild hunts (where spirits rode on spiked saddles or dressed in flesh-charring armor) were quite effective at the latter.

As we do today, the medievals varied in whether or not they believed in ghosts. Some, like Beatrice and Eleanor, thought that only saints came by occasionally for instructional purposes in dreams or visions. Others, like Wulfstan, were equally certain that less perfect souls returned to trouble the living with more malevolent intent. As for the truth, I leave that debate to others.

Since I have discussed medieval views on sexuality and orientation at some length in prior books, I will add only a short note to provide illumination on Thomas' particular concerns in this one.

His era was a warrior culture that essentially defined *masculinity* as one man's ability to conquer another. The notion of *adulthood* involved a more tribal concept of survival: taking on the responsibility of marriage, a family, and the fathering of children.

For monks, men who might fulfill a socially important function but were prohibited from doing either of those abovementioned things, a different definition had to be developed. It should not come as a surprise that the definitions for them were quite similar to the secular ones. A monk could prove his masculinity by conquering temptation with the strength of his will. Manhood was achieved when he took responsibility for leading others to God and defeating their erroneous ways with his powerful reason as any father might his children.

The battle against lust, especially after celibacy became the rule for priests, appears to have taken up almost as much philosophical time as defining heresy. There are numerous and erotically graphic descriptions of the temptations saints-in-the-making overcame. Many in the Church concluded that men and women who suffered most from sexual torments were deemed more worthy of God's grace than those who did not. It seems that Satan found mortals who didn't experience nocturnal emissions and erotic visions of many wondrous varieties just too boring to care about.

In any event, whether the monk wrestled against sexual longing for a woman or for a man was somewhat irrelevant. Winning the battle defined the man. Whether he participated in formal debates or struggled (like Brother Thomas) against those possessing a particular darkness of soul, success was the mark of manhood.

Bibliography

This book could not have been written without the help of Christine and Peter Goodhugh. Their generosity in taking photographs, answering innumerable questions on aspects of Amesbury history, directing me to the right places for other information, and countless acts of kindness is immeasurable. I am deeply grateful.

One of my joys, as an amateur in history, is the ongoing discovery of details about the medieval period. Since I know others would share that pleasure, I like to list some of the books I have found useful when I write each tale.

As always, the resources deserve all credit when I get it right. Factual errors and failures of understanding are my fault alone.

Aelred of Rievaulx, *Spiritual Friendship*, trans. Mary Eugenia Laker SSND, Cistercian Publications, 1974.

Peter Brown, *Augustine of Hippo: A Biography*, University of California Press, (new edition with epilogue), 2000.

Andrew Joynes, *Medieval Ghost Stories: An Anthology of Miracles, Marvels and Prodigies*, The Boydell Press, 2001.

Ruth Mazo Karras, *From Boys to Men: Formations of Masculinity in Late Medieval Europe*, University of Pennsylvania Press, 2003.

Ruth Mazo Karras, *Sexuality in Medieval Europe: Doing Unto Others*, Routledge, 2005.

Jean-Claude Schmitt, *Ghosts in the Middle Ages: The Living and the Dead in Medieval Society*, trans. Teresa Lavender Fagan, University of Chicago Press, 1998.

To receive a free catalog of Poisoned Pen Press titles, please contact us in one of the following ways:

Phone: 1-800-421-3976
Facsimile: 1-480-949-1707
Email: info@poisonedpenpress.com
Website: www.poisonedpenpress.com

Poisoned Pen Press
6962 E. First Ave. Ste. 103
Scottsdale, AZ 85251